Not an Ordinary Artist

A Polish Immigrant's
Challenging
and Enduring Story

By Gail Tanzer

Not an Ordinary Artist: A Polish Immigrant's Challenging and Enduring Story

All rights reserved. No part of this book may be reproduced, stored in a retrieval system, or transmitted in any form or by any means, electronic, mechanical, or otherwise, without the prior written permission of the publisher, except for brief quotations in articles and reviews.

Printed in the United States of America for Worldwide Distribution

Copyright © 2025 Gail Tanzer

Publisher: Bella Media Management

Not an Ordinary Artist

A Polish Immigrant's
Challenging
and Enduring Story

Dedicated to John and Rosealia Cieplak

To create beauty—that is what I want to do—to interpret and record the beautiful in images that will live to inspire me and the world."

—Florian Durzynski as told to
Eve Adams, newspaper reporter

"Throughout life people change, and that is one constant you can be sure of."

—Anonymous

FOREWARD

I'D LIKE TO share a little regarding the title and subtitle of my book about its subject— Florian Durzynski —who emigrated from Poland to the United States in 1929. The challenging parts of Florian's story involve the unresolved childhood tragedies that he carried with him to America and his search for identity and belonging after arriving in his new country. The enduring part of Florian's story relates to his unique art form and his hope that it would leave a lasting impression on the many children and adults who viewed it in process or after completion.

As I write each of my books about a particular person, I walk in his or her shoes and see history from a new perspective. I hope that by following Florian through his unique life you will enjoy learning more about the history of Poland, about Chicago's previously large Polish neighborhoods, and about life in the United States between 1929 and 1969.

PART ONE
1932

1

MY MORNING

It was a balmy day in 1932. My morning started like any other. Little did I anticipate what was to follow.

I sat at the edge of a long table at my favorite restaurant, Nowak's, on Milwaukee Avenue in the West Town neighborhood of Chicago. Drinking strong coffee and eating sliced bread topped with kielbasa and eggs, I thoroughly enjoyed my breakfast. Since there were so many Polish restaurants in West Town, I didn't have to go all the way back across the ocean to enjoy my favorite foods, although I wished sometimes I could.

Nowak's was about six blocks from my apartment. Its presence was announced only by lettering painted on its four by six-foot front window. Oilcloth covered four rows of tables, and the seating was a hodgepodge of different wooden chairs. Miscellaneous pictures and nick-nacks decorated the walls. Next to the door stood two unfurled flags—one Polish and one American.

As usual, I perused the Polish newspaper before and after eating. Kasia, my favorite waitress, winked at me as she whooshed by carrying two plates to a nearby table.

Krysztof, the owner, ambled over to me. Dressed as usual in his white pants, white t-shirt and white apron, he was preceded by his prodigious stomach. He liked to boast that it was a testament to his restaurant's delicious dishes. Putting a hand on my shoulder, Krysztof asked in our native Polish, "So, Florian, how's it going lately? How's your art coming?"

"I will be exhibiting a few portraits down the street at the Lewis Hotel next weekend."

Krysztof looked at me intently. "I think you said the Lewis Hotel." Sometimes even my fellow Polish people couldn't understand me.

I nodded a yes.

"That's wonderful! I bet you didn't know you'd be successful so quickly after coming here. And those portraits you exhibited at the Knickerbocker Hotel! I loved the one of Cardinal Mundelein. How'd you get to show your work there?"

"My uncle admires my art and talked to someone at the hotel who's with him in the Polish National Alliance."

"That's what we do," Kzysztof said with pride. "Poles help Poles, and that PNA group will give you a lot of connections."

Since business was slow, Krysztof sat down next to me.

Quietly, and I hoped humbly, I said, "To tell you the truth, Krysztof, even though I am making enough money working at my uncle's house painting business, I will never rest until I can become a full-time portrait painter."

"You feel like it's your calling!"

"You're so right, Krysztof."

A bell tinkled above the door, and Krysztof got up to seat his next customer.

After finishing my meal, I walked back home. Since my apartment was only six blocks away, it was an easy journey. Even though I'd been in Chicago for three years now, most everything in Chicago was still so new… and complicated. Just last year I took the streetcar to a place outside of West Town and got off at the wrong street. I couldn't find the English words to ask people at the stop for directions. Finally, a Polish-speaking person came along and helped me out.

Knowing my roommates were at work, I looked forward to a quiet day at home. My roommate Peter was soft-spoken and calm. My roommate Kazimierz was cantankerous but caring. Both were Polish like me.

Poor Kazimierz had a gruesome job. One day he tried to tell Peter and me about it. "At the stockyards the hogs are driven from their pens to the roof of our building where they are allowed to cool down a little from the fear they're probably feeling. Then they're brought to the kill floor—about 12 or 13 at a time—where a man shackles…"

Peter protested, "No, don't go any further!"

I chimed in. "Stop!"

Kazimierz laughed, "You scaredy cats! Sometimes

even children come with their parents for tours and watch the whole thing."

"Disgusting!" Peter and I groaned together.

Peter explained to me, "As disgusting as it is, most Poles who come to Chicago start by working in the stock yards like Kazimierz. A lot of others work at the steel mills. You were lucky your uncle sponsored you and gave you the job with his business. That is, until you establish yourself as an artist…"

Kazimierz grumbled, "Yeah, you're a lucky guy, Durzynski. You've got talent and connections. Our Polish brothers who ain't working in the stockyards usually have to work in the steel mills. The mills ain't much better than the stock yards. You know their blast furnaces get up to 180 degrees. One wrong move and you're cooked like a goose."

The apartment the three of us shared was, like many in our neighborhood, a brownish-red brick building with two stories and a basement. There was nothing fancy about its exterior, but my artist's eyes found beauty in its style and simplicity. Over the top of each window was a white concrete pediment; I admired the way the architect used that little decorative effect. The front porch had ten wide wooden steps that led to a small landing with a roof over it.

My roommates and I lived on the main floor. After I walked in on this memorable day, I looked into the hall's rectangular mirror that stood over our phone table. I regularly did this to see if my moustache was successfully hiding the slender red line going from my upper lip to my nose.

Looking at my reflection, I saw a slim fellow, on the short side, dressed in a frayed but nice suit, having a decent enough face with neatly combed dark brown hair, blue-gray eyes, ears that were a little too big and a nose that was a little too long—but not too bad looking overall. If only there wasn't that obnoxious red line.

Suddenly, I heard a key turn. It wasn't just any turn; the lock was going back and forth. The key turner was struggling to open the door. Since my roommates were at work, I feared it was a robber. I grabbed the nearest thing I could …a pointed, metal letter opener on top of the hall table.

When the door finally jerked open, I was horrified. A man stumbled in. He had a bandage wrapped around his head with only his eyes and nose showing.

Sensing my fear, the man said in a disgusted voice, "It's just me, Florian." It was my roommate Kazimierz. Relief washed over me! However, I detected his familiar condescending tone and didn't like it.

But I ignored his attitude and simply asked, "What happened?"

"Something at work" was all he could get out.

Kazimierz staggered towards the couch in the living room. I gently but firmly took his arm and guided him to the bathroom.

I put the toilet seat down and motioned for him to sit.

"We had a new guy on the line. When he was trying

to slit the pig's throat, he jerked his sticker my way and almost took my head off."

"Ooh." I found a clean wash rag, held it under warm water and gently mopped away the blood dripping from beneath the bandage on his forehead.

"Did they give you stitches?"

"Yeah, the company doctor did. Hurt like hell."

I didn't know if I really wanted to see what laid behind those bandages, but if blood was coming down, the stitches might not be holding.

"Do you mind if I unwrap the bandage a little?" I asked.

Kazimierz nodded. "Go ahead." Then he shouted, "Oh, how I hate my job!"

Slowly, I began the unraveling process. I found that the blood was coming from a superficial scratch to his forehead. When I cleaned it up with another washrag, it looked like the bleeding had stopped.

Then I braced myself and looked at the top of his head. I winced at the sight of Kazimierz's half-shaved scalp and the smattering of blood in his hair, but there were about 20 perfect stitches running horizontally above his forehead. So, I was happy to announce, "It looks like the doctor did a good job."

"Good. Now I must lie down," he said.

After wrapping the bandage around his head again, I walked him to his room. Kazimierz drifted towards his bed. Since it was unmade, I said, "Just wait a moment, My Friend, and I'll prepare it for you."

I straightened the covers, and pulled back his sheet,

but I couldn't stop him. With his pig-stained work clothes, Kazimierz collapsed on top of his half-prepared bed.

2

MY IMPEDIMENT

WITHIN JUST A few minutes, I heard the strident buzz of our doorbell. As I hurried to the front door, I caught a whiff of the stench coming from Kazimierz's room. Leon Walkowicz and his wife Felice were coming over for her eighth sitting.

When Leon brought Felice over for our first meeting four weeks previously, he shook my hand heartily and said, "It's an honor to meet you, Mr. Durzynski. You can see that my wife is considerably younger than me. I want a portrait of her now to remind our grandchildren someday of how beautiful she once was."

Seeing his wife frown, Leon knew he'd better follow with a compliment. "But she will always look beautiful no matter how old she is."

Turning his attention back to me, he said, "I would only give my money to a Polish artist. You may know I write for the Polish National Daily. Also, I take photographs of our Polish events, and I collect things that someday could become important history. My dream is to help establish a museum of Polish American history right here in Chicago."

Motioning for them to enter my quasi-studio, I commented, "It is wonderful what you are accomplishing for our people."

Leon turned to me and said, "I hope so. The United States was originally happy to have our Polish people and other immigrants come. We took jobs Americans didn't want. Do you know now that there are about 400,000 Poles in Chicago? Anyhow, everything changed in 1924."

By now I had motioned for them to sit on the kitchen chairs I had placed in my studio. I leaned forward and asked, "What happened in 1924?"

"A guy named Albert Johnson got on the House Immigration Committee and said he spent a week in New York and concluded that every new immigrant brings a bunch of relatives and that our country couldn't support them while they looked for work. He had very ugly names for all the immigrants. I don't want to repeat them in front of my wife. He got Congress to set up a quota system for immigrants with an outlandish 80% reduction of the yearly average before 1914. You're lucky you got in."

"I am lucky. My uncle sponsored me."

"Sorry, Mr. Durzynski, what did you say?"

Oh, that impediment of mine! As slowly and clearly as possible, I repeated, "I am lucky. My uncle sponsored me."

"Oh, I got it now." Leon smiled, looking apologetic for asking.

Again, trying my best to make myself understood, I commented, "I'm impressed with how those immigration figures just roll off your tongue."

"It's nothing." Leon's words were humble, but he puffed up like a proud rooster. "Remember I am a newspaper reporter and am dedicated to collecting and reporting facts, especially as they relate to our Polish community."

But that was four weeks ago. On this day, Leon took a seat on our most comfortable living room chair to wait for his wife. I prayed that neither of them would smell Kazimierz's room.

As usual, I planned to have Felice sit for about an hour with a fifteen- minute break in the middle.

Before we started, I asked, "And how are you today?"

"Fine. And how are you, Mr. Durzynski?"

"Fine also. I enjoyed my English class last night. I'm learning a lot there, but it's nice to be with my Polish clients like you so we can speak Polish."

"Hmm. I'm glad you are fine, but I couldn't quite understand the rest of what you said."

It happened again. Behind that line from my lip to my nose was nothing but trouble. Now that I was an adult, I could hide the line with my moustache but when I was a child it was there for everyone to see. Until I was six years old, I had no idea that I was different. But then one day on the playground a boy pointed at me, laughed and yelled, "Bunny Face! And you talk funny, Harelip!" I could hardly make it through the rest of the school day.

When I got home, I looked in the mirror and hated the line I'd always taken for granted. I asked my parents what this boy meant. They both took a deep breath. Tears welled up in my mother's eyes.

My father cleared his throat and began, "Florian, when you were born, the doctors noticed that you had a hole in the roof of your mouth. They said you had a cleft palate and that it would need repair. Your mother had a terrible time feeding you because when you drank her milk it would come out of your nose. You hardly gained any weight."

Tears dripped from Mama's eyes regardless of her attempts to push them away. Father knew he'd have to be the one to continue. "You probably don't remember when we took you to the hospital and you had surgery to sew things together on the roof of your mouth."

"Now that you talk about it, I do remember it a little but not much."

The smallest of smiles alighted on Mama's face. "I'm so glad you hardly remember, My Sweet Boy. The pain killers must have worked."

Now my mother picked up the story. "We were so relieved that you came home as happy and carefree as ever. Before the surgery, you had a wide line and indentation from your mouth to your nose, but you were so young that you didn't seem to notice, and no one said anything bad to you about it. We never saw any need to explain all this to you…until it came up."

"And now it has come up," Father said. He tried to sound brave and matter of fact as he explained, "but there were two problems the doctor said would persist after your operation. One would be that you, like other children who have the surgery, might still speak a little like you're talking through your nose. However, you'd be basically understandable. The other would be that you'd still have a line from your lip to your nose, but it would be much narrower than the wide indentation you had when you were born."

Stunned, I had always thought I was like everyone else, but now I felt "different." Begrudgingly, I accepted my lot in life. But when another tragic event suddenly upended my young life, I had questions.

I loved depicting Felice. Whenever she walked into my studio, I got the feeling of birds singing and flowers blooming. She was like a breath of fresh air. Along with bringing beauty and a soft whiff of perfume, she brought an enthusiastic attitude towards living that always brightened my day.

In addition, Felice's appearance was impeccable. She wore her brown hair short in thick, tight waves that lay flat on her head. I highlighted her hair with lighter tints for each wave. She always applied dark pencil to her eyebrows and mascara to her big brown eyes. Her brightly colored lips and the tiny cleft in her chin made the lower half of her face stand out as dramatically as the upper half.

Before sketching the basics of her appearance, I had

painted the background with a light blue almost turquoise sky. Behind her body, I put a small layer of wavy pink and purple colors that looked like mountains. That part was abstract and represented nothing. However, I did the background like this for two reasons. One was to give a bit of color that contrasted nicely with her yellowish-gold dress, and the other was to make Felice look regal.

Depicting my subjects' clothing was as important to me as depicting their face. My father, who was a portrait painter before he needed to get an office job to support our family, told me, "Have your subjects dress in their best clothes and give them the dignity they deserve."

When we finished with the day's sitting, Felice stood up, stretched, and said, "Have a nice day, Mr. Durzynski. How many more sittings?"

"Just two," I said with a smile. I knew she'd be glad to finish these inactive hours.

"Just two," she repeated, probably making sure she understood me.

I nodded my head yes.

After she left, I had to admit to myself that I was still disappointed when people asked me to repeat things, but, thankfully, there was little need for conversation when I did portraits. I had chosen the right profession.

I wanted to follow in the footsteps of my beloved father. I wanted to make him proud with my art, but when I was only nine years old, my father died in the middle of the night of a heart attack. This, along with my cleft palate, made me jealous of other children who seemed to have it so much easier. I didn't want to burden my mother or siblings with my tears. I still played outside, but I preferred sitting by the little easel my father made for me and painting pictures I'd sketched of my family. It wasn't until dark came and I laid quietly in my bed that I silently cried out to the heavens or whoever else would listen, "Why? Why me?"

3

THE LETTER

THE NEXT DAY when I came home from work, I looked in our mailbox. Mixed with a couple bills was a letter addressed to me in a familiar handwriting. Without even taking off my coat, I hurried to the kitchen table, sat down, and read:

Dear Florian,

I still wish you would have come with me to the Bauhaus School of Art and Design. Our instructors are gaining a reputation as the most innovative artists and architects of our time. I already wrote to you about Wassily Kandinsky.

Now I want to tell you about our instructor, Paul Klee. His work is so playful. He can take a face and make it into a flower. And his use of color is amazing. Have you heard of surrealism? It's the newest thing—the making of illogical scenes that supposedly appeal to the subconscious mind. Klee's work is somewhat surrealistic, but it's more fun than many other new surrealistic paintings.

But I think I know you, Florian. I bet you still like to paint things as realistically as possible—especially when you're doing portraits.

In my last letter, I told you about Walter Gropius. Sad to say, he stepped down as leader of the Bauhaus. Then we had a guy named Meyer. Now we have a director named Mies van der Rohe. His attitude towards art and architecture sums up the Bauhaus' ethos: <u>Less is More.</u>

The only thing that bothers me now is that the Bauhaus is located in Germany. At times, we see thugs in town who wear brown shirts and follow this new guy Hitler who thinks he knows everything. When Gropius was our director, he told us to stay out of the bars because the brown shirts frequently pick fights with people they think are Communists or Jews.

Anyhow, please write back and tell me all about how you are doing in America and whether your artistic style has changed any.

Regards,
Juri

I loved hearing about the new art forms and artists at the Bauhaus, but what Juri said about the unrest in Germany and those bully brown shirts made me worry about my friend. It also made me thankful that I came to America where there wasn't so much danger. Something was always boiling up in Europe.

Juri and I had studied together at The Academy of Fine Arts in Kraków which was founded in 1818 as part of the Jagiellonian University. We spent many an hour together at Kraków's coffee shops where the vibrant conversations were as addicting as the strong coffee.

My friend and I did almost everything together. We met while studying under the famous Wojciech Weiss— the head of our painting department. I greatly admired the famed portraitist and landscape artist. Seeing as how I was most interested in painting portraits, I listened and observed intently when he elaborated on how to draw a face.

He said, "You may have been taught this before, but I want to make sure you understand the basics. Start with a basic oval shape. Draw a light guideline through the middle of the face, then a cross line where the eyes might go. Then, draw a line for the nose and mouth.

This will leave your drawing divided into three sections. Next, you begin the eyes. Draw oval shapes on the eye line. Then, draw the circles for the eyeballs. Then draw in the brows. Next, begin drawing the nose, then the mouth. Now you're ready to draw the hair around the hair line that you drew previously. Remember to erase your guidelines when you're done. I will have you practice all these techniques repeatedly when you paint our live models."

We listened as if he were God speaking; this man was recognized world-wide for his expressive paintings of people as well as landscapes.

Then he looked at each of us with his flashing blue eyes that looked like they could see into your soul. "But once you are done with drawing a perfect face I want you to use your imagination."

Pointing at one of his paintings, he continued, "Sometimes you can distort or exaggerate a face or hand or use unusual colors to give off a certain feeling…like if a person is joyful or melancholic."

I had a lot of respect for Professor Weiss, so I said I would try, but I just couldn't depart from doing my realistic portrayals. I didn't need to do masterpieces.

The summer after we graduated from the academy, Juri and I decided to study for a month at The Julian Academy in Paris. Even though it was only a one-room art school, the academy was well-respected. Thinking about it brought back memories of turpentine, tobacco and sweat.

There, I discovered something that brought me joy.

My portraiture could fit into a new style. It got its name from a recent, gigantic Exposition in Paris featuring what they called "modern decorative arts." It was called "Art Deco." One of my art teachers said, "It represents luxury, exuberance, glamour and faith in the future." My portraits embodied all these ideals but on a less dramatic scale than some other Art Deco artists like the popular Polish artist Tamara di Lempicka who painted rich and famous people in a highly stylized way. Nevertheless, I felt proud to be a modern man working in a recognized style.

While in Paris, Juri and I visited the Louvre and saw some of the world's greatest art. Then we went to Montmartre—previous home of the Impressionists and now the gathering place for new artists like Pablo Picasso. The architecture in Paris showed me how art can be for all the people because looking at its buildings can bring joy to even the poorest citizen. It was like free art.

Juri and I often talked politics with our fellow university students. Even though Poland had finally achieved its independence in 1919 we doubted it would last. There was always political infighting and the constant threat of invasion by Germany, Austria and Russia.

The biggest problem for us aspiring young Polish artists was that there weren't enough people buying art. Although Poland had magnificent buildings and beautiful art from centuries ago, we students shared the belief that people in contemporary Poland had other priorities.

We concluded that poor families needed to spend all their time trying to eke out an existence from their little farms and that rich people seemed more intent in purchasing gaudy success symbols than mind-expanding works of art. Those beliefs helped us justify the fact that we couldn't sell our art. Maybe we just weren't good enough or didn't know how to advertise our work, but we didn't want to entertain those notions.

We asked ourselves where we could find a market for out art. We heard a lot about the United States. We heard that the United States was the home of the "free." We heard that it guaranteed "life, liberty and the pursuit of happiness." We never heard that the United States was invaded by its neighboring countries. So, we thought that Americans might be secure and wealthy enough to indulge in the joy of acquiring art to enrich their lives.

Our interest was stoked by letters home from some of my friends' relatives who'd emigrated and bragged about all the opportunity in America. They said there were so many Poles in certain areas that we'd feel right at home.

We discussed all this, but none of us seriously considered emigrating. Then one day our university friend Magda announced, "I am going to the United States. I figure I have a lot of years ahead of me, and maybe in America I can actually sell my art. Also, it might be fun to see a different part of the world."

The rest of us choked on our coffee and asked if this was just talk.

Magda said, "I'm dead serious. Look, the ships travel both ways. I can always come back if I don't like it there."

Magda's words had a snowball effect. One after another of my friends started seeking visas. I did too.

∽

After reading Juri's letter and reminiscing about my motivation to come to the United States, I went to my bedroom that doubled as a studio. I needed to study our English assignment for class that night.

I was lucky that my small bedroom came with a Murphy bed that I could fold back into the wall. I had an easel and a table with paints and brushes and a little desk with a chair that I got at a resale shop.

Like I did on every Tuesday and Thursday evening, I took a short streetcar ride to the nearby Erie Settlement House. By now I had been in Chicago for about three years and had attended the classes since my arrival. There was no formal graduation date for us English language learners. We left when we were ready, and I felt ready.

However, I would miss the staff at the settlement house. They all seemed to really care about us immigrants. When we made progress, a look of fulfillment flashed through the face of our English teacher, Miss Perlman. We appreciated it because we wanted affirmation that we were succeeding.

After coming home from class that night, I thought more about Juri's letter. His school—the Bauhaus—was in Germany, and my ability to speak German would have been very helpful if I attended the Bauhaus too. However, I was glad not to be bothered by the brown shirts. Also, what they started calling "modern art" like they taught at the Bauhaus still had little appeal to me.

I was thirty years old and feeling good about my decision to move to the United States. There was only one thing missing—a woman with whom I could share my life and hopefully create a family. I was afraid that my red line and my speaking difference would make it impossible, and that made me ask all the more, "Why? Why me?"

4

A NEW CLIENT

A FEW DAYS AFTER Kazimierz's work accident, he joined Peter and me at the dinner table. Peter was a good cook. He served us a meal of kielbasa, pierogi and sauerkraut. He placed everything on a lace tablecloth my aunt had given us. It felt like we were dining in high style.

Kazimierz addressed me in a surprisingly affectionate manner, "I know it's late for me to tell you this, but I thank you for helping me with my head, Florian. I snapped at you when you seemed to think I was a burglar or something, but you treated me well. I wanted to do something nice for you."

"Thank you, My Friend," I answered.

"When I went to work yesterday, the company doctor asked to see me. Said I was healing well. I told him my roommate paints people's pictures. He got excited. Said he'd been looking for someone to paint his portrait. Thought maybe his children and grandchildren would remember him after he's gone if they saw his mug every day."

I put down my fork and knife and said excitedly, "Ah, Kazimierz, you don't know how much that would mean to me."

And, so, I got my next commission.

My subject was so happy with the result that he told other managers at Armour about my portrait painting. Word even spread to the Swift plant next door.

A man named John Cieplak called me. In a voice that bespoke friendliness and refinement, he said he'd heard about my "great ability to capture the appearance and character of my subjects." He explained that he was a master carpenter at Swift meatpacking. I asked him whether he'd like to come to my little studio or have me come to his home to do the portrait.

He responded, "I would prefer to have you do most of the painting at your studio, but I'd like you to come to my house for our first meeting. It might help with the portrait."

"Yes, definitely."

And, so, on a windy, cold day, I took two streetcars to get to his home near 25th and Loomis. Although he told me on the phone that he was Polish, this was not a Polish neighborhood. Mr. Cieplak's home was one of the red brick bungalows that was becoming ever-present in the Chicago area. One and a half stories high, it had a low -pitched roof with wide overhangs and generous windows. I thought, *This man has accomplished a lot to afford a house like this.*

When I rang the doorbell, an attractive middle-aged woman answered. With a ready smile, she said, "You must be Mr. Durzynski."

"Yes, I am."

At that moment, a man who I imagined was Mr. Cieplak walked up and introduced himself.

"Have a seat with me in our living room, Mr. Durzynski," he said warmly.

As I was sitting down, a girl of about twelve and a boy in his early teens peeked around the wall separating the living room from the rest of the house.

Mr. Cieplak motioned them in to join us. "This is the man I told you about who is going to paint my portrait."

"Oh," they said in unison. The girl looked interested, the boy not so much. Mr. Cieplak introduced the children, "This is Jeanne, and this is Emil."

"So that he can paint the most realistic portrait of me, I want Mr. Durzynski to know what kind of man I am. When you and your four brothers grow up and maybe even have children of your own and gaze upon this picture, perhaps, you will sense my presence and my love."

Emil and Jeanne just nodded, probably having no perspective on what might matter to them in forty years or so. They would learn as the years went by.

Mr. Cieplak introduced his wife as Rosealia and said she was the backbone of the family.

Wiping her hands on her apron, Rosealia said, "Not just me. You are the backbone too."

Then Mr. Cieplak said to the children, "Thank you for joining us, but you can play now."

Dutifully, the children left.

I asked Mr. Cieplak to tell me a little about his background.

He said, "As a young man, I came to America for work. I was sponsored by my cousin who was employed at the Stock Yards. Two years after I arrived in America I married my lovely wife, Rosealia. I started from the bottom at work, but my bosses eventually realized I could build anything, and I became a master carpenter. I have saved every penny I could to buy this home and hope to buy more property in the future."

Mr. Cieplak took a break from telling me about his past and looked at me with ardent eyes. "On the phone, you told me you are Polish also. Then you know there is nothing more important to us than having land and a home…and, of course, going to Mass."

"You do have a beautiful home here. You mentioned Mass. I too am Catholic. Which parish do you attend?"

"St. Barbara's. I've made sure that all my children attend school there. The many activities at St. Barbara's keep the children out of trouble and, of course, give them a good Catholic education. Do you know that the church put on an addition about eight years ago that has an auditorium, a bowling alley, a billiard room and a kitchen?"

I responded, "I'm impressed. It sounds like St. Stanislaus where I go."

"Ah, St. Stanislaus—the mother church of all our Chicago parishes! What would we do without our church?" Mr. Cieplak said more to himself than me.

"Anyhow," he continued, "Perhaps seeing my house, meeting my wife and two youngest children, and knowing what I think is important will help you do a fitting portrait of me."

"Yes, for sure that is true," I said.

When Mr. Cieplak came to my apartment for his first sitting, he wore a distinguished dark gray suit with a vest, white shirt and gray tie. He struck a serious pose.

I said, "I will try to paint a fitting portrait of you, Mr. Cieplak."

"Good. This portrait is very important to me. I think you understand that even though I love my family dearly, I don't want you to just paint me as a kindly family man. I want you to show how serious I am and somehow capture my belief in the value of hard work…a quality I want to pass down to my children and grandchildren someday."

This was the kind of man that nearly every male Polish immigrant aspired to be.

I painted Mr. Cieplak in my Art Deco style. I depicted him as an accomplished man with confidence, stature, and eyes to the future. I made sure to capture the elegance of his suit and to paint a muted but lovely abstract background to give this man all the dignity he deserved. The French who originated the Art Deco style would have been proud of how Mr. Cieplak's portrait turned out.

I hoped that if my earthly father now in heaven could look down, he would be proud of me. He might be sorry for me that I hadn't married or had a family yet, but I felt he would be happy that I remained in the Catholic faith and followed in his footsteps to become a portraitist.

I was on the way to becoming a full-time artist, but I was not there yet. It would take a while to get enough commissions to give up my house-painting job. In the meantime, it was grueling to have to work all day and then paint portraits in the evenings or on the weekends. Sometimes I feared that my right arm would fail me, but it remained strong.

5

DIVINE INSPIRATION

UNFORTUNATELY, I HAD to put my hopes and dreams aside for a while because the American economy went on a downturn. More and more people lost their jobs. Fewer people came to my uncle to have their houses painted. My portrait commissions dwindled. My roommates and I worried that we'd become unemployed and wouldn't be able to afford our apartment.

Facing this grim possibility, I knew I would need to pray especially hard when I next attended Mass. St. Stanislaus was always my bulwark. Everything about the church signified strength and hope.

The church and its school took up two city blocks. Almost all the Masses were in Polish. I loved the feeling I got when I walked in. Being surrounded by so many other parishioners was like a confirmation of my faith, despite my occasional doubts. The priests sometimes mentioned, with obvious pride, that 1500 people could fit in this gigantic church, and it was usually full. The fact that hard times had hit America especially brought many of us to our knees.

The stained-glass windows were as elegant as any I had seen in Poland and France. Each one was probably 30 ft tall and had three sections all depicting scenes from Christ's life and death. Under each was a plaque announcing which family or group had donated the window. Throughout the church were statues, paintings on ceilings, and shrines that told a myriad of stories. Dozens of stained-glass chandeliers designed by Louis Tiffany ensconced the church in glorious light.

Walking into St. Stanislaus this time, I thought briefly of Juri's most recent letter, and I realized the Bauhaus would never go for a church like this. "Less is More" certainly did not apply to St. Stanislaus. However, I thought that to visually teach a person about God and to give God glory, a church should overflow with an abundance of art. A Bauhaus church with only a simple cross would never inspire me.

Before Mass, I lit a candle and prayed. After Mass, I used the kneeler for an extra twenty minutes, repeating the rosary and then offering my own little prayer: "Blessed Mother, please have mercy on me and send me more work. I desperately need more income, and I'd prefer making it from my art."

That afternoon when I got home, I decided to paint something new. I didn't know if it was divine intervention or a simple human whim. I wanted to paint landscapes—

landscapes like the ones I'd seen as a child when we visited our uncle who lived on a little farm in Poland.

I closed my eyes and tried to visualize the stately trees, the rich soil with their rows of crops, the gently rolling hills and the nearby river. Uncle always reminded me that even though the farmland in my sight line was beautiful most of it didn't belong to him.

Uncle's cows and his horse were a special delight to this city boy. I was impressed with how our Polish country people cherished their animals because of the milk and meat they provided…nothing like the way they were treated at the Chicago stockyards. On Christmas Eve, our country people even gave their cows a communion wafer.

Although I was enamored with the rural living, I knew my poor uncle was a sad man. I overheard conversations he had with my parents about how he didn't have enough land to make a good living from the crops.

I was only a child, but I asked, "Why are you so sad so much, Uncle? I love your little farm."

He put me on his knee and tried to explain, "During the partitions from about 1772-1795, Poland was taken over by Russia, Prussia and Austria. They divided our land among themselves, and our own wealthy 'big shots' in Poland found all kinds of ways to take as much land as they could from us humble farmers. We were left with so little."

Uncle added, "Finally, after the Great War in 1919 we became Poland again and got rid of our invaders, but we farmers still don't have much land."

My country has suffered so much, I thought.

∽

Landscape painting would be a totally new direction for me. To gain inspiration, I decided to find a rural area outside the city of Chicago.

I looked forward to escaping the clamorous noise of Model Ts, streetcars, elevated trains and horse carts. I looked forward to escaping the noxious smells of the stockyards and the steel mills that sometimes blew our way. I looked forward to taking what the Americans called "a vacation."

I asked Krysztof at Nowak's Restaurant where I could go within a train ride to surround myself with nature.

"Go West, Young Man, Go West!"

Seeing my puzzled expression, he elaborated. "That's famous saying in America. Anyhow, there's little town west of Chicago called St. Charles. Pretty little river there. Went ten years ago with family for vacation. It's very nice."

Thankful for Krzysztof's advice, I found out that I'd have to take the train to a town named Geneva and then board a trolley to St. Charles. Even though I hadn't gone outside the Chicago city limits since my arrival in the United States, I thought I could do that.

It only took about an hour and a half to reach St. Charles. When I arrived, I saw hills that rolled somewhat and a river that rushed somewhat. Nothing as beautiful as the countryside in Poland, but it would have to do. The problem was that St. Charles had city noises and smells like in Chicago. Carpenters yelled to each other as they nailed together wood to build various structures. Dust from their labors filled the air. Trucks rumbled up and down the dirt roads.

Having made a reservation for one night at the Baker Hotel, I asked the receptionist what was going on.

With my imperfect English and speech problem, I wasn't sure she'd understand.

She looked at me quizzically, but she seemed to get the gist of my question. "Two people in our town inherited a lot of money. So, St. Charles has become a boom town. New hotels and shops are springing up everywhere."

I shook my head in disappointment, but I smiled and thanked her for the information.

After I checked in, I brought my easel and art supplies down to the river's bank. At least, there was a river and trees skirting its banks.

I only brought pastels with me because this was purely an experimental trip to see if I could come up with new artistic techniques.

To my surprise, I found myself depicting the trees, clouds and the slightly rolling hills in a soft, swaying manner. I used light and dark greens, yellows and even pinks. In the past when I painted landscapes, I tried to make every leaf look real and to delineate every little tree knot. However, on this occasion, something else took over me. I couldn't believe that I was recreating the landscape in a somewhat abstract manner.

It almost seemed like I was moved by something

Not an Ordinary Artist

spiritual. I thought back to school when I learned about the Greek gods. Hephaestus came to mind. He was somewhat like me because he had a problem when he was born. He had something wrong with his legs. Sad to say, his parents weren't as kind as mine who loved me despite my impediment. His mother, the Goddess Hera, threw him out of Mount Olympus.

But he didn't allow his lameness to define him. He conjured up images in his mind and manifested them with his hands through artistic creations. He crafted decorative art on swords, battle helmets and even Pandora's box.

The Greeks believed Hephaestus taught creativity to people on Earth.

I knew it was probably silly, but I liked to imagine that Hephaestus was inspiring me as I depicted the landscape in such a new and different way.

Since I had been a portraitist working indoors all the time, I had rarely noticed how much nature changed over the course of a full day; how the trees looked lighter, then darker depending on whether a cloud floated by; and how the leaves wiggled then settled down as the wind increased or decreased

When the sun slowly set, the sounds and smells of the workmen dissipated. It was finally peaceful. I watched the fireflies twinkle in their golden hue, and I almost fell asleep on the riverbank.

The next day when I took the train back to Chicago, I mulled over two things. First, the story of Hephaestus. It was admirable that he didn't let his birth defect define him, but, like me, did he ever wonder why he was singled out to have his impediment in the first place? Second, I pondered my new style of painting. I visualized how I would use my paints to do landscapes with the colors and abstraction I picked up in St. Charles. I'd need a big area to make my visualization come into reality.

I got a brainstorm! When I returned home, I asked for and received the permission of my roommates to paint a large mural on our living room wall. The fellows loved it.

6

SOUTH SIDE POLES

ON A QUIET Sunday afternoon, Peter and I listened to the radio and relaxed. My roommates and I often laid on the floor listening to music with a cushion behind our heads.

Peter asked, "How about you come to my sister's wedding? It wouldn't hurt for you to have a little fun. You don't even need to bring a gift."

My first impulse was to come up with an excuse, but I was stuck. "Yes, I will go," I said unenthusiastically.

Peter said, "Come on, don't act like you're going to a funeral. You'll see how we South Side Poles do weddings. It will probably remind you of home, but there will be new things too."

I guess I still didn't look too interested. So, Peter threw out a challenge "You know us South Side Poles think you North Side Poles are snobbish."

"Really?"

I would prove him wrong.

Peter said, "All the big shot Poles are from the North Side. Think about that newspaper fellow whose wife you painted. Men like him on the North Side hold the important positions in our clubs. They own the fanciest stores. They run printing presses. But you'll see at the wedding that us South Siders are just as good as the North Siders."

I asked, "Then what made you move out of the South Side?"

"I'll be honest. I'm not proud of it, but I got into trouble. All us kids would be outside a lot. We couldn't afford to go to the movies or nothin' and our parents had most of us drop out of school at the end of eighth grade so we could work. It was so hot in our houses, and most of us came from big families, so we could hardly move indoors. We were bored; we wanted excitement. So, we boys hooked up with each other and formed clubs. We started stealing or fighting with other groups of boys. Then we said we were a gang and even gave our gang a name. I got thrown into jail overnight once for stealing. My parents worried about me…a lot. It just so happens that my dad hired your uncle to paint our walls. My dad saved for years to have that done. He was too tired from working at Swift to do it himself. When your uncle was painting, my mom told him about me and how I was getting in trouble. Your uncle said he could hire me, and they took him up on it."

"How about Kazimierz?"

"My mom knew Kazimierz's family. They lived down the street. He was getting into trouble too. She said maybe we could get an apartment together on the North Side away from trouble. Your uncle didn't need any more painters. So, Kazimierz started working at the stockyards."

I commented, "It takes him a long time to get to work, and he hates it so much. I wish my uncle would take him on."

Peter offered his opinion. "Think about it. Kazimierz is so disorganized. You see how he leaves his dirty work clothes around his room sometimes and doesn't like to wash his dishes. I can't see him being strict enough with himself to paint within the lines."

I chuckled. "That's true. Okay, you've got me curious now about the South Side. I gleefully accept your invitation to the wedding. Is that better?"

Peter laughed.

Kazimierz was invited too, and since we didn't have dates, we went together.

When the wedding came around, it was a brisk February day. Winter still had Chicago in its grip, and the temperature was about 20 degrees. Although I always tried to look nice, I put special effort into it this time. I wore my best overcoat and hat, and I polished my shoes until they radiated my reflection (even though I had to put my goulashes over them).

When we got off the streetcar and started walking to the church, I noticed that the buildings in this neighborhood were made from either asphalt siding or unpainted wood. As cold as it was, children played outside with toys they made from old tire rims, sticks, and whatever they could find.

Within no time, I could see one of the two towers of the Church of St. Joseph's. When we got closer, I saw that in the middle of the towers was the body of the building with a triangular roof. The church was made of dark red brick and, similar to those in our apartment building, white cement decorative elements. Like St. Stanislaus and the many other Catholic churches in Chicago, it was built in the architectural style we had back in Poland.

With pride, Kazimierz announced, "That's my church!" Then he pointed to an adjacent building. "I went to Catholic school there. Don't know if it did any good, but it was important to my father for me to get a good Catholic education."

Upon entering the church, I saw an opulent altar with a statue of Jesus on the cross and Joseph watching in tearful meditation. Arched stained- glass windows adorned the walls. It never ceased to amaze me how the sun took on such different hues as it beamed through the various colors of stained glass. A profusion of rich woodwork showcased The Stations of The Cross, much like at St. Stanislaus. The ceiling was arched and contained lines that accentuated its shape. St. Joseph's was lovely and provoked a meditative spirit, but I didn't think it rivaled St. Stanislaus, although I'd never say that to Peter or Kazimierz.

At first, the organ played quietly, and then it suddenly picked up tempo and volume. We all stood up and crooked our heads around expectantly. The bridal party paraded down the long center aisle. I was impressed by the mint-green dresses of the six bridesmaids and the black tuxedoes of the groomsmen. The bride's gown and veil were elaborate, and I could see that her parents really loved their daughter and worked hard to save for her wedding.

The reception was held in a room above a nearby corner bar. Kazimierz said that almost all South Side Poles had their receptions in halls like this. There was no shortage of corner bars on the South Side...or the North Side.

I never saw so much hopping in my life. The upbeat sound of the accordions lured everyone to the dance floor. I had to laugh because bent-over ladies who could hardly walk scurried to the dance floor like cripples who Jesus got to rise up and walk. Although I had only done the polka a couple times, I found the atmosphere infectious. I tapped my feet and leaned towards the dancers. When everyone at my table partnered off, I sat alone. I had always dealt with a sense of "not belonging," and now that familiar feeling clutched my stomach again.

But then I noticed a woman at a nearby table sitting alone too. She wore a dark blue dress with white polka dots. When she happened to look my way, I looked at her and gestured towards the dance floor. We got up simultaneously, and the next thing I knew we were moving to the beat just like everyone else.

We circled round and round the floor hopping like a couple of professionals. Polka music had a way of doing that to you.

We danced to about three songs, and then we gravitated to some chairs. As we sat down, we attempted to talk above the din. She introduced herself as Mary Budzinski. She was a couple inches shorter than me, had blonde hair, and bright blue eyes that looked straight into mine. I wouldn't say she was beautiful, but I certainly wasn't the best-looking person in the world myself. Mary had a bulbous nose, and her ears jutted out from her short, perfectly waved hair. However, her face and her arms were so smooth and white that they looked like Carrera marble, which I found very appealing. Mary had a ready smile and an enthusiasm I liked. We talked about trivial things, but she didn't ask me to repeat too often. My impediment didn't seem to be a problem.

7

THE COURTSHIP

At the reception, I got Mary's phone number and called her a couple of days later. I pulled up a chair by our phone that sat on the hall table. We had a long talk even though Kazimierz and Peter repeatedly yelled, "This is costing us money!" Mary told me her parents had immigrated from Poland and she was born here. She attended Chicago Normal Teachers College along with many immigrants and children of immigrants because it was close by and inexpensive but delivered a quality education. After that, she began teaching at St. John of God Catholic School on Throop Street.

I told her I was a first-generation immigrant from Poland. She was curious to hear my immigration story, but I told her I would save it for a time when we met together in person—which I hoped would be soon.

Mary was 25 when I met her. She lived with her parents and a younger brother not far from St. Joseph's. In no time, I began visiting her once a week. I was often greeted by the sounds of coca-doodle-doo from the neighbors' chickens and roosters.

The Budzinskis' house was one with wood siding. It contained a kitchen, living room, and two bedrooms. It seemed that there was a small upstairs. Her brother still lived at home as did Mary. I admired her parents because they were determined that both their children go to college...not just their son. They felt that education was the only way to succeed in America.

Mr. Budzinski was a carpenter at Swift, and Mrs. Budzinski worked as a secretary at St. Joseph's.

Sometimes Mary's family would have me over for dinner, but, as much as I appreciated it, I preferred taking Mary out to eat and then to the movies. We saw a couple of silent films, but then sound came along, and we were mesmerized by the effect.

When we walked, I liked it that Mary put her arm through mine if it was slippery. When I left her at her door, we would share a quick kiss, but that was it. I felt like Mary was attracted to me but wanted to take things slowly.

The subject of the line under my moustache finally came up. Mary caught me off guard when we were having supper together at The Chuck Wagon Restaurant. For a change from Polish food, Mary and I both enjoyed eating American food there like open-faced beef sandwiches with mashed potatoes and gravy.

She said, "I don't want to be too forward, but it looks like you had an accident once or someone injured you." And then she did something I never thought a woman would do—she lifted her hand and delicately touched my line.

I had to tell her I had a cleft palate. With sympathy brimming in her blue eyes, she said, "I've heard of that, but you seem to have a mild case."

"Yes, I do," I said with pride.

Then she said, "I noticed that you have an unusual accent when you speak English and Polish. Does that have something to do with the…the cleft palate?" Mary seemed like she almost didn't want to say those two words because it might offend me.

I feared, *Perhaps now she will not be interested in me,* but I felt I had to explain it all to her. I cleared my throat, then began, "When I was born, my soft palate didn't close tightly against the back of my mouth. So, I had to have surgery. The surgery helped, but whether I speak English or Polish, I sound different from others."

"There's nothing wrong with that. I understand you." She smiled, and we continued to eat our dinner. What a relief to have that over and to feel accepted (hopefully) for who I was.

A couple months after I met Mary, her family had me over for Easter. Mrs. Budzinski said with obvious pride, "I took our Easter basket to be blessed yesterday by the priest. Now when we eat our bread, ham, kielbasa and everything else, it will taste even better." She winked, and we all smiled. Then everyone took a slice of boiled egg, and we wished each other *Wesołego Alleluja* (Joyful Hallelujah) or Happy Easter.

These were the very same customs we practiced in

Poland. With tears in my eyes, I thought back to what my uncle had written to my mother, "In Chicago, your son will feel more like he's in Poland than he actually does in Poland." Uncle was right, but I still missed home. I found that sitting with this happy Polish family made me crave mine even more.

8

IMMIGRATION

AT ONE OF our meals at the Chuck Wagon, Mary asked me to tell her all about my immigration.

I said, "Coming to America, leaving my family was the hardest choice I've ever made. It was unbelievably painful."

Mary touched my hand. "But it might help you to talk about it."

I put down my knife and fork, thought for a while. "I'm not one to talk a lot about myself, but if you'd really like to hear, I will share it."

Mary said, "Maybe the telling will help you as well as be of interest to me. As you know, my parents came over too, but I've never asked them about it, and they've never brought it up."

"Things may have changed since they came. For one thing, I've heard that the conditions on the boat were much improved by the time I took the ship."

"Okay, so now let the story begin," she said with a little flourish of her hand.

I cleared my throat. "I'll always remember when I first got sight of her—the Statue of Liberty. It was January 27, 1929. She was taller than I expected. Her tightly set jaw and empathic eyes seemed to be telling us she believed in us. Her upstretched right arm looked stronger than any man's I'd ever seen. I believed I'd be safe with her."

"From the deck, people waved towards the shore, as if the lady would wave back. Of course, she didn't, but she held something up for us. It was a torch. I imagined it symbolized liberty. In her other arm, she carried a tablet which I hoped promised us basic human rights in our new country."

Then I paused. I moved my beef and potatoes around on my plate and sighed. "This was the uplifting part of my immigration story. The hardest part was when I told my mother I wanted to leave Poland."

I felt like I might cry, but I took a deep breath and continued, "She looked like I'd slapped her in the face. Usually, Mama was the picture of calm, but not when I made that announcement."

"Wait," Mary interrupted. "You talk about your mother, but how did your father react?"

I cringed. "When I was about nine, my father died in his sleep."

"How awful!" Mary said like my loss cut her to the core.

"Yes, it was awful."

Mary asked, "Tell me more about…about… what happened to your father, if you don't mind. I feel so bad for you."

"In the middle of the night, I heard a commotion in my parents' bedroom. Mama was screaming. My brothers and sister and I rushed to their room. Mama kept lamenting, 'He's gone, he's gone!'"

The telling of this made me put down my knife and fork. Mary patted my hand and gave me a loving smile that felt like a morning sunrise.

When I felt I could continue, I shared the thoughts which, for so long, I had kept secret. "I couldn't figure out why—why my father was taken from me when I was so young and why I was born with the cleft palate. It all seemed so unfair." I paused for a moment and then added, "But we were fortunate after my father died because we had uncles and aunts who looked out for our welfare, and my father had a decent amount of money in the bank."

Mary said, "I'm sorry you lost your father when you were so young. And the cleft palate seems unfair. I really don't understand either why these things happen…"

After Mary's voice trailed off, I continued. "When I announced to my mother my hope to emigrate to America, she furrowed her brow, squeezed her eyes together, and clenched her tiny fists. I readied myself for battle. After a few minutes that seemed more like an hour, she said more cheerfully, 'But it's not so bad here anymore, Florian. Now that we won that war with Russia a few years ago, we have our freedom.'

"I know, Mama, but at what cost? I even took a year off school and volunteered to be a camouflage artist to help with the effort, but many died or were injured, and how long will our newly gained freedom last?

"Then, in an apologetic tone, I admitted, 'Plus, I have to say that I want to see the world or at least a part of it.'

"Mama sighed deeply. 'Well, if you must go, my sister and her husband say there is something like another Poland in the city where they live. It's called Chi—something or other...

"I thought for a moment and then it came to me 'Chicago' is what it might be called.

"My mother's eyes brightened a bit. 'Yes, that's it. A big city in the middle of the United States. Your uncle is a painter there....

"'You mean an artist?' I hadn't heard much about these relatives, although I wasn't always the best listener when it came to tales about little-known family.

"No, he paints houses. He has men work for him.

"We were sitting across from each other at the kitchen table. I leaned forward and took her hands in mine. 'You can come with me, Mama, and we'll create a new life where we can truly enjoy being Polish while experiencing a new country where we don't have to worry about invasions.'

"But my mother answered with conviction, 'No, I can't leave. I can't desert your sister and brothers and my little grandchildren.' She paused for a moment, seemingly lost in thought. Then she said with a tinge of sarcasm, 'But I kind of expected you'd want more after you got your art degree, then studied in Paris…'

"I frowned. Mama seemed to be criticizing me. Words tumbled out of me in rapid fire as I tried to defend myself. 'You know you and Papa always wanted us children to achieve a good education. And remember how you had us celebrate the Feast Day of Saint Jadwiga, that long ago queen of Poland. You said she only made it to the age of twenty-six, but she accomplished so much, especially funding the Jagiellonian University. You would tell us to honor her memory by getting a good education.

"Sheepishly, Mama said, 'I remember.' Then she tried to make a joke. 'And now I have to eat my words.'

"We were both quiet. Then Mama conceded, 'But even though it's hard for me to let you go, I guess I'm glad you want more …' She was quiet for a moment, seemingly lost in thought. 'Poland still has so many problems. You are young and free. No wife or children to hold you back.'"

Mary commented, "I would find it so hard to leave my parents and brother, but I can see why you decided that Poland wasn't right for you."

"Like I said before, I know I made a big decision, a big choice by coming to America, and sometimes I wonder if it was the right decision."

"My parents made that choice too, Florian, and I'm glad they did. The United States is a good place." She paused and smiled. "Besides, I like that you came here."

I had just taken a forkful of mashed potatoes, but even with my mouth full, I could have kissed Mary.

9

FEELING LOVED

AT THAT MOMENT, the waitress brought our check. As engrossed as we were in conversation, we had somehow managed to finish our dinner. I looked around the restaurant. There was a small waiting line. I looked at my watch. We had taken up our booth for an hour and a half.

I said, "Let me walk you home. We can continue this conversation another time."

Mary agreed but also said, "Don't forget. I want to hear everything."

When we arrived at her doorstep, I leaned forward to kiss Mary, but again she just gave me the quickest of pecks.

That's all right, I thought. *This evening Mary has been a loving witness to my immigration challenges, and that's made me feel better than any amorous kiss.*

The next time we met, it was on a Saturday over Paczkis and coffee at a little Polish restaurant in Mary's neighborhood. We sat at a corner table. The place was crowded and noisy, so I didn't have to fear anyone being bothered my story.

The first thing Mary said was, "Where did you leave off? I think it was when you were discussing your decision with your mother."

"Okay, let's see…When it was finally time to take the train to Antwerp to board a steamship for America, I exchanged tearful goodbyes with my brothers and sister, nieces and nephews. Leaving my mother was the hardest part. We both cried like babies. I told her I would write often and would come back to visit soon, but we both knew that my returning would be difficult. I could barely scrape together the one-way fare to America let alone afford a round-trip ticket. But something made me believe I'd see my mother again in the not-too-distant future.

"Mama's last heart-rending words were, 'Stay the same…the same… (it was hard for her to get out the words) good, cheerful man. Don't let your…your little imperfection stand in your way. Paint, paint, paint, and hope…hopefully you will be happy in America.'

"Confusion greeted me at first when I arrived in Antwerp, the first step of my journey. People struggled with crying babies and an array of makeshift carrying bags. We were put up in hotels for a few days. Officials took groups of us to a room where we were checked for possible diseases. If any of us looked sick, we were sent back home. When I was a child, kids called me 'skinny' among other names, and I was sickly, coming down with a cough or cold the minute one of those conditions could find me. However, when I arrived in Antwerp, I felt healthy. I was warned that the inspectors looked for lice in one's hair. So, I shaved off my beard but kept my mustache…partly to disguise my line. It was winter, but thankfully the weather was above freezing. I wore long winter underwear anyhow in case I'd need it later, my best slacks, a white shirt, a woolen suit coat and a hat to make sure I stayed warm and looked good. I just hoped the inspectors wouldn't discover my little impediment.

"I could have jumped for joy when I passed inspection. Others who were thought to have a contagious disease or a serious infirmity were told they couldn't board. Their family had to figure out whether they should go ahead anyhow to America or return home with their loved one …The sorrow was so great…I couldn't wait to get out of that room."

"Wow!" Mary exclaimed. "All those difficult steps you had to take to get over here."

"It got harder," I said. It felt good to share what I had endured.

"The ticket agent at the inn where I applied for my visa told me that the SS Lapland, the ship I would take, was like a lot of other steamships. It carried exports from America to Antwerp without any passengers. After they unloaded their cargo, they loaded emigrants and wealthy travelers for the trip back to America. She also told me I was very lucky to get an Exit Visa since a law was passed in the U.S. in 1924 that called for strict quotas. She said

I got my visa approved because I had a place to live and a good job lined up by my uncle.

"The rich people were escorted to the upper levels. The rest of us were sent to the steerage or bottom of the ship. The crew served us three meals a day on long, narrow tables, and we slept on bunk beds. It was noisy, crowded and stuffy, but I worked to remain calm and pleasant. I figured this would only be a short period of discomfort. In two weeks or so, we'd arrive at our promised land.

"To escape the smells of everyone's sweat and the sounds of babies crying, I sometimes went into my own little world. This part may bore you, but one thing I did was to imagine looking at one of Kandinsky's paintings."

"Who was Kandinsky?" Thankfully, Mary still looked more interested than bored.

"Juri, my friend at art school in Kraków, enrolled at the Bauhaus School of Art and Design in Dessau, Germany. He wrote to me about his favorite teacher—Wassily Kandinsky. He said the man had a theory about colors—what feeling each evokes and which colors look best next to each other. Kandinsky created a painting with colors as bold as if they came straight from the tube. He entitled it 'Canons.' Juri said that this exciting scene featured two cannons firing across the composition in an explosive manner. The painting was abstract and non-representational. Although I'd never seen it, I imagined it was fascinating but also unsettling like the things I saw and heard around me in steerage. Going into my dreamworld and visualizing

Kandinsky's painting helped me get through some of the hardest times."

"Do you paint like Kandinsky?" Mary asked.

"No. I usually like to paint things as realistically as possible. That's why I turned a deaf ear to Juri when he encouraged me to join him at the Bauhaus instead of going to America. But I must say I'm beginning to do some partially abstract landscape painting, and I'm enjoying it."

Mary looked impressed. "You have lived quite a life so far, Florian. Your love of art, your interesting friend, your schools. But, please, continue with your immigration experiences."

Mary made me feel proud of myself.

"After a deckhand finally announced that the Statue of Liberty was in sight, I expected that our ship would pull into a dock near the statue, and we could take our first steps on American soil. Instead, tugboats and ferries come out to transport small groups of us to an island that one of the passengers said was named Ellis Island. Since there were about 1500 of us, I could see this would take a long time. Before people got onto the boats, nurses came aboard and gave everyone a shot. I heard the words 'small pox' mentioned.

"As we waited and waited to get to the Island, the cheering and dancing died down. It took three days for me to catch a ferry."

"That waiting must have been excruciating," Mary said.

"It was, and with the ship swaying back and forth in

the gentle waves, we all got a little seasick and prayed for dry land. When I finally caught a ferry, I was very relieved.

"But our ordeal was just beginning. Once we pulled into the dock, we were instructed to leave our baggage in a room at the bottom of the ship and then walk up a winding staircase that would take us to a big hall. I noticed that people who appeared to be inspectors stood at the top of the staircase. Looking down, they watched our every move.

"After people got to the top, the inspectors took aside a few individuals. They were the ones who had trouble walking. Through hand gestures, the inspectors indicated to their families that they could accompany their loved ones to a room where I imagined an examination took place. It appeared that The United States didn't want any people with physical problems who could be a financial burden to enter their country.

"Most of us made it past the staircase. Then we entered a large hall that was crowded with people who looked lost and befuddled. Inspectors checked everyone again. They were especially looking for some eye affliction, it seemed, because they used a menacing long instrument to widely open people's eyes. I heard one inspector mention the word 'Trachoma.' I got the impression that it was contagious."

"I don't think I've heard of that," Mary said.

"Terror gripped me. Would these inspectors discover my impediment? My legs shook so much I was afraid I'd collapse. When an inspector looked at my face, he hesitated for a moment. He moved my moustache, had me open wide, looked into my mouth with a small flashlight, and discovered what I dreaded.

"'You, Sir, go over there,' he said pointing to a line full of distraught-looking people. An official led us to a building next to the great hall. I remember thinking that if they turned me back, I'd rather jump off the ship than go home as a reject.

"The building was a hospital, and I sat on a long wooden bench there for three days—worrying and wondering. I tried to explain to different people who examined me what a cleft palate was, but they didn't understand Polish. Finally, a doctor came on duty who understood my condition. He patted me on the shoulder and seemed to be saying I could work, wasn't contagious, and should be released.

"Finally, I was accepted into The United States of America!"

Mary's attention never wavered. At the end, she said, "Wow! What an experience! What a piece of history! I'm ashamed that the U.S. makes it so hard for people to get in."

"Don't worry about it. I'm just thankful I finally made it."

Mary had only eaten one of her Paczkis, and she accepted a warm-up on her coffee when the waitress came around.

Throughout my long description, Mary had looked at me intently like she was painting my portrait with her eyes. I wasn't sure what to make of it until she said, "If it wasn't for your uncle sponsoring you and then your friends asking you to come to the wedding, I wouldn't have met you." Then with a shy smile, she said, "And I'm so glad I did."

Mary's words made my heart sing. I replied with gusto, "I'm happy too that God or fate or whatever brought us together."

However, God, fate, or whatever were the invisible things that made life so perplexing for me. They could bring joy or sorrow on the turn of a dime.

10

EXCITEMENT

"Eııı!" I yelled as we sped at high speeds around death-defying turns on the Bobs at the Riverview Amusement Park. My sweet Mary was the one who got me into this terrifying situation. She'd explained that this was Polish Day at Riverview. When I first saw it, the Bobs took away my breath. It was a huge roller coaster on a wooden frame. I'd been to a couple of amusement parks in Germany and Poland, but none like this. It looked like it was 70 feet high and had sharp turns that could send you flying with the birds.

After the ride, it took me several minutes to catch my breath, but when I did, I said to Mary, "That was the most exciting thing I've ever done!"

"Did you like it? Did you like it?" Mary repeated enthusiastically.

"Yes! I liked it, but I especially liked it when we got off."

We both laughed. Then I bought her some cotton candy, and we strolled along until we got to the Pair-O-Chute Ride. Mary said she had ridden it in the past and found it almost as exciting and wonderful as The Bobs. I gulped. *How much excitement could a person take in one day?* However, I felt I couldn't be a coward.

I looked at the ride's steel tower that went up a couple of hundred feet from the ground. Six parachutes ran at one time, each holding two people.

There was only a short line, so I didn't have much time to back out.

As we made the slow ascent with our parachutes, my nerves tingled with fear. When I heard KU-CHUK, I assumed we were now connected with some kind of overhead steel bar. It held us there for a couple of minutes. Rocking back and forth and feeling terrified, I still enjoyed looking down onto the city of Chicago with all its buildings, roads and cars. Then suddenly we were released and went into a free fall for about twenty feet until our parachutes opened. "Aaaah!" I yelled.

Thankfully, our landing was cushioned by a thick, rubbery mat.

I breathed just as heavily as I had after the Bobs, and

I thought, *If I didn't have to impress Mary, I'd never go on these rides.*

With a look of concern, Mary said, "I know you're not used to this. I've been going here since I was a teenager. How about just one more—The Mill on the Floss?"

"What in the world is that?"

Mary said in a coquettish voice, "You'll see."

She led me to a ride with a small boat that had six rows of seats. In each row was a couple. Before we got on, I observed that metal runners guided the boats through a long, dark tunnel. After we were seated and our boat made it under the roof, the other couples immediately began kissing. Up until then, Mary had been frugal with her physical affection—doling it out in small portions. But, in the darkness of the tunnel, Mary went right along with the crowd. I had already put my arm around her, and now she leaned into me and kissed me—emphatically. I didn't know how to react. No woman had ever kissed me like that before.

I kissed Mary back, but I couldn't respond with the passion she put forth. I reasoned that it was because I wasn't at all prepared for this opportunity. Mary kissed me several more times, but by the time I felt able to respond in kind the ride was over.

This wasn't all Mary had in store for us. That afternoon, we took a streetcar to the Polish Day parade down Michigan Avenue. Myriads of marchers and floats made their way down the wide street, and onlookers waved little Polish flags. All of this should have made me happy, but it didn't. I felt like I "belonged" but then again like I didn't. Enjoying the Polish celebrations without my Polish family was like celebrating Christmas with relatives other than your own. The food may be good, everyone is full of cheer, you even go to Midnight Mass together, but if it's not your family, you feel you don't belong.

I didn't want to deflate Mary's spirits. So, I forced a smile throughout the festivities. However, on our streetcar ride home, Mary could detect that something wasn't right.

She said, "At the parade, you tried to be enthusiastic, but your eyes said otherwise. May I ask what's bothering you?"

"Mary, you've been wonderful today, and I've truly had a good time, but I'm feeling nostalgic about my family. I wonder if your parents who were first generation over here felt they couldn't fully delight in the festivities because they left their people back in Poland. You are the second generation here. This is all you know, and you can enjoy everything with full abandon."

Mary looked at me sympathetically. "You might have a point there, Florian. I'll ask my parents about that." Then she squeezed my hand and said, "But you've got to admit that this may have been the most exciting day of your life."

I laughed heartily. "Yes, it definitely was! No pretending about that!"

On the ride to her house, Mary told me about some of Chicago's most influential leaders. She admired Mieczyslaw Szymczak who got the Naturalization

League to create fifty citizenship schools across Chicago. Then there was Emilia Napieralska whom Mary said was her personal idol. "She is a fierce Polish patriot and has been head of the Polish Women's Alliance for many years..."

I said, "Wait! My uncle takes part in activities of the Polish Alliance, but I didn't know there was a women's branch."

"They provide insurance for single women who would otherwise not be able to obtain it, but they also help needy families. Even though our Polish people just scrape by, they always seem to find a little extra for those in a worse situation, especially with Emilia's urging."

I loved and admired Mary so much. She was fun. She was knowledgeable. She was idealistic. And, if we got married and had children, she would make me feel truly a part of Polish Chicago.

11

THE STREETCAR

AFTER A FEW more dates, I asked Mary, "Would you like to go with me to The Art Institute?"

"Oh yes! I love it when you talk about your art, and

I'd like to see real paintings in the styles you describe. I went to the Art Institute once before, but I didn't fully understand why some works of art are so special."

"I'm glad you're interested. I'll come get you next Sunday, and we can take the streetcar together downtown."

"That's not necessary," Mary said. "You've already made so many trips out to my house. I'm good at taking streetcars. I'll hop on one by my house and meet you there."

No matter how much I insisted, Mary insisted back that she would take the streetcar on her own. We were supposed to meet at 1:00 on Sunday outside in front of the Art Institute by its statuesque lions.

It was a beautiful warm May afternoon. You could feel summer in the air, and you didn't even have to wear a jacket. I always loved going to Michigan Avenue where the Art Institute was located. There were so many beautiful new tall buildings; people strolled with an air of enthusiasm.

However, after Mary was a half hour late, the spell was broken. I became worried. I imagined that something bad might have happened or that she finally lost interest in me due to my impediment. I knew the second thought was probably unfounded, but it was hard for me to shake my fear of rejection.

When 2:00 rolled around, I went to find a phone booth. By now, I had memorized Mary's number. When

I called, her mother answered and told me Mary had left at 12 noon. She should have arrived by now. Panic set into both of our voices. "What should we do?" We asked each other.

Finally, Mrs. Budzinski said, "I'll have my husband walk to the streetcar stop and see if there's any problem on this end."

"All right," I said. "I'll sit at a bench out here by the museum and see if she shows up."

I bit my nails. Michigan Avenue lost its luster. *How could these people walk along so light-heartedly when the love of my life might be in danger?*

After a half hour more, no Mary. I called Mrs. Budzinski again.

When Mary's mother answered, she yelled hysterically, "Mary was hit as she got on the streetcar! Her father got there when they were loading her onto a stretcher to take her to the hospital. She was bloody and…and… didn't seem to be breathing. My husband just got home. He called a cab. We're…we're going to the hospital. It's so awful!"

I said, "I will rush to the hospital too."

"No, no please don't bother." She choked back tears and said, "We'll take care of things."

As much as I felt Mary was the one for me and as much as she felt likewise, my four- month courtship did not entitle me to go to the hospital—at least not in Mrs. Budzinski's mind. She probably cursed me anyhow for proposing the Art Institute trip.

I waited impatiently to hear from them. Three hours

later, Mr. Budzinski called. He could hardly breathe, but he managed to eke out, "She's gone."

What sound does a heart make when it breaks? I thought I heard mine do just that.

"What…what happened?"

Between sobs, he said, "A couple of bystanders told me. Mary…she was on the corner. On its edge. A car came barreling down the street from the opposite direction. It swerved to keep from hitting a child…he was crossing. It jumped the curb, hitting my poor daughter head -on."

"Oh, my God! Can I do anything to help?"

"No, what could you do? Just pray for her soul."

"I will."

∽

Even though I'd dreamed of finding a woman to love, I didn't come to America to find a wife; I didn't think that was possible considering my impediment. I came to make a living from my beloved art. Also, I came to experience a new way of life in a country far away from constant invasion. But when I met Mary, I thought my impossible dream might come true. She could be the mother of our children, and we'd reside happily ever after in Chicago. Now the specter of living without Mary was unimaginable.

That same question I'd been asking myself all my life reared its ugly head. "Why? Why me?" Why was I born with my impediment? Why did my father die when I was so young? Now, why was the love of my life taken away from me so suddenly? It all seemed so unfair.

And then I thought of Mary rather than myself. "Why? Why, Mary?" She was so young, joyful and kind. Why was she taken away so suddenly when she had so much to give?

My roommates tried to help me but couldn't. Begrudgingly, I went to work because I needed the money. I couldn't bring myself to attend Mary's funeral. I wasn't invited anyhow. I had to call her parents to find out about the arrangements. I told her mother I could understand if they were angry with me for asking her to The Art Institute.

Mrs. Budzinski told me they didn't blame me, but I blamed myself. Guilt came knocking at the door of my heart and took up residence.

I didn't attend Mary's funeral Mass. If I broke down, I would only cause more problems.

12

THE DISTRACTION

OF COURSE, WHEN I met Mary, I wrote to my mother about her. Now it was difficult to tell her what happened. I wanted to suffer in silence, and I knew that my mother would overflow with sympathy…repeatedly.

Just as I expected, she doubled the frequency of her letters. Now they always started with "My dear, sweet Florian." I wanted to tell her not to treat me like a child, but that would hurt her feelings. I had enough guilt to contend with.

My roommates kept urging me to go out with them and do something. They played baseball with the St. Stanislaus church teams and loved it. They enumerated the many things I could do through the church like sing in the choir or be in their drama club or their literary society, but I didn't care.

Every day after work I immediately went to bed and let my mind sink into oblivion. One day Kazimierz had the nerve to disturb me.

He yelled down the hall, "Ya got a telephone call, Durzynski!"

When I replied with a moan, he yelled, "Get your ass out of bed and answer the phone."

"Okay, okay," I said as I forced myself to get up.

The caller introduced himself, "Hello, Florian, this is Bruno Zulaski. I'm sure you'll remember doing my portrait."

Coming out of my comatose-like state, it was difficult to recall him. I pretended. "Oh, yes, yes,".

"I know a very famous lady, a movie star who wants her portrait painted, and she told me she wants you to do it."

"What's her name?"

"Pola Negri."

"What!" I yelled. "<u>THE</u> Pola Negri…our Polish

screen star. I saw her in a silent film…" Then a wave of sadness hit me. I thought of how Mary and I held hands during the movie.

"Yeah, she's beautiful, ain't she, Kid?"

"Yeah."

"And she's rich, so she can pay well."

I thought for a moment, and then I asked myself my so-frequent question but in a positive way, "Why me? "

Zulaski said she was a big fan of Leon Walkowicz, the news writer who had me do a portrait of his wife Felice. "She stopped in town last year to thank him for all he's done for our Polish people, and lately she got the bright idea to have someone paint her portrait and give it to him. The only problem's that she wants it done in a week."

"A week?" I spat out in alarm.

"You can do it, Kid, I know you can."

"I'll have to…I mean I will."

Like a new man, I was full of enthusiasm. My roommates were amazed at my transformation. I knew that painting this famous woman would not fill the void left from losing Mary, but I thought it would be a distraction.

A week later, Zulaski brought Pola to our apartment. I made the appointment for a Thursday when my roommates were at work. Otherwise, they'd be gawking like lovesick teenagers.

Before Zulaski brought Pola, I made sure everything

was clean and orderly. When the doorbell rang and Pola entered, I was surprised to see her without makeup. She still looked beautiful. Every one of her delicate features fit together into a perfect whole.

Not waiting for introductions, she said "Hello, Mr. Durzynski. I hear that you're a Pole just like me. It'll be nice to relax and speak my favorite language with you."

"That will be a pleasure for me also," I said as we stood in the hall.

She looked puzzled. I knew she was thrown off by my unique speaking style.

I ushered the two of them into the living room. Immediately, Pola was attracted to my mural. After studying it for a couple minutes, she said, "Beautiful! I could sit here all day and feel completely at peace. This makes me glad Bruno said you should do my portrait."

Zulaski said he'd wait in the living room as I escorted Pola to my studio.

When she entered, she said, "Before we get started, I want to tell you something…can I call you Florian?" When I nodded, she continued, "I am a very active woman. I will not be able to sit still unless you entertain me."

Breaking into a smile, I said, "I'm sorry I can't dance and sing while I paint."

"No, no, of course, I don't mean that. What I want is for you to describe each step you take—from the way you make the background to the way you capture the expression on my face. I used to love to draw. When I was a child back in Poland I suffered from tuberculosis.

I had to stay still for long periods and begged for pencil and paper to draw things. But when I got better, I couldn't wait to be more active. I studied ballet and acting in Warsaw. The point is I love art, and it's hard for me to sit still. So, please keep me calm by telling me every step you're taking in your painting."

"Okay, sure," I said agreeably.

"You can see I'm not dolled up today. I just wanted to get these things straight before we started."

"That's fine, Miss Negri. You will need to come in every day for the next week if you are in a hurry."

"Could you repeat that, Florian? There's something unusual about the way you talk." This was a woman who got to the point.

I repeated it slowly.

Without apology, she asked, "What's wrong with your speech?"

I was glad Pola Negri was so brash and that we could get this situation clarified right away. "I have a cleft palate. When I was born, the skin from my palate didn't meet with the back of my mouth like it should."

"Okay, good, now I understand. I may have to ask you to repeat things sometimes. Is that okay?"

"That's fine," I smiled.

"I can tell you're a good man, and I think it will be a pleasure sitting for you," she said in the softest tone she'd used since she entered the apartment.

On the next day, Pola showed up alone in what I thought of as her femme fatale look. She wore a chiffony wrap that allowed her low-cut negligée top to display a considerable amount of her alabaster skin. Her black eyeliner and purple eye shadow made her eyes look sultry. Capping her eyes were long, thin, dark eyebrows. Bright red lipstick covered her little lips. Her straight black hair went down to her shoulders.

After I ushered her into my studio, I had her sit at an angle near the window where I had pulled up the shade. I explained, "I want the light to cast a shadow on your face making the portrait more dramatic."

Pola liked that idea.

Also, I had clipped the pastel drawing I'd done in St. Charles to an extra easel that would be in her line of sight. I said, "Looking at this could help you relax."

"Ah, yes."

Once again, Pola demanded that I tell her about each step of my work "And don't worry about your pronunciation, Flor (I liked that she nicknamed me). I'll figure out what you're saying. I'm not supposed to talk anyhow, am I?"

As she sat in her pose, I told her that the first thing I was doing was sketching the main elements of her face with red pencil. It was very important to get the correct location of her eyes, nose and lips. I held up the protractor I would use to help me do this. When I finished that, I told her I would do the underpainting—using yellow ochre with plenty of paint thinner to make a thin wash to put over the whole background. The pencil marks would show through just enough to begin the painting.

Within about a half hour, I finished part of this

process and suggested we take a break. "Can I smoke?" she asked.

"Certainly, but if you're using a match we should go in the living room, away from the paint thinner."

She complied, and as we sat together, she pulled out a long cigarette holder and quizzed me about why I came to the United States. "So many of our people left to make enough of a living to feed their children. When I come to visit Leon and his wife, I see a lot of Poles in Chicago. It's like a little Poland here."

"It definitely is, and that's very comforting."

Pola proceeded to tell me her immigration story. "My reason for immigrating was a little different than most. I came for big money, and I got it. In my late teens, I was acting and dancing in Berlin. I made a film entitled *Passion* with the German director Ernst Lubitsche. It was so successful that it was optioned in America. Lubitsche and I were given contracts to work in Hollywood."

Blowing smoke rings, she added, "I signed with Paramount. I hate to brag, but I was the first actress from Europe ever to get a contract in Hollywood."

"Wow, I'm impressed, and you have every right to brag." But then, looking at the clock, I said we needed to get back to work.

When we got situated again, I explained, "I am putting down a dark base on your face in some of the areas where there are shadows. Later, I will add lighter colors to give your face definition."

Pola continued to sit, and I continued to work until I suggested another break.

In the living room again, Pola pointed to the wall and said, "Staring at your country scene, my mind wanders back to the days of my youth. I loved my father so much and he loved me, but he was an unhappy man. He was utterly disgusted with the Russians occupying the eastern part of our country. So, in 1914 he joined up with Józef Piłsudski ...you've heard of him?"

"Oh, yes, he is a hero to us Poles."

"Well, as you probably know, Piłsudski got together a little army to rise up against the Russians, and my father assisted him in recruiting men. A guy who must have been a Russian spy found out and reported him. In the middle of the night, two Russian soldiers banged on our door and pulled my father out of bed. My mother cried and begged to know what the reason was. One soldier said, 'He is bad man. We take him to labor camp in Siberia.'"

Two fat tears fell from Pola's eyes. Wiping them away, she said, "I never saw my father again."

I hated to see a woman cry, and from reading the newspapers I remembered that Pola Negri could be very emotional. From my pocket, I pulled out a clean handkerchief and handed it to her.

She accepted it.

"You're proba...probably...afraid...afraid...I'll fall apart now like I did when my Rudolph...Rudolph Valentino...died. I'm sure you heard about that...People were so critical...It is difficult for a foreigner coming to America... It was particularly difficult for me, a Slav. My emotion seems exaggerated to Americans." Then angrily she added, "I cannot help that I haven't their Anglo-Saxon restraint."

I nodded without saying a word. The newspapers had shown pictures of her prostrating herself on Valentino's casket and fainting two times. At the time, I took Pola's side: Pola's being so emotional was what made her a successful actress.

Comforting a crying woman was not something I was accustomed to. However, I patted her hand and quietly said, "It will be all right, it will be all right."

Once Pola pulled herself together, I suggested we get back to work.

"I can't," she said. "Look at my makeup now."

I urged her to just freshen up a bit and try to keep posing. One week was such a short time to do a portrait.

On our last break of the day, Pola said between puffs on her cigarette that this was the second time she came through Chicago. She told me what Zulaski had already explained—that she had come the first time to meet Leon Walkowicz. "Even though he lives here, Leon has always been an outspoken advocate for Poland. Someone told him about my father's efforts to recruit an army to overthrow the Russian occupiers, and he wrote an article about it for your Chicago papers. A relative sent it to my mother. The article made me appreciate my father's sacrifice and I wanted to thank Leon personally. At Leon's house, I saw the portrait of his wife that you painted. That's why I came to you. I will give my portrait as a gift of appreciation to Leon and Felice."

I was so impressed with this woman. Although she was famous and wealthy, she still thought seriously about many issues and wanted to recognize people who had shown her and her mother respect in their difficult times.

On the fourth day of our portrait work, I put on some music before we started. When Pola walked into my studio and sat down, she emitted a sigh of contentment. "Maybe you don't need to explain anything to me today, Flor. I can just get lost in your Chopin music."

I smiled. Poland's great pianist had that effect on people.

On the next day of her sitting, I put on music by Ignacy Paderewski. Immediately, Pola recognized the piece. "Ah, Paderewski, what a pianist! And I so admire how he worked for our country. Didn't he give up his music for a while for Poland?"

"Yes, Pola. I was about 18 at the time. We praised him for going to the U.S. to influence President Wilson to make the creation of an independent Poland part of the Treaty of Versailles."

Pola recollected, "I remember my mother talking about how he was briefly our prime minister and then went back to giving piano concerts. He didn't need the political limelight."

When, after one week, I completed her portrait, Pola studied it. "This is so much more striking than any photo of me. You captured me, Flor! You show my glamour but also the sadness that lurks within me, and the background you created gives me the regal look I like."

Pola gave me a half hug. It was nice to experience a little human touch again.

I invited Pola and Bruno to come over Sunday morning to pick up the portrait. I said to Pola, "Would you like to go first to St. Stanislaus, maybe with my roommates if they promise not to leer at you too much? Then you and Bruno can come back for coffee. I know a bakery that makes great Paczkis."

They accepted my invitation and during the service at St. Stanislaus I saw Pola dab away tears behind the black veil she wore to disguise her identity. Back at the apartment, she said, "It was so nice to be at a Polish Mass again!"

When she took a bite of the Paczki, she looked like she was going to cry again. "This reminds me so much of my mother. She made us Paczkis every Tuesday before Ash Wednesday. God rest her soul."

The whole experience with painting Pola's portrait was a healthy distraction from my grief and a sentimental journey back to Poland for Pola.

13

MARY AND CERMAK

As much of a distraction as Pola was, I kept thinking about Mary. She was in every breath I took, in every paint stroke I made, and in every encounter I had with a blue-eyed person. But when darkness fell, she withdrew, and I was alone.

After a couple of days, Kazimierz and Peter came to my darkened room. Lying on my back with my hand over my head, I squinted towards them. How two people—two Poles—could be so different was beyond me. They not only looked different but also smelled different. Kazimierz was as big and hairy as a bear and smelled like one. Peter was as fair-faced and petite as a woman and, with his after-shave lotion, smelled like one. It ran through my mind that you should never clump individuals from one nationality into a group and think you know them. Every individual in a group is different. Why such a pensive thought came to me at that moment I don't know. Maybe it was the dramatic way the hallway light framed the figures of these two men in an almost spiritual manner.

Kazimierz interrupted my thoughts. "Are you going to waste your whole life layin' around?"

"Yes, may…maybe," I stammered. My conscience still stung like a paper cut. "It's the guilt. If I wouldn't have…" I tried to protest.

Peter said as sternly as he could, "Listen, Florian, you weren't the one who got in a car and ran over her, were you?"

"Well, no, not exactly."

"Right. You absolutely weren't. So, don't crucify yourself."

Kazimierz grabbed my shoulder and ordered, "Now get up. Our favorite radio show is coming on. Forget about yourself and think about what's going on in the world."

I got out of bed like an arthritic old man. After we went to the living room, Peter turned on the radio and moved the tuner to The Polish Hour of Education. It was 6:00PM, just the moment when the show began.

"News Flash! News Flash!" the announcer squawked. "The mayor of Chicago, Anton Cermak, has been shot!"

Stunned, we leaned towards the radio as one. The announcer said, "Cermak was in Miami hoping to convey Chicago's needs to President-elect Franklin Delano Roosevelt who just returned from a Caribbean fishing trip. Roosevelt signaled to Cermak to meet him at his car. Just as Cermak reached the car, a man took a gun out of his pocket and fired it towards Roosevelt, but it hit Cermak. A woman named Lillian Cross saw it and knocked the man's gun out of his hand. Roosevelt was fine. Lillian Cross was unscathed, but Mayor Cermak was seriously injured."

Our mouths dropped open. Peter said, "We finally got a mayor who isn't Irish, and now what happens!"

Kazimierz said, "The guys and me talk at work. Cermak ain't at all uppity like Thompson was. We love Cermak. He's Czech. Came over on the boat like us. He even hates Prohibition."

I didn't care personally if they banned liquor or not, but I read in my Polish newspapers that Prohibition led to organized crime and a decline in taxes that could be raised from legally selling liquor. There were speakeasies all over Chicago, and my roommates probably went to them. I didn't ask, and they didn't tell where they were when they occasionally came home drunk.

More important to me was my recollection of something Mary once told me: "Mayor Cermak cares about us teachers. Luckily, I get paid by the Catholic schools. It isn't much, but it's better than nothing. Lately, Chicago Public School teachers haven't gotten paid because of the Depression. Mayor Cermak is very concerned about the teachers' welfare."

I thought that perhaps Cermak was going to talk with the President about that very issue when he took Roosevelt's bullet.

∽

Now, instead of lying in bed, I tuned in with the fellows every evening to The Polish radio station to hear how Cermak was faring. Reporters said he still obsessed about political matters while he laid gravely wounded in a Miami Hospital. One reporter snuck in to see him and recorded something Cermak said. "I do not know if I'm going to get well. I hope whoever succeeds me will make his first duty the money owed the teachers. If this will have helped me get loans…I am glad I was shot. This bit of lead is not too burdensome for me to carry. For a long time, I have had lead in my heart over the teachers' distress."

Mary was right about what a good man Cermak was.

A few weeks later, Anton Cermak died. When we heard the radio announcement, each of us showed our feelings in a different way. I winced. Peter cried. Kazimierz cursed.

14

THE RETURN

From the moment I came to the United States, I saved every penny I could because I wanted to use my savings to visit my family in Poland. Despite the challenging financial times, Uncle's painting business was holding on, and I still had a dribble of portrait commissions.

Peter's words about me not being responsible for Mary's death made an impression on me. I gradually shoved Guilt out the door. Even though it left behind an odor that hadn't quite disappeared, I felt I had a right to be happy again.

One stroke of good luck was that I met a gentleman at Nowak's who ended up being a client. You couldn't miss him when he strode into the restaurant. A tall man dressed in an expensive suit and tie with perfectly quaffed hair, he didn't quite seem to fit at a humble place like Nowak's. Apparently Krysztof knew him. He brought the man to my table and introduced us.

"I think I saw you on the opening night of your exhibit at the Lewis Hotel. I think you mainly did portraits." the man said.

"I'm sorry there was so much going on that I'm afraid I didn't see you."

"My name is Benjamin Kane, and I'm the soon-to-be proprietor of a restaurant going up down the street..."

Still standing with Mr. Kane, Krysztof interjected, "This man could be a rival...I guess that's how it's said in English...but his restaurant will be much different from mine."

"Yes, that is true, Krysztof. You close at 4:00PM, and my establishment doesn't open until 6:00 PM. We have a dress code, and our food will be expensive." He put an apologetic arm on Krysztof's shoulder. "No offense, I love your Polish food here."

Mr. Kane proceeded to explain to me, "Mr. Durzynski—is it?—I've been coming to Nowak's for a few months because I've been trying to get my restaurant organized and I need a place to eat lunch. I'm not Polish, but you can't beat the Pierogi, cabbage rolls and pork cutlet here."

"I wholeheartedly agree," I said ,wondering how long these fellows were going to stand next to my table.

After finally asking if he could sit down by me, Mr. Kane said, "I'm glad I've met you. I've been thinking I'd like to have my portrait painted. I'd want it to be nice and big, and then I'd put in in the restaurant."

I perked up. "It would be a pleasure to paint you, Mr. Kane. How about if you come to my home studio this Saturday, and we could discuss it, if you'd like?"

Benjamin Kane did just that. When he arrived, I told him, "I want to depict you as the successful businessman you are. For your sittings, please wear your very best clothing and jewelry."

When he came to pose for the first time, Mister Kane wore a tuxedo and a formidable gold ring. He sat back with a smile and a look of self-satisfaction. I painted him as the handsome man he was and endowed him with the extra weight he carried because of eating and drinking well. I made it clear in my portrait that this man had achieved what he wanted in life. I thought to myself, *Yes, I truly do paint in the Art Deco Style!*

Benjamin Kane loved the elegant way in which I depicted him. I felt good that he liked the portrait, and his payment would give me more much-needed money for my upcoming journey.

When I was able to take my trip back to Poland,

I took the Mauritania cruise liner and enjoyed staying in the upper quarters this time. By now my mother was living with one of my brothers and his family in Bydgoszcz, located on the Vistula and Brda rivers in Northern Poland. The city had a beautiful waterfront, exquisite Art Nouveau buildings, and a thriving economy—all of which told me I didn't have to worry about my mother.

When Mama first laid eyes on me, she yelled, "Florian! Florian!" She kissed me and hugged me so tightly I thought she'd never let me go. The whole family came from nearby cities and villages and wined and dined me for the two months I was there.

I thought back to a quote I had written down in my little notebook of great quotes. Cesare Pavese, a young Italian novelist, said in one of his short stories, "We do not remember days, we remember moments."

The days flew by, but the moments I remembered were seeing my father in the features of my nine-year-old nephew, savoring my sister's exquisite pierogi, attending Mass at the 500-year-old St. Martin and St. Nicholas Cathedral, and crying with my country uncle who lost his farm and had to move to the city.

And I remembered the moment when one of my brothers and I sat outside taking in the beauties of the Vistula River. He said to me, "You know you could come back here to live. We have our freedom now, and you can see that things aren't so bad."

"I still don't trust the Germans or the Russians. You've probably heard of that Hitler guy…"

"Oh, yes, we all have. But let him do what he wants in Germany. I think he'll have his hands full there."

Anger welled up in me. "I remember our mother lamenting about what the Germans did in 1915, though. How they ordered the destruction of Polish factories that might compete with theirs. Many of our laborers were reduced to starvation, but the Germans didn't care."

My brother scratched his head and frowned. "I forgot all about that. It didn't happen around where we lived so I didn't see any evidence of it. I was only about fifteen at the time. Too busy chasing girls, I guess."

I explained, "From a young age, I've paid attention to what they call 'politics.' I miss you folks greatly, but the United States doesn't have neighbors who are constantly trying to invade, and the people in Chicago have purchased my art. That's what I wanted, and I haven't been disappointed." Holding back tears, I added, "I can't fully enjoy living in America because you and the family are not with me"…Choked up, I paused… "but forgive me for wanting to remain there."

My brother took his drink and raised it in a toast, "Don't feel bad, Florian. I congratulate you. You've convinced me that you made a wise choice for yourself, and we'll be all right here."

PART TWO
1933-1938

15

DOWN, THEN UP

No sooner did I return to the States than really difficult financial times hit America. I was glad I took the trip back to Poland when I did.

Hardly anyone was interested in getting their portrait painted, and the few who could afford the luxury probably knew they would look grim. In addition, since many people lost their jobs, they couldn't afford to get the exterior or interior of their houses painted. So, just working for Uncle a couple days a week, Peter and I got thinner. One evening we showed each other how we literally had to tighten our belts to keep up our pants. Kazimierz worked fewer days also because the advent of refrigerated railroad cars and trucks made it more economical for people to slaughter their animals on-site rather than send them to the stockyards.

∽

Now when I went to Nowak's, I ordered oatmeal or museli because it was cheaper than my usual Polish favorites. I tried to find a used newspaper. I'd be sneaky about it, wanting to hide that I couldn't afford the few cents for a new one. Without words, Krysztof came to understand that I was almost broke. He started making a big deal of not wanting to let used newspapers go to waste and would deliver an abandoned one to me as if I were doing a heroic deed by reading it.

However, in the midst of my worrying, something wonderful happened. I'll never forget the date—December 15, 1933—when I opened the paper and read a story that seemed too good to be true. The Works Progress Administration (WPA) was adding a new branch in Illinois to employ men and women. It was an arts program for talented but unemployed artists, and it mainly would have the artists paint murals. I exclaimed "What!" and got so excited I spilled my coffee.

Dishtowel in hand, Krysztof dashed over, looking concerned.

I said, "Luck has found me! I'm going to get a regular job as an artist!"

Rising from my chair, I hurriedly put the money for my breakfast into Krysztof's palm. When I looked back, I saw Krysztof staring at me with his mouth agape.

Almost slipping on the ice a couple times on my way home, I walked as fast as I could. Then, I put on my three-piece suit and scurried to the elevated train to take me to downtown Chicago. The article said applications were being taken that very day in Room 1135 of the Field Building on 135 S. LaSalle.

Turning the corner at Jackson and looking towards

LaSalle Street, I was surprised to see people lined up outside the building. When I neared the group and heard them talking about how they hoped to get into Illinois' WPA program, I felt defeated. *With so many other applicants, how could I ever get a spot?* As I shuffled along in the slow-moving line, I looked up and marveled at the height of the Field building. It must have been fifty stories high. The exterior was made of limestone and, as I saw when I entered, the interior was full of Art Nouveau style black granite walls and decorative elements around the elevators and mailboxes. Other than those details, all the building's lines, inside and out, were straight—so modern that even Mies van der Rohe from the Bauhaus might approve.

    I couldn't believe that a government work program for unemployed artists was officed in such an elegant place. As I neared Room 1135, I got nervous. *Would I be able to make myself understood?* But I had no reason to worry yet because the man who managed our line said that meetings were closed for the day. He gave me a slip of paper for an appointment in January. It was just a few weeks away, but I feared that by then all the positions would be filled.

    Four weeks later, I returned to the Field Building.

    When I walked into Room 1135, I was surprised at how spare the office was in comparison to the rest of the building. However, I knew it would be irresponsible for the government to invest in fancy oak desks and elegant chairs when they were supposed to be funding the work of us down-and-out artists.

A middle-aged woman with a conservative-looking suit, makeup-free face and hair pulled back under a simple but stylish hat sat behind a large metal desk.

She smiled and said, "I am Increase Robinson, and I manage the Illinois Arts Program."

She looked at a piece of paper on her desk. "And you, I believe, are Mister Durzynski. Am I correct?"

I responded with a nervous "yes."

"Pleased to meet you, Mr. Durzynski. We are really looking for mural painters, but they are hard to come by in the Chicago area. We've made it known to schools, post offices and other public institutions that we could do murals for them because the WPA is supposed to make art that is available for public viewing. But we need qualified artists to do them."

Increase frowned. She looked like she'd been trying her best—unsuccessfully—to hire muralists for the WPA. "What kind of artistic experience have you had?"

"I studied under Wojciech Weiss in Poland …"

"My goodness! I hate to interrupt, but through my work in the arts, I have learned of Weiss' wonderful expressive portraits and landscape painting. I am impressed, Mr. Durzynski. However, I interrupted you. Please tell me more about your experience."

"I have been painting since I was able to tie my shoes. I went to the Kraków Academy of Fine Arts, studied in Paris and have done numerous portraits for the last seven years."

"I'm sorry, Mr. Durzynski. I didn't quite understand what you said."

I thought, *How can I explain my impediment? Will Increase Robinson respond as kindly as Felice Walkowicz and Pola Negri?* Each word with my terrible diction could destroy whatever chance I had to succeed.

However, I forged ahead. With my hands tightly clutching my chair's arm rests, I spoke as clearly and slowly as possible, "You may not have understood me because I have a cleft palate. I had surgery for it when I was a child, but I still have problems speaking clearly. I'm so sorry."

Increase became apologetic. "Oh, no, no. I am the one to be sorry. I didn't realize what was wrong…or maybe I should say why I couldn't understand you. I will listen with the utmost of patience from now on, and please forgive me if I ask you to repeat something."

I breathed a sigh of relief. Increase proved to be one of the people I met in my adulthood who would support someone who admitted an inadequacy. Perhaps these individuals also had an impediment or a serious problem that wouldn't go away. Like me, maybe they asked themselves, "Why? Why me? Why do I have this issue?"

After I repeated what I said about my artistic background, Increase responded with the utmost respect, "I am quite impressed about your studies with Weiss and your accomplishments in portraiture, but do you think you'd be able to do murals?"

I thought for a moment and then spoke as distinctly as possible. "Why don't you come to my apartment and see the large painting I did on our wall?"

Two weeks later, Increase came to see it. As she

looked on admiringly, she said, "You've painted a lovely artistic scene of our Midwest. If you add some people working together harvesting crops or just enjoying the beauties of nature, you will have what it takes to be the kind of muralist we want." Then speaking as if from a textbook, she said, "We are looking for artists who will depict The American Scene in a way that radiates optimism and hope as well as the value of hard work. I think you can do that."

I could have kissed Increase Robinson.

But then she added a caveat. "However, first I want you and all the other accepted WPA artists to research mural painters—especially the Mexican muralists—to see how they did their wall painting. The United States has not yet had a mural tradition. I hope that our WPA artists will change that!"

I began reading everything I could about the theories and murals of Diego Rivera and David Sigueros. Rivera's work was in the news a lot. Sometimes it evoked controversy. In my desire to see more of the country as well as to get the WPA job, I decided to take a train Northeast to the Detroit Institute of Art to see Diego Rivera's latest murals.

The day before I left, I received a letter from Juri. Not having heard from him for a while, I tore it open and read it while still standing inside our front hall.

Not an Ordinary Artist

Dear Florian,
May 11th, 1933

I've been painting at a studio rented by a few of us former Bauhaus students here in Berlin. We are actually selling our work, but something terrible has happened in Germany. I told you about those brown shirts and that guy named Adolph Hitler. Germany's chancellor, Hindenberg, gave all his powers to Hitler a couple months ago. Hitler's a dictator and a cruel one at that. In March, he set up something called a "work camp" in Dachau for political prisoners—people who challenge his authority.

I hate that. But now I hate something else even more. Just last night Hitler ordered a book burning, targeting "un-German" authors. I heard that a book by one of your Americans was even burned...a book by Helen Keller who championed disabled people and women's rights. Hitler thinks disabled people are inferior and should somehow be done away with so he can create a pure Aryan race. What an idiot!

Although my art is selling well in Berlin, I've got to get back to Poland. I can't stand the atmosphere here, but I'm afraid to return home because who knows how the Nazis will start influencing things there? You know how much trouble we've had with Germany and Russia in the past.

And so, I'm taking an outside chance by asking you something. Could you possibly sponsor me to come to the United States?

Don't worry if you can't. Thankfully, I am not Jewish so my life is not in danger with those damned Nazis.

I'm glad to share with you, Florian, that people here seem to like my art, but I am sorry to have such dismal news about the political situation. Hopefully, this will all blow over. Hopefully, the Germans will recognize Hitler as an evil tyrant and get rid of him somehow.

Regards,
Juri

Juri's desperation jumped from the page. He was so miserable and had so little hope for the future. I wanted to grant his request, sponsor him, and create a home for him here, but I had no steady income. Even though the WPA held promise for work, it seemed like it would be sporadic. In one of the clauses of my contract, the WPA said they would only hire people who had been in America for three or more years. So, Juri couldn't get a job with them. And work with my uncle had slowed to a trickle.

An immigration clerk would probably never deem me able to provide financially for my friend. And Juri couldn't claim that he'd have immediate, steady work as an artist.

I grieved for my friend, but I also grieved for Berlin. It was a special city. How tragic it was that Hitler was ruining it and all of Germany! Although some of my German classmates were cruel because of my impediment, many were nice, and I had made some good friends there. The city itself was always bustling with excitement and glamour.

Father said he moved us to Berlin because the economy was so much better there than in Poland. Many other Poles came to work and live in Berlin. The city was only about 90 miles from Poland's border.

Hearing about Hitler, I thought, *I'm glad I chose to come to the U.S. Even though I miss my family I am happy I am living in a democracy where a president or chancellor doesn't have the power to do whatever he wants. People here would never put up with that!*

I wrote to Juri that my heart broke for him, but I couldn't sponsor him because I didn't have enough income and couldn't get him a job. However, I reassured him that he wasn't in imminent danger because Hitler and those Nazis didn't seem to bother people who weren't Jewish or disabled. While explaining all this, I squeezed my handkerchief so tightly that my fingers hurt for the next couple of days.

The first step in getting to see Rivera's murals was taking a streetcar downtown to Union Station. With its tall Corinthian columns and marble staircases, the station was beautiful, but it dredged up bad memories... memories from my immigration experience. My uncle was supposed to meet me in New York City when our ship docked, but while I was kept in that hospital for several days, he gave up on me, thinking that maybe I'd missed the boat. I had his phone number and called him when I finally was released. He had his brother-in-law who lived in New York come to explain to me in Polish how to take a train to this very place—Union Station. I was wound as tight as a drum all the way on the trip from New York, and as I got off the train, I wondered if my uncle would be there. *What did he look like? Did he know where to find me? Would he understand me with my impediment?* Thankfully, in the train lobby, I saw a man holding a little sign that said "Florian," and I knew I was safe. Uncle wrapped me in his arms, and we departed. As beautiful as it was, Union Station evoked anxious memories.

Departing Union Station to get to Detroit, I was relieved to gradually leave behind the sights, smells and sounds of the city. Within no time, I could see how much open space and fertile land existed in the U.S. This scenery didn't have the rolling hills and the charm that I found in my native Poland, but, nonetheless, this was the type of landscape that Increase wanted us to capture in our murals.

After my train arrived in Detroit and I took a cab to

the Detroit Institute of Arts, I went up a short flight of stairs that ushered visitors into a gigantic space called The Garden Court. The room must have been forty feet high and thirty feet wide. Scenes from Rivera's murals covered every inch of the four walls.

With the English I had acquired over the last four years, I could easily read the sign that explained the murals. It said they were commissioned by the Ford Motor Company. Diego Rivera was called upon to make auto-manufacturing look majestic. Between April and July of 1932, Rivera toured and sketched Ford's River Rouge plant and other industrial sites. He made thousands of preliminary drawings called cartoons. Then he used the fresco method of painting the murals on a coat of plaster.

Rivera and his assistants depicted people involved in all aspects of the industry from architects looking at blueprints to line workers pensively performing repetitive tasks. As I studied Rivera's masterpiece, I got so excited that I felt like a bird was fluttering in my chest.

I didn't think I'd ever have to create anything as tall as Rivera's murals. However, as time went on, I found the WPA had other plans.

16

CHOICES

ONE EVENING I received a long-distance call. An obnoxious crackling noise immediately irritated my ears, but I could tell it was my brother Ignatz. He sounded calm at first. So, in an enthusiastic manner, I said, "Hello Ignatz, how are you?"

"Not too well, Florian. I have bad news." He stuttered, "Our dear…mo… mo…mother died yesterday."

I had been standing, but now I slumped down on the chair by the hall table. I dropped the mouthpiece, and it dangled by its cord. I vaguely heard, "Florian, Florian, are you there?"

In a daze, I picked up the mouthpiece.

"Yes, I'm here. What happened?"

"A week ago, Mama started coughing a lot. Thought she just had a cold. Then had trouble breathing. I took her to the doctor. The doctor said I should take her to the hospital. Said her pulse was weak. He gave her tests."

I interrupted. "Why didn't you tell me this when it was happening?"

"We thought it was something she'd recover from. She could sit up and talk and everything. But when the doctor got the test results back, he said she had something called Congestive Heart Failure."

"Oh, how I wish I could have talked with her."

"We do too, Florian. You know you were very special to Mama. Yesterday, the nurses put her into a wheelchair, and we took her to the telephone on her ward to talk to you. As we wheeled her along, her head fell forward, she took two big breaths, and she…you know what I am going to say…"

"She passed," I said, feeling as bereft as when my girlfriend Mary died.

When I regained my composure to some extent, I said, "I could try to come for the…the…funeral."

Ignatz's voice tightened. "Things aren't looking good for Poland right now. All this stuff with Hitler…I think you should wait…especially since Mama's gone now…"

I was consumed by memories of Mama—from the way she cooked to the way she looked, from the way she scolded me to the way she comforted me. It was unfathomable that I'd never see her again.

I was tempted to cry out like when Mary died, "Why? Why my mother?" But this was different. Mama was much older and had her turn to lead a full life. I knew I would grieve, but I couldn't question why she was taken from me. People die when they got old. That's all there is to it.

Yet, I still took to my bed.

As I went into my third day of mourning, Peter came to my room. Quietly, he sat on the simple wooden chair next to my bed.

I shared with Peter, "I made a really big choice coming to America. I knew I was giving up a lot back home…and now I couldn't be with my mother before she died. Choices change lives, and it's so hard to know if you've made the right one."

Peter scratched his head. "We make choices every day…big and little. You made a big choice coming here, but you had important reasons for it, I bet."

I sat up in my bed. "I did have reasons, but when I made my choice, maybe I didn't think enough about the consequences—like not being there for Mama when she needed me."

"But she had your sister and brothers and all your nieces and nephews."

"Yes, they were there for her, but selfishly speaking, it would have made me feel better to hold her hand in her last days. It's so hard not to be able to say…to say goodbye."

And that's when it became fathomable: I would never see my mother again. I sighed deeply.

Then Peter said, "You're making me think about my choices. I'm 27 years old. Should I be happy just being a house painter or should I want more?"

I thought for a while, then said, "You know what I think, Peter. There's a certain joy in making a room look prettier than it was before."

"I admit I do like that feeling and how people's faces light up when they see the results of my hard work." Then Peter paused, and a laugh boiled up in him. "And I do like painting in the lines. I'm remembering how we talked about how Kazimierz could never paint within the lines."

"Yes, I remember it well. He makes a fine hog butcher, but painting within the lines would probably not be for him. In your case, if you like your job and do it well, you're probably making a good choice by sticking with it," I assured Peter.

"Thanks, Florian. That sets my mind at ease. Talking like this has helped me and hopefully you. Let's go in the kitchen and make a pot of coffee."

Peter sprung up from his chair, and I slowly made my way out of the bed. It helped me to try to help Peter. It helped me almost as much to the see the sunshine streaming through the kitchen window, to hear the birds chirping, and to smell the coffee brewing.

17

THE PROCESS

Increase Robinson sent me a letter informing me of when to come to her office for further instructions. When I arrived, I was surprised that others were present also. Two fellows were already there, and then a woman and two men joined us.

Increase began in her deliberate but sincere tone, "I welcome all of you to be mural painters for the WPA."

Our relief was palpable. "Oohs" and "ahs' escaped from our mouths. We got hired!

At that point, Increase sneezed and looked in her desk drawers for a tissue. This gave me an opportunity to glance at the others. They seemed to be between 20 and 45 years old. Their clothes were casual. Their hair looked like it had barely been combed. Their shoes looked like they had rarely been polished. Wanting to understand them and not judge them, I concluded that these people probably valued ideas more than appearance. I wore my usual three-piece suit. Going forward, I wanted to continue giving the subjects of my portraits a majestic look, but I thought that to "fit in" with my fellow artists it wouldn't hurt for me to look less formal.Increase continued, "The Illinois Arts Council has sent out letters to many public institutions like schools and post offices. We said we would happily offer them inspiring and decorative murals painted by talented artists. If they accept our offer, we will meet with their representatives to find out what they want. The institution's only expense would be the cost of supplies, but in these hard times it may be difficult for them to come up with the money. We don't want to turn away any interested group, but it may take a while from signing a contract, to getting the funds, to beginning the project."

A cheerful- looking young guy, with a thick head of black, curly hair and an affable grin, asked, "How would you decide which artist would work with which institution?"

"That's a good question, Mr. Goldman. By now, I have met with you all of you individually and know each person's style. When I receive a request, I will figure out which one of you might be best to meet that institution's needs. Then I will set up a meeting with you and a committee from the institution to find out their preferences for subject matter and theme. Once those ideas are crystallized, I'll have you make up sketches. I'll submit them to our advisory board, and if they approve, the artist and I will bring them back to the institution in question. Sometimes one or more changes will be requested, and we will ask our artist to make them."

After this thorough explanation, she took a deep breath, hesitated and then asked, "Do you have any questions?"

First, the woman spoke up. She was short and slender with black hair that she brushed up in a porcupine-like style. She wore a white blouse, and—unusual as it was for a woman—pants. "What if we need help? I know when I've executed large paintings, it's been nice to have someone with me if I'm on a ladder to hand me a different brush or something."

"Miss Piotrowski, we may hire at a reduced rate some assistants, but it may be that you can help one another in between murals, and we will pay you also at a reduced rate."

After a minute of silence, Increase said, "Well, if there are no further questions, wait to hear from me. It won't be long. I'll call you as soon as we find an institution that wants something in your particular style."

Mr. Goldman raised his hand.

Increase asked, "Yes?"

"Where and when do we collect our paychecks? And, if I should be so bold to ask, how much will we get paid?"

Increase shook her head and looked like she was reprimanding herself. "I'm so sorry. I did leave out that very important part. You will start as a Grade Two artist and make $87.60 per month. If your work is of high quality, you will graduate to Grade One and receive $94.00 per month. Those who linger in Grade Two will be assigned to teaching responsibilities like at Hull House or the Howell Settlement House where the WPA will give art classes to children and adults. That is not a punishment but an important job that gives others the opportunity to create art. Miss Augusta Savage in New York City runs the largest WPA program in the country, and her art classes have produced some new, highly regarded young artists."

"Thank you," Mr. Goldman said.

Then Increase gave us a downtown address and said that the WPA offices would be moving there very soon. "This elegant building was only a temporary site for us to begin our work. You will probably see a lot of each other, and I am excited as we go forward together in this great endeavor."

And then in her proper way, she dispatched us. "Now, goodbye and have a nice day."

We walked as a group back to the front entrance of the building.

Goldman said, "Hey, I know a place around the corner where we can get coffee. Wanna go?"

Two of the artists said they regretted that they had other commitments, but we all agreed we'd probably see each other again when we picked up our paychecks or worked on a project together.

With my impediment, I felt shy around new people. However, I wanted to join the remaining group. So, I did.

The porcupine-headed woman, Miss Piotrowski, said, "This is quite a posh area with the Board of Trade building right across the street. Take me to a cheap coffee house!"

Goldman said, "Yeah, but let's take a moment to

appreciate The Board of Trade. It was just completed a couple years ago, and it's the tallest building in Chicago now."

As we looked from the bottom to the top of the huge slender building, one of the guys said, "Do you see the setbacks at places to emphasize its verticality? It's amazing! Inside, I hear it's got black and white polished marble, and supposedly the world's largest light fixture. Seems to me it's done in the Art Deco style."

I smiled to myself because I knew my portraits were in the Art Deco style also. It was so nice to feel I was in such good company with The Board of Trade.

Goldman pointed upwards. "See that huge statue on its top. I heard it's made of aluminum. It's Ceres, the goddess of grain. I like the way Art Deco uses modern materials…no bronze statues here."

One of the other fellows said, "Oh, and this street's called the Board of Trade Canyon, because the trade building sits at the end of the street perpendicular to the other buildings. Everything begins and ends here. This is the only street in Chicago like this."

"You know Chicago's been called the Architecture Capital of the World," said Miss Piotrowski. "I, for one, feel lucky to live here—to be able to see all these new, modern buildings."

I was entranced with Chicago's architecture, but as we walked towards the coffee shop, I couldn't help but notice individuals in the recesses of buildings holding out an old hat or a tin cup in hope of receiving a handout. One person had no leg, one looked blind, and one had arms that didn't grow all the way. That all-too-familiar question popped back into my mind, "Why?" but this time it was "Why them?" In the case of these individuals, they had infirmities that were worse than mine, but, since they were begging on the streets, they probably had the extra impairment of not having family to love and help them. It seemed so unfair that some had it better than others from the time they were born. "Why? Why them?" I felt I could not rest until I found answers to these questions.

While ruminating, I searched in my pocket for change. A skinny man with a too-large, three-piece suit, urged me quietly, "Please. For my children."

This was the case of a man who fell victim to the bad economy. Although it was somewhat of a sacrifice for me, I was happy to give him a nickel. I thought, *But for the grace of God go I.*

Those heavy thoughts quickly left my mind as we entered a little, run-down coffee shop just a few blocks from the Field Building. The moment of truth was coming: I would probably have to speak with my companions for the first time.

After getting our coffee and sitting down, we made introductions. Miss Piotrowski's first name was Sophie. Goldman's first name was Isaac. The other fellows were Ethan and Richard.

When they got to me, I hesitated, then plowed ahead, "I'm Florian."

Everyone looked at me with an encouraging smile, and Isaac said, "That's an interesting name."

Sadly, this would take some explaining. "Florian is the patron saint of firefighters in Poland. There's a long story about it, but once a woman invoked his name when her house was burning down and supposedly the fire suddenly stopped."

Because I was nervous, I spoke rapidly. My audience furrowed their brows, nodded their heads as if they understood, and then made one or two comments like 'Wow' or 'Good Story,' but I don't think they fully understood me.

Isaac piped up and told us his father was a rabbi and that he wanted Isaac to become one too. Isaac said he wouldn't mind, but his need to paint was so great that he couldn't consider any other career.

Sophie said that her father was an artist. Her big family lived in Pilsen. Sophie didn't mention her heritage, but I heard that Pilsen was another neighborhood with a large concentration of Polish as well as Spanish people.

Ethan and Richard both went to the Art Institute and were grateful for the WPA because they just graduated and didn't have commissions or a job yet.

I made a few short comments as we conversed, but I could see that people looked perplexed. I decided I might as well clear the air. So, I laid it out. "If you notice, I can be hard to understand. This is because I have a cleft palate and I still have a strong Polish accent. I just came here in '29."

Speaking as slowly and clearly as possible, I added with a smile to put people at ease, "If you ever can't understand me, let me know and I'll repeat myself."

Everyone seemed to relax. Now that they understood my condition and felt free to ask me to repeat things, they quit looking at me so nervously when I spoke.

18

CITIZENSHIP

WITHIN NO TIME, Increase called and asked me to do a mural for Greenman school in Aurora, Illinois—a short trip from Chicago. She said that the Greenman School PTA had advanced the money to the school to pay for the mural.

The murals were supposed to depict scenes about early Americans who went out West and ended up in what became Aurora. I thought it was strange that I, as an immigrant from Poland, was asked to depict such a specific period in American history. I went to our local library and studied book after book with pictures and stories about people going out West in covered wagons, etc.

One evening Peter saw me pouring over the books and remarked, "This is hilarious. You just came here, and you're supposed to become an expert on a part of American history that you probably never heard of back in our homeland."

I smiled, "Yes, it is kind of comical when you think about it. But I've always liked studying history. The history of Poland is so long. United States history is very short, but I find it fascinating."

This job entailed creating two framed murals on large canvases. When I completed and installed them, the Greenman School held an open house, and hundreds of students, parents and teachers attended. I was touched by the fact that the Aurora community cared enough about art to raise the money for the murals and then came out to see them. I hated that I could not attend, but I came down with a terrible cold and cough. A news photographer sent me a paper with pictures of the festivities, and Increase said more jobs would be coming my way.

After that, I had nothing to do for a while. So, I had time to think, and think I did. I pondered whether I should become a U.S. citizen. I decided to go to City Hall to obtain more information.

A clerk showed me a blank application for naturalization.

He asked, "In what country were you born?"

"Germany," I said without enthusiasm.

"Then you would have to renounce all loyalties to The German Reich," he responded.

I felt my face break into a smile. "Gladly. Can I sign on the dotted line now?"

"No, not yet. Let me explain everything else to you. Then you can take these papers home and fill them out at your leisure."

The line behind me lengthened. I didn't want to inconvenience people, but the kind clerk insisted on being thorough.

"I will read the official explanation. 'Naturalization or becoming a citizen, is a two-step process that takes a minimum of five years. After residing in the United States for two years, an alien can file a declaration of intention (first papers) to become a citizen. After three additional years, the alien can petition for naturalization (second papers). If the petition is granted and a test is passed, a certificate of citizenship is issued to the new citizen.'"

Walking out of City Hall with my paperwork in hand, I felt I was on the brink of making a momentous decision.

∽

I became sentimental about my life back in Poland. Although I'd been in the U.S for six years. I felt like Poland was my true home. I had one foot in America and one in Poland, and straddling the two was difficult at times. I wanted to make a choice and quit straddling.

Then I received another letter from Juri.

Dear Florian,

My heart aches because some of my fellow graduates from the Bauhaus are being treated cruelly by the Nazi regime. I correspond with Otti Berger who, I think, is one of the most innovative textile artists of the twentieth century. She opened a very successful business in Berlin. Companies across Europe came to her for modern window coverings, upholstery and rugs, but, because she is Jewish, she has been banned from practicing her art in Germany. Yet, she says it's almost impossible to get out because the Nazis will take 80% of all your assets, and other countries will not take in a Jewish immigrant. She writes that she is suffering immeasurably as she tries to figure out what she can do.

Things are definitely getting bad in Europe. You made a wise choice by emigrating to America.

Regards,
Juri

Juri's letter made me think about how I'd recently heard some individuals on streetcars or at coffee shops complaining that Jewish people wanted to escape from Germany but that these immigrants could take away their jobs in the U.S. I wanted to tell them, *How foolish you are! Would it kill us to have one more textile designer? Perhaps a person like Otti Berger could even create more American jobs by launching a successful business.*

Nevertheless, I thought that although the U.S. was imperfect, it had more pluses than minuses for me. Be that as it may, something in me told me to wait to apply for naturalization.

19

OH, NO!

"Whew! How did I ever agree to this?" I said to myself.

I heard Isaac laughing but didn't want to look down.

Two weeks earlier, a man named George Thorp called me. He said Increase Robinson was assigned to another position, he was my new boss, and he had a job for me. I cursed him as I stood on a ladder 30 feet above the floor. I felt like I was Diego Rivera, but I didn't want to be.

Painting the mural at this school—Newton Bateman—was far more difficult than I'd expected. Dealing with the height was terrifying. There was no way out, though. It was the culmination of numerous designs, proposals, and meetings with the school's representatives.

As far as Increase Robinson was concerned, I heard that she still worked for the WPA but was put into a more administrative position. I respected her for her organization, her clear sense of mission for us, and her kindness to me with my speech problem. I hoped that George Thorp would be cut of a similar cloth.

Thorp and I had met with the principal and two teachers at Bateman. During our long meeting, Bateman's committee said they wanted a scene depicting nature in a pleasant, optimistic way that would be a backdrop for their school plays. It seemed that procuring the money for this mural project was not a problem.

Then they took us to see the wall for the mural. After we walked up a short flight of stairs, I found myself on a stage with curtains pulled to the side. As I turned to study the wall, I gulped. This would be a very tall mural. It would be in a dark area about fifteen feet from the front of the stage. So, to get the attention of the onlookers, I would have to paint my country images in more vibrant colors than was true of real nature. I could certainly do that, but, oh, that height did not appeal to me.

The first time I climbed the ladder I felt my stomach turn. Children ran around screaming below because the seats were removed from the auditorium for their recesses. I feared that a child's earsplitting cry could startle me and make me fall.

Fortunately, George Thorp assigned Isaac and a couple of beginning WPA artists to assist me. I bumped into Isaac often when we artists congregated at 211 N. Michigan to pick up our paychecks. I was drawn to this friendly guy who oozed confidence, intelligence and good humor.

In preparation for this project, I had drawn a picture

of exactly how I wanted the mural to look. In my home studio, I divided my drawing into squares.

At the school, I needed to replicate this drawing onto the gigantic theater wall. But first, my assistants and I had to piece together individual canvases, because the largest canvas one could buy was only 72 inches by 36 inches. We would have to glue the canvases together onto the wall and make sure they butted against each other perfectly.

So, while the children played, Isaac, my two assistants and I climbed the tall ladders to brush the glue onto the highest section of the wall.

"Eeyou!" a spine-tingling scream rang out followed by a loud thud. I looked down to see my assistant Jake sprawled on his back. We immediately climbed down our ladders, went to him and yelled, "Are you all right? Jake, Jake, are you all right?"

Jake moved his body delicately. Then said, "I think I am."

In his left hand, Jake still held a jar filled with glue. His right arm, along with his glue-filled brush, hit the floor full force. Isaac picked up the brush and got a rag with some turpentine to wipe up the glue.

"Here, take our hands, and see if you can move if we slowly try to pull you up," I said.

Looking dazed, Jake responded weakly, "I think that will work."

Isaac and I each took a hand and pulled. Jake gradually got to a standing position. "I'm okay… I think. Maybe that glue made me dizzy."

We each put an arm around Jake and slowly walked with him to the front office. Looking very worried, one of the secretaries said she would call a cab for him when Jake said he felt well enough to go home.

In a shaky voice, Jake said, "I'm so sorry to disrupt our work today, Florian. I think I'll be well enough to come in tomorrow." He hesitated for a moment. "I need the work."

"Call me tonight at my home number. If you're too stiff or sore to make it in, I'll just sign you in anyhow, and no one will need to know."

As conscientious as I was, I believed this was the right thing to do.

Still reeling from Jake's accident, the rest of us had to get right back up on the ladders and attach the canvases to the glue before it dried.

By the time we finished, we were spent. My right arm ached, and my nerves were a wreck. But when we went down to the auditorium floor to assess our work, I was pleased. All the canvases fit together perfectly, not a seam showing. Then I launched a silent prayer to the Holy Mother that Jake would fully recover.

Isaac said, "It's too bad about Jake, but I think he'll be all right. We really accomplished something here today! Why don't we go out to celebrate?"

I said, "I'm not much of a party-er."

"I know how to party, Florian, but I can tell you're not the raucous type. My idea for celebrating with you is very subdued. We could have a light dinner and then you could come to my house and chat with my parents. I think you'd like them."

"Okay," I said wearily. "That sounds like my kind of partying...especially today after all that work."

Isaac said, "My idea may entail more streetcar riding than you'd like. It will take about thirty minutes to get from here to a place I'd like to go for dinner. Then we'd have to take a streetcar to my parents.'"

"What's the name of the restaurant?"

"Nathan's Deli. They have great kosher food as well as other dishes you might like."

"Ok. It might help me unwind and get my mind off everything."

"That was a sticky business today," quipped Isaac.

We both chuckled and began our celebration with a spring in our step. But I added something, "Let's not tell your parents about what happened with Jake. It's not going to help to dwell on it."

"Good idea, Florian."

I loved Nathan's Deli. I wasn't familiar with some of the foods on the menu like matzo ball soup, Gefilte fish, and lox, but Isaac convinced me to at least try the soup with a pastrami sandwich on rye. I did just that, and my taste buds enjoyed the new, unfamiliar flavors.

Isaac's family lived in a beige frame house with brown shudders and reasonably well-maintained landscaping situated under a canopy of neighborhood trees. I think Isaac said we were in the Edgewater neighborhood. When Isaac opened the door, his father was reading a book. As he slowly pushed himself up from his easy chair, his face lit up, and he immediately stretched his hand out to greet me.

After Isaac explained that I was a friend from the WPA and that we were working on a mural together, Mr. Goldman said, "So glad Isaac has brought home a fellow artist. Welcome, and have a seat. I'm afraid Mrs. Goldman is down the street visiting her mother."

Looking directly at me, he asked, "How was your day at work?"

"A bit scary," I said. "Had to get on tall ladders."

Isaac's father reacted like everyone else when they first heard me talk. He cocked his head to one side, looked at me pensively, and tried to make sense of my words.

"Don't worry, Mr. Goldman. I will try to speak slowly and clearly. Everyone has the same reaction when they first hear me talk. I have a cleft palate."

Mr. Goldman winced ever so slightly, looking like he hurt for me, but he quickly hid his reaction.

I smiled to relax him. "Now if I speak like this, can you understand me?" As slowly and as clearly as I could, I said, "We had a frightening, sticky day today. Isaac can tell you the rest."

"Yes, I did understand you this time, Young Man."

And so began my relationship with Rabbi Goldman.

The next day at Bateman I brought my design to the school. I asked Isaac to take a pencil to the canvas with me, and we split the gigantic canvas into squares to copy onto them what I had on my drawing. We used rulers and wide lead pencils. This took all day. The children quit shrieking so much when they played in the auditorium at recess. Wondering why it was so quiet, I turned around and saw a multitude of eyeballs focused on us. I guess this is what the WPA meant about producing "art for the people." These little people were involved in the process, even if it was only to see how an artist worked.

20

THE OLDEST QUESTION

AFTER THIS CHALLENGING day—which happened to be a Friday—Isaac called and asked me if I'd like to come to his house on Sunday evening for dinner. "My father was so enthused about meeting you that he wanted my mother to meet you too."

"How can I refuse?" I said joyfully.

"My mother says she will make beef brisket. I bet you can handle that."

I anticipated that arriving at the Goldman house for the second time in a week would make the first few moments of conversation easier. By then, Isaac and his father would have explained about my speech problem, and Mrs. Goldman wouldn't be surprised.

Isaac's mother was short and chubby like her

husband. She wore a white apron and a red and white scarf that covered everything from three inches above her scalp and a couple of inches below where her graying black shoulder-length hair ended.

The beef brisket along with an assortment of cooked vegetables was delicious. I profusely thanked Mrs. Goldman. She encouraged us to have another helping and got up a couple of times to replenish the serving bowls.

After I thanked her again, I asked if I could dry the dishes, but she said with a smile, "No, I am happy to take care of things myself."

Mr. Goldman took us to his study. The walls held shelves with more books than I'd ever seen in a place besides a library. Mr. Goldman said, "I always tell my wife I'll help with the cleanup, but she seems to like doing it herself."

Isaac, his father and I began talking about a wide range of subjects from the U.S. press' poor coverage of Hitler's actions against Jews to recent attempts by stockyards workers to strike for better hours and conditions. Just like the first time I met him, Mr. Goldman impressed me as a man who was very knowledgeable and cared about others.

Out of the blue, I found myself blurting out that question I'd repeatedly asked the air but not a real person. "Mr. Goldman, you are a rabbi, and in your work, you must meet many people who are physically or emotionally sick. Many have had a crisis—like they lost a limb, or their child was still-born. Do they ever ask you, 'Why? Why me?'"

Mr. Goldman nodded. "That's the oldest question since the beginning of time. Many people have had occasion to ask themselves that. They feel they are good people and don't deserve what has happened to them."

"That sounds like me. I'm sure you can figure out that I'm asking because...because of my impediment. And then my father died suddenly when I was only nine."

Isaac frowned in sympathy, and a new crease appeared between Mr. Goldman's eyebrows.

"I'm so sorry about that," the rabbi said.

I often say to myself, 'Why was I born with a cleft palate? Why did my father die when I was so young? 'Why? Why me?' I haven't spoken out loud about how I feel because I haven't wanted to make my parents and friends feel bad."

Mr. Goldman took a deep breath and began, "I'm glad you chose to share this tonight, Florian. Many of us have questions or demons in the dark recesses of our soul, but if we bring them to light, they lose their power over us. Otherwise, they stay bottled up and we feel like we're going to explode. Sometimes people do explode, and the outcome can be bad."

A warm sensation of relaxation spread over my whole body. "It does feel good to finally talk about these things."

I think that Isaac and his father were both observing the change in me. We sat together quietly.

Then I went back to my original question. "But I still ask 'Why? Why me?' why have I been dealt two tragic blows."

"As far as the speech impediment is concerned, I am surprised this is still a difficult issue for you. And I'll tell you why. When we first met and you noticed I reacted to your unique way of speaking, you didn't get flustered. You simply explained it in what I thought was a calm manner, and then we went forward. I would think that some people who have not dealt with their cleft palate would become shy and not want to engage."

I said, "A couple people have shown acceptance when I explained it to them, and strange as it may seem, Increase Robinson was the most recent one." I looked at Isaac because he had complained about Increase's demeanor once or twice.

Isaac groaned. "She seemed so stern to me."

"But you must admit, she got things done. She hired a lot of us and found schools that wanted our murals."

"Okay, that's true," Isaac said. He seemed to consider looking at Increase in a better light.

I expressed my developing philosophy. "I think that as life goes on many of us have been dealt a bad hand in one way or another. Out of pride, people often won't admit what has gone wrong, but when they see someone else with a problem who admits he or she is suffering, these people can empathize. At some point, they probably have asked themselves, 'Why? Why me?'" I paused. "Maybe Increase is one of them."

Rabbi Goldman fingered his short salt-and-pepper beard. "Let me get this straight. You haven't found the answer to your question. Yet, you are learning how to be open and honest about what you call your impediment. And then you find that many people are understanding."

"Yes, I guess that's what I'm saying."

"That's a good thing, but maybe too you need to talk also about losing your father at such a young age…so suddenly."

I took a deep breath and tried to stay calm, but it was momentous…for better or worse…to finally delve into that subject. "I didn't want to share my sadness over my father's death. My mother tried to be strong for us, but I often saw her wipe away an unexpected tear, and sometimes I heard her crying in her bedroom."

"That must have been so hard and lonely for you, Florian."

"Yes, it was." Again, it felt good to share my feelings and have them acknowledged.

Ring! Ring! At that moment the living room phone startled us out of our reverie. Mrs. Goldman answered and came into the study. "Bella Deutsch had a heart attack today. Her children want you to come to the hospital. They say this may be her last hour."

As much as he could, Mr. Goldman sprang to his feet. "I am so sorry, Boys. Especially to you, Florian. Let's return to this subject soon."

21

VICTORY

Back at Bateman on Monday, I was ready to lay paint to the mural, but I still needed the help of Isaac and the other two fellows to hand me things and keep the ladders steady. Jake had returned to work and, though stiff and sore, he was determined to do whatever it took to be of assistance. But this mural was mine now to make wonderful or horrible.

When I mixed the colors, I had to remember that when colors dry they always look darker. So, with this knowledge and the fact that the mural would be in a dim location, I made my colors as bright as possible.

Isaac and my assistants put down drop cloths and the newly invented masking tape around the edges of the canvas. Then I began.

I started painting the top left square and then the two sections to its right. After that, I went down to the next three sections below until I went all the way to the bottom of the mural. Then I went up to the top and began the process again. My assistants handed me fresh brushes when I changed colors. This was very time consuming and demanded perfection, but at the end of the day, my assistants and I studied the mural and agreed we were off to a good start.

Again, many of the children paused in their play, stood quietly and observed. One little girl watched us the whole time. I figured she was an artist in the making. I wanted to talk with her, but I hadn't been around children for so long that I didn't know what to say. Also, I wondered if she'd be able to understand me.

After five weeks, we were finished. The four of us went to the auditorium floor and looked up and out to the back of the stage. I got tingles up and down my spine. I felt we had created an imaginative, colorful, and delightful country scene.

To evaluate the mural, George Thorp from the WPA came out and met with me and the school personnel who'd suggested its content. Together, we went to the auditorium to view it from afar, and then we climbed the stairs to the stage and studied it up close. Smiling widely, the principal shook my hand and said, "Well done." Thorp said he would contact the newspapers to take pictures and write up a statement about the mural. I found that I liked George Thorp as much as Increase Robinson.

As our last day of work was concluding, Isaac asked me to come to his house again to celebrate. "I know you won't do anything more exciting, Florian."

We surprised his mother and father who were listening to the radio and relaxing.

"Welcome, welcome," Mr. Goldman said as he went

through his slow, measured movements to pull himself up and out of his chair.

He said, "How nice to see you again, Florian."

After a discussion of how well the mural ended up, Mr. Goldman said, "Let's retire to my study and have a Manischewitz. This calls for something more potent than a glass of apple juice."

In the study, Isaac said, "This is as close to partying as Florian is going to get." Then he downed his little glass and poured himself another.

We enjoyed the wine and told Mr. Goldman how challenging the mural was. Both of us said we didn't know if our arms would ever stop aching.

"I am so happy for you two. Very few things are as satisfying as getting completely involved in a project and then having it turn out well."

Isaac and I nodded our heads in agreement. I even had a second glass of wine. Then Mr. Goldman said, "Are you in the mood to continue the conversation we started last time, Florian, or is it too serious for this night of celebration?"

Remembering why we were interrupted the last time, I asked, "If it's all right, may I inquire as to how Mrs. Deutsch fared?"

Nodding his head and frowning, Mr. Goldman said, "Not well. She died before I got to the hospital."

"Oh," I groaned. "Hopefully she's in a better place."

"Hopefully…" Mr. Goldman's voice trailed off. "But we were talking about your difficulties, Florian, and how they led you to ask, 'Why me?'"

"Yes," I said, earnestly hoping I would find some answers.

"Last time I said that at least you have developed a good way of coping with your speech challenge. If somebody doesn't understand, you explain why you have a different way of speaking, and most people respond well and are patient as you converse slowly and distinctly."

I responded, "Yes, but there are instances when I don't have time to explain and people just look at me with a puzzled expression. Like if I'm at a store and inquire about the price of something. Or even," I turned to Isaac, "Remember that little girl who kept watching me paint?"

"Oh, yeah, she was really interested."

"I had to concentrate on my work, but I would have liked to engage her in a brief conversation. Then I thought 'Forget it, it will take too long to make myself understood.' Those are the times when I ask myself that 'why' question."

"I've been thinking about your dilemma, Florian, and I've come up with a theory."

"Oh, good." I leaned forward eagerly.

"My answer is a non-answer. We need to accept that some things happen for no reason. As humans, we strive for connections. We desperately try to make sense of all that happens. Often, we magically ascribe an unexplainable tragedy like the premature death of a parent or a birth defect as having been caused by us personally. We may think things like God is trying to teach us a lesson or we are responsible in some way—rather than accept the randomness."

"That makes sense. Over the years, I've often wondered what I did to deserve this or if God had a reason for my impediment."

"You personally did nothing to deserve these difficulties at such a young age, Florian. They just happened."

Just like the last time we were together, we sat in silence for a while. Isaac and his father knew how to let new thoughts sink in.

"Something else comes to me," said Mr. Goldman as he fiddled with his little beard. "Do you think your tragedies led to you becoming the accomplished artist you are?"

I gave him a puzzled expression.

"Some of the world's highest achievers became that way because they escaped thinking about tragic events by becoming very involved with mental or physical activities that took their minds off their problems. Again, I don't think that God or some mystical force sent your difficulties to you for that reason, but the bi-product of suffering can be this absorption in something else—like art—that in the long run brings joy."

Thinking about how content I was after a day with my brushes, I responded, "You have a point."

Then Mr. Goldman said in a sweet, soothing voice like my mother used when I was a child, "Appreciate any good that your suffering has led to, and, if you find yourself thinking about your tragedies too much, say to yourself, 'Let it go. Bad things just happen to good people for no reason. It's been like that since the beginning of time, and it will continue to be like that forever.'"

Out of nowhere, Isaac broke the mood and said, "Okay, enough of all that philosophizing for now. I'm going to take Florian to my room and play my new Louie Armstrong album for him. We need to have some fun tonight!"

Reluctantly, I said, "Okay, but Rabbi Goldman, I want to continue with our conversation again soon. I find it very helpful."

The rabbi looked disappointed that his son interrupted him mid-conversation. It didn't seem right, but I'd noticed that many parents acquiesce to their children when they become adults. However, seeing as how I still was not a parent, I didn't have room to judge.

When we went to Isaac's room and he put on the album with Armstrong's trumpet and gravelly voice, I was impressed with these sounds—the likes of which I'd never heard before. I told Isaac that I liked Armstrong's style.

Isaac explained, "Yes, he's the king of what we're calling jazz now in America. He often plays in a club in Chicago." Then he changed the subject. "Listen Florian, I know I was rude down there, but while my father was sharing his insights—and I do agree with him—I was thinking about another possibility. I'm wondering if you still could do something about your speech challenge."

Holding Armstrong's album cover in my hand, I asked, "What could that be?"

"Believe it or not, Florian, at one time I thought I might like to be a singer. I have a pretty good voice. I found out about the Sherwood Music School at the Fine Arts Building in downtown Chicago. I studied under a man named Marcel Roger de Bouzon. He is known internationally for his singing voice, but he also teaches diction and elocution. I wonder if maybe—just maybe—he could help you with your speech."

I shrugged. "Isaac, I know you are well-meaning, but isn't it too late for that? Nowadays, I hear about children going for speech help, but adults? I don't know."

"You could give it a try. I still stay in touch with Marcel. I can give him a call."

"Okay," I agreed half-heartedly, thinking this path would lead to a dead end. However, the day had been a good one. I was so proud of my gigantic mural that I saw everything through a victorious lens.

22

SO MANY EMOTIONS

HUMMING A HAPPY tune when I returned home at about 11PM, I found our apartment empty, but, within no time, my two roommates bounded through the door.

Peter said, "We were down the street."

"Yeah," Kazimierz joined in. "We were talking about our futures." I caught a faint smell of beer on both his and Peter's breath, but not as strong as usual on a Friday night.

"That's always good," I said. "To plan for the future."

The guys took off their coats and put them onto the coat rack in our hall (I insisted we buy it shortly after I moved in because otherwise the guys strewed their coats around wherever they could).

Peter said, "Let's sit at the kitchen table and talk."

That sounded ominous.

When we got to the table, Kazimierz lit a cigarette and turned to Peter. "You explain it, Peter. You're better with words."

"You know how our country is in this Great Depression?"

"Do I ever!"

Peter continued, "You have your WPA job even though it's not regular. My work with your uncle has almost come to an end. Nobody has money to get their house painted..."

I waited for some big announcement.

"And you know how much I like my girlfriend, Tassia? Well, I am going to ask her to marry me, but I want to save some money for us. So, I'm thinking I'll move back to my parents' house and live there, hopefully get a job at the steel mills or something. I can't afford this rent..."

"Oh," I groaned. It hit me; the fellows were going to leave.

Kazimierz cleared his perpetually hoarse throat.

"There's not much work at the stock yards either anymore. My mother wanted me to move to the North Side here so I could get away from the gangs, but now I'm older. I ain't interested in gangs anymore, and I'm pretty sure they've forgotten about me."

"So, you want to leave too?" It was hard for me to say the words.

Kazimierz's eyes radiated an unusual tenderness. "I got to go too, Florian. You've been a great roommate, but I'm sure you can understand."

"Yes, sadly I do. Our lease is up in four months. Can you give me time until then to figure out where to move? I won't be able to manage this rent alone."

Peter said, "Sure, sure, Florian. Four months. Okay, Kazimierz?"

"Yeah, sure," Kazimierz said.

"We'll just have to keep tightening our belts a little more," Peter said half-jokingly and half-dolefully.

When I went to bed that night, I thought, *This has indeed been a day of great highs and lows.*

On the one hand, I was still thrilled with how my mural turned out and by the enthusiastic response of those who viewed it. On the other hand, I didn't want my living arrangements to change. How could I live without my breakfasts at Nowak's? How could I live without my chats with my Polish neighbors? How could I live without attending services at my beloved St. Stanislaus? I concluded that I'd try to find new roommates in West Town, but in the deep recesses of my mind I realized that might not be possible.

Sleep illuded me. With so many emotions roiling around in my head, it was difficult to focus on any one.

23

NEW BEGINNINGS

I SIGHED WITH PLEASURE as I stood on a ladder at the Francis McKay School at 6901 S. Fairfield. I thought, *Aah. It's so enjoyable to have come up with so many different shades of green.*

Three representatives from McKay said they had read about my Newton Bateman mural and wanted my artwork in their school; a newspaper art critic had given it a positive review, saying my landscape was "undulating and sensuous."

Because the McKay hallways were so dark, the reps specified that they wanted, most of all, for my murals to be colorful. They wanted a landscape scene shown from four different points of view in a way that would appeal to the children.

Each of the four murals was to be eight feet tall and 4 feet wide, and they wanted them painted on wood instead of canvas so they could hang them and move them if desired. Seeing as how I had always painted on canvas, I had to do some research.

On a warm Friday afternoon when I waited in line to pick up my check, I asked one of the other WPA artists about this. He told me to talk with a fellow back in the line who had just finished painting on wood.

The fellow said, "You must seal the wood to keep out moisture, and then prime it to strengthen adhesion between the paint and wood panel."

He emphasized, "It is imperative to sand the wood. Do it after you put on the primer and before you put on the sealer. Otherwise, your surface will be uneven. And make sure to put a good varnish over your painting when it's done. Raymond Shiva from the art supply store should be able to help you get the right stuff."

I heeded my fellow artist's words. Preparing the wood was tedious, but by now in my artistic career, I realized that many steps had to be followed before one could actually paint.

So, on the ladder now, I continued painting my trees. This time I made them differently than I did at the last school. I still had my tree leaves billowing in bunches, but I made the individual billows look almost three-dimensional by shading each one in a thick blue that made them look like globs of glue. Each "billow" had a combination of green and blue gradients. I made the higher bows or "billows" darker than the lower ones.

I was totally lost in the process. Painting made my life worth living.

The Greek god Hephaestus would have understood.

However, after I took the streetcar home that evening, I knew I had to face two challenges—figuring out where I could live and planning with Isaac to meet Marcel Roger de Bouzon.

I put off thinking about finding a new place, but I did call Isaac that evening to plan the meeting. I was always shy about meeting new people, but maybe this man could help me.

Two days later Isaac had us meet outside at the Art Institute. He said, "I wanted to meet here, because I thought maybe you'd have a good view from here of the Fine Arts Building." He pointed at a tall building across the street and said, "That's where the Sherwood Music School is housed and Marcel has his room."

Indeed, this was a good vantage point.

"Romanesque," I said, as I recollected what I had learned at the Kraków Academy of Fine Arts.

"You're right. See its massive quality, thick walls, round arches, and sturdy Corinthian columns. Just one of the many buildings that makes Chicago the Architecture Capital of the World. Thank God that Mrs. O'Leary's cow knocked over that lantern in 1871..."

"What? In one breath, you're talking about architecture and in the next about a cow. I don't understand."

"When she kicked over the lantern, most of the buildings in Chicago burnt down, and so that's why the city was rebuilt in such new, architectural styles. But now let's go across the street for our appointment."

After walking through the Fine Arts Building's ornate lobby, Isaac had us enter the elevator. Operating the elevator was a woman who wore white gloves and sat on a round chair.

As we got off on the sixth floor, I heard a disjointed combination of musical sounds from various rooms up and down the hall. Noticing my surprise, Isaac said, "This isn't called the Fine Arts Building for nothing. The Sherwood Music School has many recital rooms here, but other performing artists rent practice rooms too."

Isaac brought me to Marcel's room and knocked on the door. A sonorous voice called, "Come in."

As we entered, Marcel put down a sheet of music and rose to meet us. He was the most handsome man I'd ever seen.

Marcel Roger de Bouzon was dressed in a beige linen suit with a white collarless shirt, perfect for this warm Saturday summer morning. He had a full head of brown hair and combed it in a modern style. God gave him perfectly formed features. His chestnut brown eyes looked at me with an intensity I'd seldom experienced meeting someone new.

After Marcel and Isaac exchanged pleasantries, Marcel said, "Isaac told me a little about what you may want, but could you put it in your own words?"

"I'm sure Isaac told you I was born with a cleft palate. In about 1907, a doctor in Berlin sewed up the hole in the roof of my mouth and did a pretty good job,

I think. However, I still have trouble pronouncing some words, and I talk in a slushy, nasal way." After getting out my story, I took a deep breath. "Isaac tells me you are a master of elocution and thought maybe you could help me speak better."

Marcel asked, "May I look into your mouth, Mr. Durzynski?"

I opened wide like I was going to the dentist.

"Tilt your head back a little so I can get a good look," Marcel said.

"I can kind of see what you have there, but maybe I'll bring a small flashlight next time and get a better look. Regardless, we can get together again. I'll figure out which sounds are most difficult for you, and I will try my best to help you improve your elocution. Does that sound agreeable?"

"Oh, yes," I answered eagerly. "May I ask what your fee would be?"

"Since Isaac was one of my favorite students and is now blessing our nation with his beautiful art—as you are—let me do this for no charge. Anyhow, there's no guarantee that I can help you. I've never taken on this type of challenge before."

No matter what he could or couldn't do for my pronunciation I knew I was drawn to this man and would be happy to see him again.

We were finished with our meeting by 11:00AM. Isaac and I both had the day open, so he suggested we go to the Chicago Public Library main branch located just a few blocks down on Michigan Avenue. Isaac wanted to look up mural techniques used by Sigueros in Mexico.

Isaac raved, "Sigueros' work is amazing."

"I'd like to research his work too, but I think I'd better look up information on cleft palate."

As we walked through the building, I marveled at the design of the library. Its exterior was done in the Romanesque style like the Fine Arts Building, but its interior was what took my breath away. I was amazed by its gigantic dome made of translucent glass and its hanging stained glass lamps.

Isaac said, "We studied this building at the Art Institute where you know I went to school. The famous Louis Tiffany designed the dome and the lamps."

"I could tell. The lamps are like the ones at St. Stanislaus." The library's beauty overwhelmed me so much that I almost forgot about the unsavory task of reading up on my cleft palate.

But Isaac and I got to work. We sat together at a long table. With the help of a librarian, I gathered up five books and journals having to do with cleft palate. One journal explained how early cleft palate repairs employed heavy sutures and focused solely on anatomical closure, neglecting principles of palatal function. This resulted in a short, immobile palate that, in many cases, impaired speech production. It said that newer techniques used principles that lengthen the soft palate and completely cover the hole. If a gap was left after the sutures were made, one's speech would be better than without the surgery, but it could never be totally improved. Earlier surgeries had this problem, but the good thing about even those earlier surgeries was that the bearer, like me, had only a slender line going from the upper lip to the nose.

It was frightening to read all of this. I just hoped the doctor hadn't left a gap when he did my surgery.

24

ART FOR THE PEOPLE

I SPENT THE NEXT day—Sunday—at Mass and then tried not to obsess about my library findings. Monday rescued me. As usual, I got lost in my art. Back at McKay, I painted the top sections of the panels with mainly tree branches and abundant leaves,

As I worked my way down, I painted the trunks in bright, yellow-gold colors which you really don't see in tree trunks. I used cadmium orange for the occasional knots and striations on the trees. I made the upper branches look almost like hands reaching to the sky. I felt I was giving the trees a human quality; the children might like that each tree had its own personality similar to ones in children's books.

When the committee came to see my finished product,

I was nervous. Every artist feels like I did when waiting for the judgment of others. However, I had nothing to fear. The members gave me abundant accolades, saying my landscape depictions brightened up the narrow hall just like they wanted them to do.

What a relief it was to have my work approved! I felt like my future as a WPA artist was assured.

One thing that still bothered me, though, was my interaction—or lack thereof—with the little girl back at Newton Bateman. I felt guilty that I had let my impatience with my speech problem interfere with this child's possible need to derive inspiration from an artist like me. So, I made up an excuse to return to the school. I called the secretary and said I wanted to come look for a container of paint brushes that I left behind.

Knowing that the little girl always watched me during the 9:30 recess break, I visited at that time. I pretended like I was looking for the container by the mural. Then I went to the front of the stage searching for my supposed lost container.

I was delighted when the interested girl came and peered up at me from the gym floor. "Hi," she said.

I smiled widely and gave her my full attention. "Hello to you."

"You did that real big painting on the wall, didn't you?" she asked.

"Yes, I did. Do you like to draw or paint?"

"What?" she asked. I knew I had my speech problem, but the noise of the kids running around the gym didn't help.

I said, "Wait a moment."

I hurried to the side of the stage and down the stairs to the gym. I leaned down and spoke as slowly and distinctly as I could. "Let me ask you again: do you like to paint or draw?"

"Yes, I do…soooo much."

"What's your name?" the girl asked without reservation.

"Florian."

"That's a strange name."

I went into the whole story about Saint Florian, although I don't know how much of my speech she understood.

"What's your last name?"

"Durzynski."

"Ooh, those are some hard names to remember. Flor…Flor…Durz…Durz."

"If you ever forget, just look at the right lower corner of my mural and you'll see where I signed my name. Okay?"

"Okay. My name is Ella Leonhart."

"That's a nice name: Ella Leonhart. It has a special lilt to it."

I smiled. "An artist should always have the supplies she needs so she can use her gift. Do you have pencils and paper?"

I asked this because her clothes were tattered, and there was a little hole in the arm of her blouse. Art supplies might not be high on this family's list of priorities.

"I have two pencils, but I can't find much paper."

"I'll tell you what: why don't I come back again this Thursday, and I'll bring you a little package of pencils, erasers, paper, water paints, and brushes."

The girl hopped up and down a few times like I'd seen some of the other kids do. "Really? That would be great!"

Two days later I came at her recess and brought the package. Ella's eyes lit up when she peeked and saw the assortment of art supplies. Overcome with emotion, she could hardly get the words out. "Thank you so much, Mr. Dur..dur...."

I helped her with my name. "Durzynski."

That night when I went to bed and reviewed the day, I felt my heart would burst with joy from making Ella so happy. My heart actually felt warm but not in a bad way. No words could adequately describe the feeling. And I realized more than ever the value of creating public art for everyone's enjoyment and, perhaps, inspiration.

25

THE GAP

MARCEL CALLED ME and asked if I'd like to come to the Fire Arts Building that Saturday for an elocution lesson. "Great," I responded and looked forward to seeing him.

This time Marcel wore beige slacks and a matching vest along with a striped shirt and a tie which he'd loosened. I admired him for his style. I always thought that how one dresses can be a form of art.

Marcel was sitting in his chair next to a stand that held sheet music, and he motioned for me to sit across from him. Leaning towards me, he said in a kindly manner, "I thought for our first session we should become better acquainted. I'll tell you a little about myself and then maybe you can tell me a little about yourself. Is that all right?"

I nodded. "Of, course."

The timbre of Marcel's baritone voice was so strong yet comfortable that I could listen to him talk all day. He explained, "I was born in Trieste, Austria of French and Italian parentage. I studied languages at the University of Budapest, and then I studied voice at two different conservatories. I love to learn and obtained a Doctorate of Philology. I have performed solos at many concerts and am fluent in Italian, French, German and Hungarian."

"Wow! That's quite a resume."

"Even though I've accomplished a lot and love my life, some say I should go outdoors more and maybe think about marriage and a family. But music and learning have possessed me, and I can't escape their hold."

I responded, "I guess I'm like you, although I haven't accomplished quite so much. I love painting and especially thinking about how I am going to depict something. From the beginning to the end of a project, I am consumed by it."

Marcel was studying me. I knew he was listening for my enunciation.

"So, tell me a little more about you, Florian…where you were born, etc."

Painting with a broad brush, I told Marcel about my childhood in Berlin, my speech issue, my years in Poland, my education with Weiss, my immigration to the U.S., my joy with living in a Polish-Chicago neighborhood, and my work with the WPA.

Then I said, "Let's stop there. I'm pretty sure you're assessing how I pronounce certain things…"

Throughout my story, Marcel stared at me intently. "Yes, that's partly what I was doing, but I am also amazed at how much you accomplished so quickly when you came here. Within no time you were exhibiting, doing portraits, and now painting murals for the WPA."

Then Marcel got into his analysis. "From what I heard while you talked, I felt like you have the most trouble with letters or combinations of letters that call for a buildup of pressure. Those would be the b's and t's."

I should have known that to be the case, but I'd never made the effort to be so specific about my speech problem. Nor had anyone else.

Marcel continued, "I brought my little flashlight today. How about if I look into your mouth again?"

I gladly—but fearfully—obliged. What would Marcel find?

"Hmm, I am no expert at these things, but it looks

like the surgeon did a wonderful job," he said. However, Marcel kept looking—which concerned me.

"The problem is that there is still a gap—a very tiny one. That's probably what accounts for your difficulty."

My heart fell to the floor. "Does that mean I can't be cured?" I began speaking rapidly and emotionally. "I never thought I could speak normally, but Isaac got my hopes up."

"Not to worry," Marcel said in his soothing baritone voice—which settled me down a little. "Why don't you come back at this time next week. In the meantime, I'm going to do research to figure out what I can do."

From my visit to the library, I knew what that little gap meant. With the anticipation of a cure and then the letdown, I trembled.

As I stood up to leave. Marcel must have noticed how shaky I was. "Hey, it's 1:00. Any reputable man can have a drink at this time. There's a restaurant that serves drinks just a few buildings down. Care to join me?"

"Sure…I guess," although inside I was still reeling.

Marcel and I had a couple glasses of chardonnay. I enjoyed talking with this learned, sophisticated gentleman. Hearing about all his travels in Europe and the United States also helped me relax.

When I returned home in an alcohol-induced numbness, I was determined to push away my fear.

26

OPPORTUNITY KNOCKS

BUT MY DETERMINATION could not tamp down my anxiety. Now I kept thinking about my speech problem. Oh, if only Isaac hadn't gotten up my hopes! When I woke up in the morning, it took about fifteen minutes to put my emotions aside and get on with the day.

On Tuesday morning when I woke to that assault again, I heard the phone ring. My roommates both had gone to work, and so I climbed out of bed and ambled to the phone.

It was George Thorp. "Good morning, Florian. Do I have a job for you! It will be one of the biggest challenges and opportunities that our WPA mural painters have ever encountered. Get this: Chopin School wants two murals, each to be 84 feet wide and 5 feet tall."

The announcement took my breath away. "I am quite pleased, but why me?"

"The principal at Chopin knew you did that gigantic mural at Newton Bateman and did it so well that you would be the man for the job. Plus, he wants half of the mural to feature the namesake for their school—Frédéric Chopin—and he thought that you as a Polish man might have an affinity for Chopin."

"I undoubtedly do. I have the deepest admiration for his music."

"They want the other mural to depict Stephen Foster, a great American songwriter. Since it will all be in their large auditorium where they have many musical presentations, they wanted the murals to glorify one of our own musicians as well as one from Europe."

At that moment, my obsession over my defect disappeared—at least temporarily. My waking thoughts changed to how I would depict the work of these great musicians on a very wide wall.

Then Isaac called and told me about something that piqued my interest. László Moholy-Nagy from the now defunct Bauhaus School of Art and Design was to speak at the newly formed artist union in Chicago. How exciting! I would find a way to attend this meeting. I immediately penned a letter to my friend Juri to tell him about it.

27

THE MEETING

I TRIED TO BLOCK out my trepidation about meeting with Marcel, but the day had to come. Upon entering his office, I saw that he was wearing a checkered brown blazer, beige slacks and again a white, open-collared shirt. He looked very dapper, but his snappy ensemble did not match the expression on his face.

Although I feared I was being too intrusive, I asked, "Are you all right, Marcel?"

"I am fine." Unwittingly, he put a slight emphasis on the word "I."

"You're fine, but I guess I'm not. There's no hope for my speech problem, is there?".

Marcel paused and seemed to have difficulty getting out his next words. "Right, and I feel so guilty for leading you on to think I could help." Then he inquired, "But how did you know?"

"I went to the library and discovered that if someone has a little bit of open space left after the surgery his speech will be better than it would otherwise have been, but it would never be completely normal. I still was hoping for a miracle, but…but…"

"Yes, sad to say, it's true. I contacted my friend Nan Sally who is a speech therapist. She broke the news to me."

Marcel still looked forlorn. I felt I should comfort him, but when it came down to it, I couldn't. I went from being calm to agitated all within thirty seconds. I said, "The bad thing for me was that I became attached to a woman who seemed to really love me and accept me for who I was…speech problem and all. I know in my heart of hearts that this will never happen again."

I suddenly began to tear up. Marcel reached for my hand and held it.

"What happened?"

"She was killed. A car hit her."

"Oh, my God! So tragic!"

I took a couple gulps of air and settled myself down. Only slowly did Marcel pull his hand back.

I continued, "It took me a long time to recover. Knowing I would never find someone to love me like that again, I couldn't get past questioning, 'Why? Why me?' Why did I have this terrible speech defect, but then when I found love, why was my dear Mary taken away?"

"Oh, Florian," Marcel's voice overflowed with empathy.

Words tumbled out of my mouth as fast as a runaway freight train. "And why did my father die suddenly when I was only nine years old? I've been searching and searching for answers. When I met Isaac and he introduced me to his father—a rabbi—the man seemed wise, so I looked to him for answers."

"You've certainly had your share of losses." Marcel paused. His face was etched in pain like he was taking on my suffering. Then he said, "Try to take a deep breath and then tell me what the Rabbi came up with."

I was quiet for a moment. I knew I felt better after talking with Rabbi Goldman, but I hadn't really digested what I learned from him. Then it came to me. "The rabbi taught me that nature is random. We look for regularity, but when bad things happen it is often random." I felt my voice shaking. "He said I…I… hadn't done anything wrong to deserve my speech problem or the sudden loss of my loved ones. I guess…I guess… I could just as easily ask 'Why not me?' Others suffer from random events also."

"That sounds like good thinking," Marcel said in a steady tone, probably intended to calm me down.

I kept going. "So, I think that rationally I understand better about these unfortunate events in my life. And, through my talks with Rabbi Goldman, I've learned some other things."

"Which are?"

"On the positive side, I've learned that when I put my heart and soul into something—like this Chopin mural I'm doing—I forget about my impediment and my losses."

Marcel sat there quietly, waiting for me to continue.

"Also, if I worry less about how I sound and think more about helping others, I feel better." Ella Leonhart was my teacher there.

"And Isaac's father complimented me on explaining to people, like I did with him, why it is difficult to understand me. I've found that when I do, most people are very understanding."

Marcel said, "So, you've found some very effective ways to cope with your issues."

"Yes, I guess you could say that." I smiled weakly. "The only problem is that I'll just have to accept that I'll never find someone who loves me the way I am."

Marcel commented, "I wouldn't be so sure."

Then he said, "Why don't we get together socially once in a while, Florian? I think you'd enjoy meeting some of my friends. They are very educated like you and are in artistic professions. You'd have a lot in common with them…and it would probably be good to get out and do things with people so you don't dwell so much on your speech issue or your losses."

"I would enjoy that." Even though he'd been the bearer of bad news, something about Marcel made my insides lift.

∽

All my life I felt like a dark cloud followed me. Sometimes, it was at the very edge of my sight line; sometimes, it was front and center. Now it seemed to disappear. I didn't grieve so much about the death of my father and my speech impediment. I felt free. I asked myself *What made the difference?*

I turned over various possibilities, and then I came to this conclusion: "Talking things out," as Rabbi Goldman called it, seemed to be what changed me. Opening up with Isaac, his father, and now Marcel—that really seemed to help. At least temporarily, the dark cloud disappeared, but I feared it would return.

PART THREE
1936-1938

28

THE CHOPIN MURALS

Now I had even more energy than ever to concentrate on my art. I spent the rest of my weekend thinking about how I would do the Chopin School murals.

I decided I wanted the two murals to be homogenous. So as not to overload the viewer's senses, they would be similar in content, color and design. I started with the mural about Chopin since I already knew so much about my country's favorite musician.

Beyond that, I was stumped. *How do I depict an auditory thing like music in a visual way?* I went out in the hall and made a telephone call to Isaac. He had no answer.

Luckily, Peter overheard me. When I walked back towards my studio/bedroom, Peter beckoned me into the kitchen where he was making potato pancakes. I wasn't a big eater, but my mouth watered whenever I smelled the potatoes, onions, flour and egg frying to a crispy, golden brown.

Turning a pancake, Peter said, "Hey, Florian, I heard

you talking to Isaac. I've got an idea for you. Music makes people want to dance, right? Remember how even you got up and polkaed around the room when the accordion music played at my sister's wedding?"

Wistfully, I said, "How could I forget?"

Peter offered his idea. "Why don't you paint people dancing to Chopin's music?"

"Hmm, you may be onto something," I said.

Peter continued, "We did the polkas at my sister's wedding, but did you ever see people doing mazurkas too?"

"I sure did. Chopin created many piano pieces for mazurkas. I remember going to my uncle's in the country. Those people barely had enough to eat, but for feast days they somehow had matching costumes and danced the mazurkas like they were the luckiest people in the world." I became nostalgic. "Actually, I was a little jealous."

"Well, there you have it. Paint pictures of people dancing the mazurkas."

Although I was more familiar with Chopin's concertos, I remember my father playing his mazurkas too back in Berlin. He said more than once, 'Chopin was such a gifted musician representing our Poland. The lyrics in his mazurkas always make our country sound like the best place in the world.'"

After enjoying a couple of Peter's potato pancakes, I rushed to my room to play Chopin's music. I had a wide array of his work from which to choose.

Then it hit me. I could paint Chopin on the left side

of my wide horizontal mural with paper and pen in hand composing his music. Because he was so gifted, I would have a long flowing wing of an angel on his shoulder, but the wing would almost look like a gigantic leaf: I loved incorporating nature into my murals. Behind Chopin, in a corner, I'd have lightly painted depictions of musicians who inspired him. Then I'd paint a landscape with a path on which a row of country girls with their beaus would dance the mazurkas. This row would gradually transform into a group of female ballerinas standing on their tiptoes with one at the head of the group in a majestic pose with a male ballerina.

The colors would sing like music! As I listened to the sometimes sharp and sometimes lilting nature of Chopin's music, I felt inspired to use bright pink in some spots and maroon and soft pinks in others. I would use violet for the trees on each side for balance and then I'd use various shades of brown to temper the livelier colors.

Still, I thought I needed one color to be consistent throughout the mural. But I didn't know what it could be. I took a break and walked to Nowak's. Krysztof greeted me with a "Hello, where have you been?"

"Paining, painting, and more painting," I said with what was probably a tired smile.

"That job with the WPA has paid off, hasn't it?"

"Oh, yes, but I'm stumped about one thing." Then I saw it: a scarf around a patron's neck in the most striking shade of teal.

"What is it?" Krysztof asked with his usual concern. "But before you tell me, let me bring you some kolackies straight from the oven. I know they're more for dessert, but all your hard work calls for a special treat."

"That sounds wonderful, but I must rush back to my studio."

"Why this running off?" frowned Krysztof.

"I'm sorry, but I must fly when inspiration hits me." I pointed to the lady's scarf, and Krysztof looked puzzled.

"That color will work beautifully in my latest mural."

"Now I understand. Glad it's not that you're just too busy for us."

I wanted to savor those kolackies with their cream-infused dough and jam filling, but I had to keep my eyes and my mind on that teal color. Wrapping the cookies in a paper napkin, I flew out of Nowak's.

When I returned home, I mixed my paints until I got just the shade I wanted. I would use the teal in both the Chopin and the Foster mural. Then, I put the paint aside until I began my murals at the school.

Exhausted, I took a long nap, and, just as I was awakening, I heard the phone ring. My roommates were both at work. So, I went to answer it.

Putting my ear to the phone, I heard Marcel say in his captivating voice, "Hello Florian. I hope you are doing well. Some of my friends are having a small party this Saturday evening, and I wonder if you'd like to attend."

"Of course," I said.

It dawned on me that I would be entering new social territory in a place without my Polish people, and that both tantalized and frightened me.

29

THE PARTY

I was nervous about the party because Marcel would be the only person I knew, but I went anyhow, partially following Marcel's advice that getting out socially might be good for me.

Upon entering the host's apartment, I was greeted by plumes of smoke and the sound of laughter and tinkling glasses. A short, slender man wearing a velvet smoking jacket and white shirt greeted me with a pleasant smile and shook my hand.

"Hello, I'm Cyril and whom do I have the pleasure of meeting?"

"I'm Florian. I was invited by Marcel Roger de Bouzon."

The friendly man laughed. "He's simply Marcel to us, but I'm glad to meet you, Florian." He put a cigarette holder to his lips and took a deep drag. "Let me bring you to Marcel. He's in the kitchen."

The apartment was even smaller than the one I shared with my roommates. We made our way through the crush of people in the living room, and then I saw Marcel leaning against the kitchen sink. He was embroiled in deep discussion with another man.

When he saw me, Marcel straightened up, and he looked at me with that warm expression that always stole my heart. "Hello, Florian! I'm so glad you made it. Did you have any trouble finding the place?"

I said, "No, everything went fine," although that was a far cry from the truth. The apartment was at 54th and Harper in Hyde Park. I didn't want to admit that when I got off at the nearest streetcar stop, I had turned the wrong way on 54th St. and entered a courtyard that had no outlet. Nervous already about going to a party with strangers, I got a little panicky, but when I followed 54th St. in the opposite direction, I found the address easily. The problem was that it was windy, cold, and snowy. Not a good evening for a walk of any kind.

"Let me introduce you to our friends," Marcel said, and he did just that after first pouring me a flute of champagne.

As Marcel told me previously, his friends were mostly artists of one kind or another. One was a set designer for a small theater, two were music teachers at the Sherwood Academy, one was a haberdasher, one was an art critic, and the one who hosted the party was an art history professor at the University of Chicago. Additionally, Marcel made a special fuss about a man who he said was a soloist this month at The Civic Opera House.

Our host turned up the volume on the phonograph. Swing music permeated the air. It was early—about

Not an Ordinary Artist

9:00PM—and, so, it took a while for the guests to loosen up. But as the night wore on people began to dance, and, to my surprise, a few men danced to "slow" dances closely—like couples. Marcel didn't dance. There were only two women, and they were heavily engrossed in a conversation.

Marcel mingled with everyone, and at one point he came by me and gestured for us to sit on two chairs next to the women who were talking.

He said to one, "Maribel, how've you been doing? Are you still going to the theater a lot?"

"Definitely, Marcel, you know that's my passion."

Marcel introduced me and then went back to mingling.

I enjoyed talking with the ladies about plays and especially the exhibit they'd recently viewed at the Art Institute. Even though the host kept offering me drinks, I tried to restrain myself. I had about six blocks to walk and a streetcar to take home.

When I got ready to leave, Marcel came over to me, put his arm on my shoulder and said, "I hope you had a good time." Even though he didn't spend much time with me, he still made me feel special.

"Oh, yes, I had a grand time!" was what I said, but on the way home on the streetcar, I mulled over a few things. Even in Kraków where I attended all kinds of parties, I had not witnessed men dancing with each other in an intimate way.

Something suddenly entered my mind. Standing in line one day waiting for my paycheck, I overheard some artists talking about a man with the last name of Carlson. They said he was a personnel director at the WPA office in Rockford and that he was found guilty of having sexual relations with another man. He was sentenced to prison on what was called "a morals charge." Tragically, he killed himself in jail while waiting to be transferred to a state prison.

Sending that man to prison seemed so wrong! While it perplexed me to see men being physically close to one another, I didn't think it should be a crime.

Oh well, America—the home of the free! From what I'd heard the U.S. guaranteed that everyone has the right to life, liberty and the pursuit of happiness. I felt like Carlson was denied those gifts.

Anyhow, the good thing about the party was that I got to see Marcel (although I wished he'd spent more time with me), and I hardly thought about how I talked. I didn't worry about my speech ahead of time, and the music was so loud that we all had to repeat things. Maybe that dark cloud had really vanished.

30

THE FOSTER CHALLENGE

THE NEXT MORNING, I was too tired to go to Mass. I woke up at 11:00AM.

As I sat in the kitchen and sipped my coffee, Kazimierz and Peter were just returning from St. Stanislaus. Kazimierz smirked, "Now that you got a little bit of a social life, you can't fit God in, can you? Peter and I go to Mass even if we're so pickled we can hardly walk."

Peter laughed and said, "Don't let Kazimierz get to you, but I am curious. Tell us about the party."

I told them about its location—Hyde Park—and the individuals at the party. The men dancing with each other was not a subject I wanted to broach.

"One was from the University of Chicago, huh?" Kazimierz said. "I imagine there weren't any Poles there."

"I don't think so, but does it matter?"

Peter shot an angry look at Kazimierz. "That shouldn't be a big deal, Kazimierz." Then he looked at me. "I'm glad you finally had a little fun, Florian.".

"Just don't get too big for your britches," Kazimierz said in a warning voice.

I chose not to respond. Instead, I rinsed my cup in the sink and said, "Now, if you fellows will excuse me, I must retreat to my room and get back to planning my Chopin School mural."

Like at Newton Bateman, Chopin School wanted me to put together canvases and glue them onto the wall. This process would take twice as much patience and precision as at Newton Bateman because it involved two walls. Also, the murals might only be five feet high, but they didn't start until six feet up from the floor, and they extended to the ceiling. Again, I would need three assistants and a healthy dose of concentration to face those heights with glue and canvas in hand.

I had already figured out how I would paint the Chopin mural. My daunting challenge now was to envision the Stephen Foster mural. The committee at Chopin told me everybody was singing his tunes. Born and raised in Poland, I knew nothing about Foster or his music. Filled with eager anticipation, I went to the Chicago main library.

In the library's encyclopedia, I found that Foster was born in 1826 and died in 1864, only living 38 years. Chopin died young also, at the age of 39. Foster was born in Pennsylvania and only once went into Kentucky or any Southern state, but he liked to create sentimental songs about life in The South and American life in general.

I read the lyrics of Foster's most famous song, My Old Kentucky Home. The encyclopedia said the song has a soft, melancholic tone that has appealed to Americans for years. Foster and his nine older brothers and sisters originally lived in a very nice home, but the rich relative who owned the home lost all his money and the family suddenly had nowhere to go. They moved from house to house but never attained the lovely environment they had in their original home. That is why Foster supposedly composed such a sweet, sentimental song like My Old Kentucky Home.

The encyclopedia went on to explain, "He absorbed musical influences from the popular, sentimental songs sung by his sisters; from Negro church services he attended with the family's servant Olivia Pise; from popular minstrel show songs; and from songs sung by Negro laborers at the Pittsburgh warehouse where he once worked."

I had learned in my world history class back home that the owners of what were called Southern plantations enslaved Africans. Coming from a country where we didn't have slaves, I was revolted by the idea of slavery, but, since I was asked to do a mural about Foster, I needed to look into his heart and mind.

Turning to the encyclopedia section about Slavery in the United States, I learned that the slaves were freed in 1865. I had to remember that Foster was born in 1826—about 40 years before much consideration was given to letting the slaves become free, and that he probably never saw a slave, since he lived in a northern state.

The lyrics of many of Foster's songs showed a respect for these Negro men, women and children and a consideration that they had the same feelings as White people about their homes and families. Foster probably didn't realize the suffering that slaves experienced.

So, the library visit gave me some ideas, and, when I returned home, I started sketching. Similar to what I did in the Chopin mural, I drew Foster on one side gazing into the distance with a piece of paper in his hand, trying to figure out what music to compose.

From my reading at the library, I had discovered that the banjo was the musical instrument used in most of Foster's tunes. So, I sketched a banjo player on the left merrily strumming away. Just like in the Chopin mural, I depicted a landscape again with a path. On one side of the path, I drew the "Southern Belles" I had read about in the encyclopedia—women with varying shades of pink and red hoop skirts—clapping demurely to the music. On the other side, I drew a couple of women with beautiful white dresses. In the background, I sketched men and women with plainer outfits dancing to the music. I used the teal color that I saw at Nowak's in small details throughout both murals.

Then, in one large group, I depicted Negro men neatly dressed in work outfits, easily lifting bales of cotton, and looking the picture of health and strength. In another group, I sketched Negro men dressed in matching finery and cheerfully carrying top hats for their masters. From my research, I knew that this was not realistic, but this is the way Foster seemed to perceive things.

Although I tried to portray everything in Foster's idyllic way, I inserted two images that reflected my personal feelings. First, I drew a big tree separating an older Negro man and woman from the rest of the action. The couple stared longingly at a wishing well; I wanted people to conclude that they wished to be free. Second, I painted an image of a ship in a large body of water. It could be seen as a boat to transport the bales of cotton, but I wanted it to symbolize a ship by which the Africans were transported as slaves to the United States.

Although this thinking and research exhausted me, it was a good exhaustion. I felt I succeeded in making the two murals harmonious in color and composition. Most importantly, I thought they told the story of Chopin's and Foster's music. The only problem was that I still hadn't heard Foster's songs being sung.

I decided to contact Marcel… Maybe I was just looking for an excuse to see him again.

31

SONGS AND CITIZENSHIP

ON THE PHONE, I told Marcel about the mural and asked him if he'd ever heard Foster's music. "Of course, Florian. Why don't you pop over to my room at the Fine Arts Building next Saturday and I'll sing a couple of his tunes for you?"

I loved visiting Marcel not only to see the man himself but to gaze upon the Fine Arts Building's rich interior. From what I knew of architectural history, the décor was in The Art Noveau style with it ornate, organic details. Lamp holders, elevator doors, large clocks and mailboxes—all were decorated with intricate, lovely plant designs in a variety of materials—bronze, wrought iron, glass, wood and marble. I had to resist the urge to finger the elaborate newel posts at the end of the staircase railings.

When I arrived, Marcel was situated next to a stand holding a sheet of music. He radiated his usual enthusiasm. Shaking my hand, he got right down to business. "Hello, My Friend! Have a seat. I am trying to recall exactly how a couple of Stephen Foster's songs go. Even though the man's been dead for 70 years, people in America still love to sing them, and I am somewhat of an expert in American folk songs."

"But you weren't born here in the U.S. How do you know his songs?"

"I've been here for quite a few years. As you know, I give many concerts across the United States, and I sing what I'm hired to. Some pieces are operatic, and some are popular American folk songs like Foster's." Marcel gestured to his music stand. "I was just practicing one of his pieces. This one I can sing without hesitation."

And, so, like it was as simple as tying one's shoe, Marcel began singing in full voice, "Oh, the sun shines bright on My Old Kentucky Home…"

I stared at him with awe. *How could someone have the courage to just start singing with no accompaniment or other signers joining him?* And the way he sang—with such beauty and sentimentally; it brought tears to my eyes.

Then Marcel got out a second piece of sheet music. "I don't know if you've studied this one, but it too is a very popular Foster song."

He began singing, "Oh Susanna, oh don't you cry for me, I come from Alabama with a banjo on my knee."

This was a lively tune, and the reference to the banjo player reinforced the wisdom of my idea to place one in my mural.

After Marcel sang the last few notes, he said, "Maybe the Poles in West Town don't know these, since they're just trying to master English, but listen when you're in streetcars or restaurants, and you'll occasionally hear a couple of people quietly singing or humming Foster's songs."

I laughed. "If I started humming the American songs myself, my roommates would really give me a hard time. They already accuse me of losing my Polish-ness."

"What? That's ridiculous!" Marcel said indignantly as if they had insulted him.

"Now that I'm associating with you and Isaac and other non-Polish people, they think I've somehow lost my loyalty to Poland."

Marcel's tone became pensive. "It is a bit of a quandary when you feel stuck between one national group and another, but I figure we're all the same people deep down inside." Appearing to be lost in thought, he said more to himself than me, "I'd rather expand my wings than cut them."

I was silent as Marcel continued, "I've studied, taught, and sung in so many different places in America and overseas that I feel no strong national identity. I've been living in the U.S. since I came here as a young man. I like the U.S. and became a citizen, but I don't feel any special allegiance to any country, and no one pressures me to do that."

"You've accomplished so much, and what a life you've led!"

"Yes, but it's been somewhat of a lonely life traveling all over to do solos and teaching at one college or another depending on their enrollment. Now that you tell me about your Polish friends, I'm almost jealous of the solidarity they feel with each other and you."

It was my turn to become pensive. "Yes, I have been fortunate to live in West Town in Chicago. I feel like I'm still in Poland, and I find that comforting and enjoyable—the food, the language, the history we share. But I don't want anybody to box me in. My roommate Kazimierz is the one who badgers me. A while back, I picked up an application to become a naturalized U.S. citizen, but something made me hesitate. Maybe, in the back of my mind, I questioned myself just like Kazimierz does: will this make me less Polish?"

"Heavens no! It absolutely won't, but if you don't decide, you'll have one foot in a bucket of water representing Poland and the other in one representing the United States. You'll stay in that position for the rest of your life and not be able to walk."

"I've made a similar comparison myself."

Marcel moved from his position at the music stand and sat down on a chair facing mine. His piercing eyes communicated with me as pointedly as the words he spoke. "If you eventually want to return to Poland and live the rest of your life there, you shouldn't become an American citizen. But, if you feel it is wiser for you to lead the rest of your life in the United States, I say you should become an American citizen."

"I love both countries equally, maybe even Poland a little more. But I can't live there. Too many problems."

"Yes, and now I hear that Hitler and his Nazis are thinking about invading Poland," Marcel said.

"No, not another invasion!" I shouted. "I can't believe it. Are you sure?"

"That's what I hear. For some reason, they want to recapture what they think they lost after the last war."

I dug my palm into the arm of my chair and started shouting again. "Recapture…what they lost…Rubbish! We never belonged to Germany or Russia." I put my head in my hands, then looked up again. "That does it! My main reason for coming to America was to get rid of the constant threat of being invaded by Germany or Russia. I worry so much about my loved ones and friends, but…but…"

"But what, Florian?"

"I've made my decision. I will apply to become a U.S. citizen!"

I stood up. Then I thought of something. "I need two people to vouch for me that I would be a good American citizen. I could ask my physician to be one, but would you be so kind as to be the other one?"

Marcel said, "Certainly."

I thanked him profusely for singing Foster's songs and rushed home to find my naturalization form and submit it. If Kazimierz said I wasn't Polish enough, that was his problem. I thought, *Even if I become an American citizen, I will still remain a Pole in my heart!*

32

WALKOWICZ AND NAGY

Leon Walkowicz called me on the phone. "Hey, Florian, remember how I've collected historical items so that we'd have a Polish museum in Chicago?"

He was so excited that he didn't let me respond. "Well, guess what? The museum is finally opening, and Felice and I want you to come to the grand opening."

I said, "Certainly! Thank you so much for asking me.

Not an Ordinary Artist

I noticed they were working on that building at 984 N. Milwaukee."

Leon crowed, "Yep. The Polish Roman Catholic Union of America has constructed a gigantic room for the museum within its headquarters. I love that the museum is right in the heart of West Town. Just a few blocks from where you live."

"I would be thrilled to attend the grand opening," I re-iterated with utmost sincerity.

I asked Kazimierz and Peter to join me. They refused. Kazimierz said, "I bet there'll be a lot of speech-makin.' And I hate to get dressed up unless it's a wedding."

Peter said there was a playoff round for his dart league at St. Stanislaus, and the guys would be mad if he missed it.

I smirked and said, "And who is the real Pole now?"

Kazimierz pretended like he didn't hear. Peter just smiled.

The museum—called "The Museum and Archives of the Polish Roman Catholic Union of America"—was packed. Hundreds of people, wearing their best attire, crowded into its large, main room. We all ooh-ed and aah-ed at the Polish artifacts, exhibits, embroidered folk costumes, and works of art. It was a proud night to be a Pole.

Leon beamed, and many people congratulated him. Felice stood proudly at his side. After all, this was Leon's heart's desire—to establish a museum to honor all of Poland's contributions to the culture of Chicago and the world. Many of the pieces in the museum were items he had personally collected and donated.

A week later, I discovered that László Moholy-Nagy from the Bauhaus was coming to speak on Thursday at the newly formed artists' union in Chicago. I thought about the difference between Walkowicz and Nagy. One represented reverence for the past, and the other represented vision for the future. I thought that both were worthy of humanity's attention.

I didn't know much about the artists' union and didn't particularly care since I was just thankful to be gainfully employed. When I entered its storefront office, I saw Nagy sitting behind a long, narrow table that held blown-up photos sitting on pedestals. Behind him was a screen.

The room was crowded. I got one of the few remaining seats. Then someone introduced Nagy. "We are ever so privileged to have with us tonight a noted professor from the former Bauhaus in Dessau, Germany, László Moholy-Nagy. He and the artists of the Bauhaus have come up with so many artistic innovations that they would be hard to number. Suffice it to say that they have created what is coming to be known as 'modern art, architecture and interior design.' I don't want to get too political, but you may know that the German government, for no good reason, recently ran them out of Dessau!"

The audience gasped. Most of us had heard of the Bauhaus, but some did not know how much Hitler was trying to control everything—even the art—in Germany.

The moderator continued, "Now Mr. Nagy is trying to begin what is called The New Bauhaus in the United States. We invited our illustrious guest tonight to show us what innovations he could bring to industrial design in the U.S. So, without further ado, I present to you László Moholy-Nagy."

Everyone clapped heartily.

I wasn't sure what "industrial design" was, but I expected I'd find out.

Nagy stood up and began speaking quickly and energetically. His impeccably tailored suit, his perfectly coiffed hair, and his uniquely designed glasses radiated an attention to detail. I thought, Each aspect of his appearance means something to him and probably comes from his outlook on art and design.

Immediately, Nagy got down to business. "In the past, objects were created by individual artists in small workshops, but today we have factories where we are beginning to mass-produce objects, even of an artistic nature. Industrial design is determining a product's form and features which will be duplicated over and over again. This process could apply to designing furniture, upholstery, lighting or even a pen or hairbrush."

He gestured to the back of the room, "I will now have my assistant start a soundless movie while I speak. It will give you a view of the Bauhaus building and its teachers and students who have innovated many of the 'modern' designs about which I'll tell you."

In the movie, I looked intently for Juri, and to my great joy, I saw a brief snippet of him painting with other students in one of the workshops. I also looked for the woman from the weaving workshop about whom he had written—Otti Berger. I saw several women in the workshop but, of course, I didn't know which one she was. The looms on which the women worked were gigantic, and I was impressed with how they handled their hand tools and floor pedals with such dexterity.

As he let the movie run, Nagy talked about how the Bauhaus invented new materials that could be used in design for the modern age. This included such things as devices for hot and cold forming of plywood and the use of plastic in the weaving process. At this point, he had his assistants turn off the movie and begin to show slides.

Nagy expounded on the Bauhaus philosophy. "We from the former Bauhaus believe that form should follow function, that 'less is more,' and that sleek design is both efficient and beautiful." Some people frowned. It seemed they were not ready to move out of the decorative phase.

"I have spoken with influential people about putting together a new industrial arts manual for Chicago public schools. This would include teaching students how to use wood, metal, textiles, photography and graphic design in new and exciting ways."

Some groaned while others exchanged nods of approval.

After two hours, I left. Later I heard that the meeting eventually moved to a nearby bar and continued until closing time. Months later, I heard that Chicago public school administrators rejected the manual that Nagy developed because they didn't want to retrain teachers or change their basic way of operating. So much for progress!

That disappointed me. I considered my own artistic style. From hearing Juri's views on abstraction, I had somewhat altered my approach. Although I did not become as abstract as other up- and -coming artists, I had turned from trying to get every detail right in my murals towards putting forth a certain impression that I wanted to get across.

I wrote to Juri about Nagy's presentation and the stodgy audience. I praised Nagy's multi-media approach that, among other things, allowed me to get a brief but clear look at him, my dear friend.

33

POLISHNESS

ONE SATURDAY I got up at 7:30AM, dressed, and ate breakfast. Peter came to the kitchen table just as I swallowed my last sip of coffee.

"What are you doing up so bright and early?" Peter asked matter-of-factly.

"I'm working in my room, putting the finishing touches on my drawing for the Chopin School mural. Then

I'll begin my mural about an American musician named Stephen Foster." I looked at Peter and continued, "Your parents came to the States right before you were born. Did you ever hear or sing anything by Stephen Foster?"

Kazimierz drifted into the kitchen. "Stephen Foster? Who the heck is he?"

"He wrote songs like My Old Kentucky Home, Camptown Races, Oh Susanna."

Kazimierz laughed. "Are you kidding? Never heard of them, and I bet Peter hasn't either…"

Peter shook his head "No."

Kazimierz adopted the bossy tone I didn't like. "You know, Florian, I'm worrying even more about you now. You've been hanging around so much with that guy called Marcel and that Isaac fellow and all those artsy people, and now wanting to sing those American songs. I think more than ever that you're losing your Polishness."

For one of the few times in my life, I spoke up for myself. "You've accused me of that before, and I don't like it. I will always be loyal to Poland, but I'm going to remain living here and, in fact, I am now seeking U.S. citizenship!"

The guys' mouths dropped open. I'd never talked in such a defiant tone. And this was the first time I mentioned becoming a citizen.

"That's great!" Peter said. He came to where I stood and gently slapped me on my back.

Leaning on the doorway, Kazimierz said, "I'm not so happy for you. Maybe I'm jealous. Peter was born here so he had citizenship right away."

I knew it wasn't easy for Kazimierz to admit he was jealous, so I changed my tone. "You can still apply for citizenship," I said encouragingly.

"It would be too hard."

"I could help you study…"

Kazimierz plopped down on a kitchen chair. "You don't get it, Florian. I can hardly read."

Lighting a cigarette, Kazimierz changed the subject. "I ain't going to worry about that now. I've got a new girlfriend, a nice Polish girl from Pilsen where there are a lot of Polish along with Czech and Spanish. Why don't you come with me to Pilsen sometime, Florian? She has a brother who's looking for someone to room with. It'll be just three more months now till our lease is up."

"I've been trying to ignore that fact, but you're right. I'll have to find another roommate soon…"

Peter cracked a couple of eggs and put them into a sizzling frying pan. "Kazimierz's making a good point there. Maybe you should go to Pilsen and meet this guy he knows. You might like living in Pilsen."

I said, "Maybe… I'll think about it, but I've got work to do now."

34

STUDENT REACTION

Now that I had my drawings prepared for Chopin School, I was ready to execute. I had three assistants again—two fellows and Sophie Pietrowski. I remembered Sophie was from Pilsen, and I filed that away for possible conversations about the neighborhood.

The murals were for a large auditorium, and the rows of seats had not been removed like at Newton Bateman. In this area, classes were taught, plays were rehearsed, and musical instruments were played. I was prepared for the challenge of keeping myself and my assistants calm even if we heard a sour note from a trumpet or a dramatic scream from a play.

In one way this mural would be easier than the big one at Newton Bateman because I had experience with applying the glue and then sticking the canvases together. However, I knew it would be physically more demanding because there was such a wide expanse to be covered.

First, we did the wall with the Chopin mural.

I wondered if the students knew anything about Chopin. This had to be a Polish neighborhood because I heard most of the kids speaking Polish, and the fact that the school was named after Chopin spoke volumes.

One day a boy came up to me after I had descended the ladder to mix a new batch of paint. He had straight brown hair that came forward in bangs and brushed his eyebrows. He wore a long sleeve shirt, knickers and suspenders—all of which looked like they'd seen plenty of outdoor play.

He said, "Hello. I don't speak good English, but…"

"Do you speak Polish?" I asked in Polish.

His face brightened. He pointed to my half-finished mural and spoke to me in our native tongue. "I see people dancing the mazurkas like we did back home."

"Does that make you happy?"

"Oh, yes. We came here two years ago, but I still miss my friends and even our cow. Her name is Angelique."

"I understand. I came here not too long ago, and I still miss my family back in Poland."

I pointed to the part where I had painted Chopin. "This man was Polish, and he wrote music for the mazurkas."

The boy's eyes widened with excitement. "Really?"

I continued to speak in Polish. "Yes, his name was Frédérick Chopin. He was the most famous pianist and composer ever in Poland. People danced his mazurkas, but they also did ballet to his music in fancy theaters."

As he listened and looked at what I had painted so far, the little boy's eyes became as wide as saucers. He sighed and said, "Thank you, Mister." Everyday thereafter he studied what I painted, and when he did, he always smiled.

When I began working on the Foster mural, the students watched again. There was only a handful of Negro students at the school, but after I made considerable progress, a Negro boy and girl approached me. They were not smiling. Instead, they wore pensive frowns.

I asked them what was on their mind.

The boy said, "It looks like you have some Negroes in your painting."

"I do."

"We've been watching how you paint them. I'm Willie, and this is my sister Ivy. We came here from Mississippi with our folks a couple years ago." He pointed to the Negroes with the cotton bales and then the ones carrying the top hats for their masters. "Are those Negroes supposed to be slaves?"

"Yes."

Ivy piped up, "You make those slaves look happy, and they wear nice, clean clothes. They look like they get plenty to eat and love serving their masters."

Willie frowned and spoke with conviction. "My grandma was a slave and she said it was nothing like that. She picked cotton for hours in the hot sun all bent over, thirsty and hungry. The masters were mean to the slaves. They mainly ate whatever was left over in the kitchen from the masters' meals or had to hunt whatever they could."

I cleared my throat. I could understand what these children meant, and in most cases, it was as bad as they said. I had to explain why I painted the slaves like that. "Our two murals were supposed to show achievements in music. So, the directors wanted us to have Chopin who was Poland's most famous composer on one mural, and Stephen Foster who is said to be the Father of American Music on the other one."

The children looked puzzled. To make sure my speech was not the problem, I took more time with my words. "Foster only visited the South once. He was from Pennsylvania and lived in the days long before the Civil War and before people thought about freeing slaves. He seemed to believe that the slaves and their masters got along pretty well down South and that the masters treated the slaves decently."

Willie spoke up defiantly. "Oh, no they didn't!"

"I agree with you, Willie, but I'm just trying to depict Foster's songs in a painting. I think the good thing about Foster was that he seemed to see the slaves as equal to their slave owners because his songs are partly about their having joys and heartaches just like their masters."

The children no longer frowned, but their lips were still tight. Obviously, they felt Foster got it wrong.

I was quick to add but still slow in my speaking. "However, I'm not as innocent as Stephen Foster was. So, I inserted my own views into the mural." I had the children walk with me to the left side of the mural. I pointed upwards. "Here I put up a divider, and to its left is an older Negro couple looking at a wishing well."

Ivy said, "And I bet they wished to be free."

"That's right! And I want people to understand that."

A thought passed through my mind: Art is like magic because it takes an idea and turns it into something you can see; that's just what I was trying to do with the wishing well concept. Then I brought them to the middle of the mural. I had them look up. "Do you see that ship? To me, it symbolizes the ships that kidnapped the Africans and took them to America."

Ivy nodded. Willie said, "That was so bad."

Time was running out. The kids had to scurry to their next class, but I wanted to add one more thing. "Even though you and I think Foster was misguided about slavery, he created songs that many Americans like to sing." I rattled off the names of his songs, and the kids had to admit they sang a couple themselves. I pointed out that although Foster saw the relations between the slaves and their masters through rose-colored glasses—very unrealistically—the contents of the songs did not disparage or belittle the Negro slaves. Foster seemed to respect them.

I knew I was speaking rather formally and that the kids probably only grasped part of what I tried to convey. So, I asked, "Do you know what I mean?"

They shook their heads "Yes." Willie said, "I understand. You did all right."

Ivy produced a small smile, and they rushed away to their next class.

∽

There were so many children at the school that the auditorium had to be used for a variety of classes throughout the day, and that included English classes. One morning, the English teacher approached me.

He said, "I notice that the kids have a lot of questions for you as they go in and out. Would you be willing to give a talk to my class about your murals?"

I hesitated. Although I felt a lot better about my speech difference, it was still challenging for me to speak to strangers—let alone to a whole class. However, I tried to recall all I had learned from talking with Isaac's father and Marcel.

"Yes, I will do it," I finally said.

And, so, I spoke to the class. I started right away by telling them that sometimes it might be hard for them to understand me because I still had a Polish accent and because of my cleft palate (I explained what that was). I welcomed them to raise their hand if they couldn't understand something. I told them everything I told the Polish boy as well as the brother and sister. They all listened earnestly as they kept looking at select parts of the murals when I described them.

A few times I could see the students looking confused—like they had no idea what I was saying. So, then I repeated myself. At one point when they got that bewildered look, I smiled and said, "Oh, that speech problem of mine! None of us has a perfect body or voice." I shrugged and said as jovially as possible. "We just have to make the best of what we've got, right?"

The kids nodded in agreement. A boy who had to use crutches every day and a girl in a wheelchair grinned.

As I concluded my talk, I saw George Thorp enter

at the back of the auditorium. Oh no, I thought. He had never shown up in the middle of a job before.

As he witnessed the children clapping after my speech, Thorp smiled from ear to ear. When I walked to where he stood, my boss stared at the murals and shook my hand. "I just want to compliment you. Your murals are beautiful, and I have recently realized that these two horizontal murals are the largest continuous narrative scenes in the Chicago Public Schools. We are so proud and blessed to have you as a WPA muralist."

35

CONFUSION

MARCEL CALLED. To me, hearing his voice was like listening to an aria. Just a simple, "hello" and "how are you?" from this gifted baritone was enough to put me into a state of bliss. I couldn't help my reaction, but I thought maybe it was strange for a man to be affected like this by another man.

Anyhow, Marcel invited me to a second party. One of his friends was having a get-together on Friday around the corner from where Marcel lived.

"It will be informal, but there will probably be more

people than at the last one. Perhaps you'd like to come to where I live first and we can go together. You'd probably feel more comfortable that way. His place is on Cedar Street—only a short walk from my residence."

"Oh, yes, that would be wonderful!" I responded enthusiastically.

"I reside at 1040 N. Lake Shore Drive. You seem to have no problem with public transportation. So, I assume you can figure out what streetcars to take."

"Definitely."

"Let me tell you a little about my residence. It's a large rooming house with mostly professional people. I'm so busy that I like having my meals prepared and my room cleaned as they do for me here. So, this setup is very satisfactory, and it's not far from Sherwood Academy. When you enter the building, I'll be waiting for you in the parlor." In his tone that always made me feel special, he added, "It will be nice to see you again."

Marcel was so kind and caring. He had a hold on me. I couldn't resist it.

When I approached his residence, I saw that it was a multi-storied, limestone building. On the side near the entry way was a tall tower with a turret on top. There were three or four stories, and each had a veranda. After entering the building's imposing double doors, I walked into a large parlor with somewhat old-fashioned but comfortable-looking couches, chairs and lamps.

Marcel was sitting on an easy chair and immediately

rose to greet me. Dressed in a navy-blue jacket and beige pants with a white shirt, Marcel looked as handsome as ever. I had purposefully purchased a new up-to-date, casual jacket and had a colorful handkerchief in my breast pocket. So, I felt I cut kind of a dashing figure myself.

We walked the few blocks to the party. It was held in a sophisticated-looking brownstone building. After the host buzzed us in, we walked up to the third floor. As the door opened, a clamor of voices and a haze of smoke greeted us just like at the last party. Oh, how I hated the odor of that smoke! But I had to be tolerant. Everyone I knew seemed to smoke. Marcel was one of the few exceptions.

"Greetings," the host said as he kissed Marcel on both cheeks. "And this must be your friend?"

"Yes, this is Florian Durzynski. He is a gifted artist and is creating a bevy of murals for the Chicago public schools."

The host reared back and said, "Well, I'm impressed. Come in you two, and have a drink."

Walking us through the apartment's large living room and dining room, our host turned to me. "I regret that I can't introduce you to everyone seeing as how we have such a large crowd, but maybe Marcel can have you meet a few art aficionados."

I noticed about six men sitting on a couch and chairs in one corner. They seemed to have formed couples, with some laying their arms on each other's shoulders or holding hands. Two women were dancing cheek-to-cheek to a slow song. If the lighting was not so low, people could probably see me blush. Again, I felt like in Poland this would have never happened…at least not where everyone could see.

Marcel brought me to a group of four men standing together rapt in intense conversation as they smoked their cigarettes. After he introduced me to each of the men, Marcel walked away, telling me he went to make me a drink.

The men readily welcomed me into their conversation. It had to do with new developments in Chicago architecture. One of them—a debonair, nattily dressed fellow—looked at me intently and said, "I'm John Harper and I work with the architectural firm, Baker and Baker. Have you heard of it?"

When I said I hadn't, he gestured for me to sit on the couch with him. He asked, "Have you heard of Mies van der Rohe?"

"Of course," I said proudly. "My friend attended the Bauhaus and told me all about his architecture."

"I'm not sure if I like his minimalism. His work is taking over the downtown Chicago landscape. I think…"

The man launched into a rambling soliloquy about what he liked and didn't like about Mies' style. The music, talking and laughter were so loud I had to lean towards him to hear what he said.

Eventually, Harper came up for air and moved so close to me that our faces almost touched. He said in an affectionate tone, "You have beautiful eyes."

At that moment, Marcel came into the living room with two cocktails in hand. Immediately, I stood up and walked towards him.

The drinks were in triangular glasses with long stems and contained a cloudy liquid with olives on a little stick. Still reeling from John Harper's advance, I asked nervously, "What kinds of drinks are these?"

"They're becoming the latest rage in Chicago—martinis."

Marcel probably didn't know it, but he saved me. He looked at John. "I hate to interrupt, John, but I told Florian that I must continue to take him around to meet everyone."

"Nice meeting you, John," I said without an iota of enthusiasm.

Mumbling so quietly that Marcel probably couldn't hear, John said bitterly, "I've got better people to talk to anyhow."

As we walked towards the kitchen, Marcel said, "John can come on pretty strong, but he's basically a nice fellow and is an especially talented architect.".

After he introduced me to a couple more people, some of his friends waved Marcel over from the other side of the room. He looked at me apologetically. "Excuse me, Florian, but I've got to talk to those folks."

I tried not to be noticed. About a half hour later, Marcel came next to me. "You're not having a good time, are you?"

Before I could answer, he said, "That's enough for one evening. How about if we leave?"

Those words were music to my ears. I couldn't get to the bedroom fast enough to look through the pile for my coat. Marcel did likewise. As we walked home, he told me about some of the conversations he had with people and asked if I spoke with anyone interesting.

"Well…" but I had nothing to say. I really hadn't mixed much.

We walked a half block in silence. Then Marcel said, "I don't think you 've liked these parties, but I'd like to stay in touch with you."

"Definitely," I answered.

When we got back to his building, I said I wanted to catch what I thought would be the last streetcar to my neighborhood. Marcel said he understood, took a gentle hold of my shoulder, looked me in the eyes and said, "So nice to see you again, Florian."

On my way home, I thought about what kind of man Marcel might be. He associated with many people who were clearly homosexual, and he was very nice to me—another man—but he never made overt displays of affection to me or anyone else at the parties. I was flummoxed.

36

BORYS AND QUEEN JADWIGA

When I finally finished the Chopin School murals, I needed rest. My right arm was sore from holding a brush upwards and sideways for long periods of time while standing on a ladder. I hoped Thorp wouldn't call me soon to do another mural. I wanted to take time not only to recuperate but also to look for an apartment and a roommate.

One Sunday as Kazimierz, Peter and I walked home from St. Stanislaus after late Mass, I turned to Kazimierz, "I'm ready to visit Pilsen." Kazimierz stopped and slapped me on the back so hard that he almost sent me sprawling. "Good! You are coming to your senses! After all, maybe you'll keep your Polishness!"

I turned to Kazimierz and said with conviction, "Let's not start that again."

"Okay, okay," Kazimierz chuckled.

By the time we entered our apartment, Kazimierz had hatched a plan. "I know how much you like our Polish churches. St. Stanislaus is the greatest, but St.

Adalbert's in Pilsen is amazing too. Why don't we take the streetcar next Sunday to see it? Maybe we can meet my girl Monika and her brother Borys for Mass there and then go to their house afterwards? Borys is looking for a roommate."

On the next Sunday as we walked to St. Adalbert's from the streetcar stop, I was reminded of when Kazimierz and I walked together to St. Joseph's for the wedding. Although this church had the trademark two towers of our Chicago Polish churches, it was much taller and more baroque than St. Joseph's, and its towers were topped by beautiful copper domes. St. Adalbert's buildings were massive and took up a lot of land. It appeared that the church had a large school.

I was amazed by what I saw when we walked in. Marble was everywhere. Beige-and-grey pillars with gold capitals lined the aisles and the nave. White marble (probably Carrara from Italy) was used for the handrails, pulpit and altar.

Perhaps because he had attended Mass here once before and perhaps because he didn't have artist eyes, Kazimierz was not dazzled like I was. He was more intent on finding Monika and her brother Borys. He spotted them sitting near the front. Ah, I thought, it will be great to sit in the front because now I can study the copious amount of art around the altar.

As solemn organ music played in the background, we said a quick, quiet hello to Monika and Borys. Then my eyes gravitated to a large, darkly painted mural behind the altar. I didn't pay it much attention until the middle of Mass when my mind wandered. On the left side of the mural, a marriage ceremony was taking place. A youngish woman was being married to a much older man in an elaborate, ancient setting. The more I examined it the more I believed it was the wedding of Queen Jadwiga of Poland and Grand Duke Jogaila of Lithuania. Seeing as how Queen Jadigwa was her idol, my dear mother would have loved seeing this!

After Mass, we took a two- block walk to where Monika and Borys lived. They resided within the first floor of a three-story nondescript red brick building.

I noticed on the way that some of the other buildings had architecture like our residences in West Town: brick with white pediments above the windows and doors. The brick in Pilsen was red, though, whereas the brick in West Town was usually a chestnut brown. Pilsen's buildings seemed shorter too. They had a bottom floor below street level just like some in West Town. Numerous buildings had storefront restaurants and shops with Polish as well as Czech signs above them.

Monika and Borys' parents, Mr. and Mrs. Ostrowski, greeted us at the door. Their mother looked traditional in her babushka and shawl. Although their father was very bent over in what looked like a painful posture, he wore a cheerful smile. Mrs. Ostrowski had prepared a bounteous breakfast for us and, of course, we all spoke in Polish.

At one point, I asked, "Was that Queen Jadwiga pictured in the mural at the church?"

Borys and Monika gave me blank stares. Mrs. Ostrowski spoke up vigorously. "Yes! How I adore her!

She didn't live long. Had no children but tried to help everyone."

I said, "She restarted the defunct Kraków University, and my mother said she sold her jewels to help buy property to expand it."

Monika looked interested, but Borys looked like he could care less. All he had to say was, "Could I have more coffee, Mother?" And then he changed the subject. "It's good to see a blue sky out the window for a change, isn't it?"

I couldn't help but think, Boris is so boorish. He may not be my kind of roommate. But, then again, he might be all right, if he was pleasant, fairly clean and paid his half of the rent.

After we ate, Borys and Monika invited us to sit with them in the living room. Their parents went to a back room. Kazimierz sat on the sofa with Monika and gently held her hand. The two of them spoke in a low, affectionate tone. My face burned with jealousy. How had Kazimierz found someone to love him while I remained single? But then a thought hit me. I have a new friend named Marcel who could possibly fill that void. He may not be of the opposite sex, but he does seem to really care!

Borys and I had one thing in common. We didn't want to sit with the happy couple. We raised our eyebrows to each other, and I said, "I heard you might be looking for a roommate. You want to step outside and talk on the front steps?"

"Yeah, Florian. Let's put on our jackets. Maybe I could show you a place I have in mind."

Although the sun was shining brightly, it was chilly outside, but it was better than being inside with that couple who were obviously getting quite warm with each other.

Borys said, "There's a place a block away where an old couple died, and their married kids—who I know—want to rent out their apartment. Wanna look at it—at least from the outside?"

"Sure," I said, smiling and trying to whip up some enthusiasm.

As we walked down the block, the cool, autumn wind kissed our cheeks. I loved this time of year. A flurry of dried leaves swirled into a whirlwind. Whenever this happened, I liked to believe it was something spiritual—that one of my parents was communicating with me from the dead. What could they be saying today?

However, I had to stick with the here and now to avoid being run over by the activity on the sidewalks. Children ran up and down, playing tag or throwing balls. A family all dressed up in their Sunday best came out of a store-front restaurant; the husband and wife were arm-in-arm. Some spoke Polish. Some spoke Czech. A few spoke Spanish. So far, I didn't like Boris very much, but I felt at home in this neighborhood.

Down the block, a fellow sitting on his steps called out in our direction. "Hey, Borys, my friend, good to see you!"

"Same here. I'm bringing my friend Florian to see your apartment."

When we got to where the guy was sitting, Boris said to me, "This is my friend Stosh."

Stosh said, "Lucky for you, I'm here and can let you in."

He brought us down some stairs to what was a basement apartment below street level. "You will love this! Perfect for a couple of single guys," he crowed.

As the door creaked open, it was like we were entering a dark cave. Stosh flicked on a switch by the door and the light exposed a bare room with linoleum flooring and dirty walls. A sagging couch and a nicked-up coffee table were left behind by the last residents. When Stosh brought us into the kitchen, we were greeted by the sound of a trickling water faucet. Against the wall was an ancient-looking Formica table that would only fit a couple of people. The two small bedrooms had no windows and, therefore, no source of natural light.

Borys was undeterred. In an upbeat voice, he said, "Look, we will each have our own bedroom for when… well you know what I mean."

Returning to what you could call the living room, Borys said, "Not bad for two single guys, right? In America, they call it a bachelor pad. All we'd need is to paint the walls and get some furniture from the second-hand store down the street."

I felt like saying, You can't be serious, thinking this is a decent apartment?

Trying to figure a way out of the situation, I feigned sickness. "Oh, yes, Borys, it is quite nice, but suddenly I am getting a stomachache. Must be from eating something bad yesterday. I need to get home quickly."

And that was the end of my foray into living with Borys in Pilsen. I gave Kazimierz my illness excuse too, and I was successful in getting him to make a sudden dash home with me. I told him in the streetcar how dismayed I was about the apartment that Borys thought was so promising.

Kazimierz sighed and shook his head. "It's just because you're an artist."

"Perhaps, but I don't apologize for that. Our apartment now is quite nice. It has adequate light, and Peter painted the walls. I added the finishing touches—decent furniture, the pictures, lace curtains…"

"And your mural," added Kazimierz.

"I can tell that Borys has no desire to do anything with that place." It almost made me laugh to think about how Borys believed the ladies would flock to our so-called "bachelor pad."

"Okay, I understand," Kazimierz said. "But I still hope you can find something in one of our Polish neighborhoods."

I didn't respond. I wished Kazimierz wouldn't be so insistent on that. I had to find a place, but I didn't know how or where.

37

MARCEL AND SIGMUND FREUD

ALTHOUGH I SPENT a lot of time worrying about where I would live, my thoughts also kept returning to Marcel. At night in my bed, I would fantasize that I had lost a loved one and Marcel took me in to comfort me. I laid on an extra bed he had, and he stroked my forehead, uttering words of support. When I had this fantasy, it felt so good. However, I wondered: was I a "latent homosexual?" I heard that Sigmund Freud—the famous psychoanalyst from Austria—was writing a lot about latent homosexuality. He seemed to believe that while some people think they like the opposite sex, deep down inside they are attracted to people of their own sex.

Freud also talked about the importance of dreams. I thought that if I really was attracted to Marcel in a sexual way, I might dream of doing sexual acts with him. However, I didn't have any such dreams.

Ah, Life! I thought. You just resolve one set of problems and then another comes along. I felt I'd finally gotten over my bitterness that my father died so early, and I'd finally come to terms with my speech problem, but now I had this sexuality thing to figure out.

No matter what, though, I decided to call Marcel. I had nothing special to say. I just wanted to talk with him. So, when he answered in his always melodic, cheerful voice, I simply said, "Hi, how are you?"

"Florian, how nice to hear from you! How have you been?"

I looked for a topic that might be of interest. "I'm fine. I went to look at a possible apartment in the Pilsen neighborhood."

"Wait! I didn't know you were thinking of moving."

"I have to. My roommates are both going back to live with their parents. You know how tough times are now. They don't have much work, and they feel they can save money that way."

"So, now you are in a quandry. I imagine you couldn't afford to pay the rent yourself where you are."

"No. I can't."

"So, how did it go in Pilsen? Did you like the apartment?" As usual, Marcel sounded very interested.

"No, it was a disaster. Tiny rooms, no light, dirty walls. It wasn't for me."

"I'm so sorry to hear that. Why don't we get together and maybe I can give you some ideas?"

"Great!"

I was glad I took the leap and called Marcel even though there was no special reason for it. We decided to meet in a few days at the café next to the Fine Arts Building.

But first I felt I needed to talk with someone…alone. Of course, Rabbi Goldman was the one to whom I would turn.

PART FOUR
1938

38

CONFIDENTIAL

I CALLED ISAAC, AND he said I could come over the next day at around 2:00 and he would tell his father I needed to talk with him alone.

Mr. Goldman's greeting was as effusive as ever. "Welcome, Florian. So good to see you again! Mrs. Goldman is at the grocer's now. Isaac said you had something you needed to discuss with me, so I told her this was a good time for her to do the shopping."

I was surprised at something rubbing against my leg. A cat!

"Isaac is like a little boy. He found this cat a couple days ago. You can see he's very thin and still hasn't cleaned himself up properly, but he loves affection."

"I like cats," I said. "We had one when I was a boy in Berlin."

Mr. Goldman offered me a cup of coffee, but I declined. Even though the cat temporarily distracted me from my problem, I was so anxious that I was afraid my hand would shake when I put the cup to my mouth.

"Mr. Goldman, I have another problem now."

"Life is like that, isn't it?" he responded with a twinkle in his eyes. "That's why it is so interesting."

"But also difficult," I said.

Mr. Goldman's cup was always half full and mine was often half empty.

"This problem is very personal and confidential. It's difficult for me to talk about."

A short silence ensued, and then I continued, "But I'm going to plunge right into it. I like a man…a lot… Sigmund Freud's been talking so much about 'latent homosexuality.' I'm just afraid..." My voice trailed off.

"I'm glad you are sharing this. I imagine it's hard to discuss, but I can see it's weighing on you. Try to relax." Mr. Goldman looked at my leg that was bouncing up and down. "Let's try to figure this out together. What do you like about the man?"

"He's very warm towards me. He always looks so intently at me when we talk, and his eyes are so captivating. I don't know how to explain it, but he seems to think my feelings and comfort are of utmost importance."

Shame-faced, I looked down at my hands folded on my lap. "And he is handsome too."

"Do you have things in common?"

"In general, yes. The arts. He has a college education as do I. He also is an immigrant like me, but, unlike me, he holds no firm allegiance to any one country because his family moved around when he was young."

Mr. Goldman pondered this information for a while. Then he launched into his opinions. "First of all, I admire Dr. Freud because he is trying to help us understand human behavior. However, I think he is too negative. Everything we do seems to him a deep problem seated in some terrible trauma that we experienced as a child, even though we can't remember it. And I think he unnecessarily troubles a lot of people with his latent homosexuality theory."

My confidante fingered his beard and, with a laugh, said he was tempted to shave it off just because it reminded him of Dr. Freud.

"Now let's look at each factor you brought up about your attraction to this man." Mr. Goldman sounded like the rabbi or teacher he was. "Do you have other people in your life who are good listeners?"

"Mary was one, but she's gone. Isaac is one." Thinking, I stared off into space. "And really that's about it. My roommates seem to care, but they're not good listeners."

Goldman said, "Tell me more about what you two have in common."

"We both like art, music, and things of the mind."

"Do you have other friends like this?"

"Only your son, Isaac."

Goldman asked, "And you say this man is good-looking?"

"Yes, and that's what concerns me. The fact that he is handsome in addition to being so caring and interested in me makes me worry about...you know..."

"Your sexual proclivities."

"Yes," I admitted with such gravity that you'd think I'd killed someone.

Goldman twiddled his thumbs, took a deep breath, and said, "I hope I'm not being too forward, but let me ask you another question. Do you fantasize about doing explicit sexual acts with this man—anywhere from kissing to other things?"

"No, I really don't," I said with complete honesty. Then I told Rabbi Goldman about my fantasy concerning Marcel comforting me after a terrible loss. "But," I said, "I never think about doing anything sexual with him."

Mr. Goldman' gray eyes reached out to mine with heartfelt compassion. "I know how much you've had to manage on your own, coming alone on the ship from Poland, trying to establish a career here, negotiating a life with roommates. It must have been and still is difficult and, at times, lonely."

I pushed back the tears that suddenly stung my eyes. "I…I… have been lone…lonely many times. Since leaving Poland, I've had to do everything…on my own… without my mother and family to fall back on."

Mr. Goldman called the cat to his side. "Here, Kitty, Kitty." The cat had been bathing himself with his paws but sauntered with a regal indifference to Mr. Goldman who picked him up. Then the rabbi gestured as to whether he could put the cat on my lap.

I nodded yes, and after Mr. Goldman delivered the furry creature. At first, the cat didn't seem to want to settle onto my lap, but when he finally did, I immediately enjoyed the warmth of another living being. The cat's loud, rhythmic purring made me feel even better.

Then Mr. Goldman returned to his teacher mode.

"In 1907, a man named William Walker Atkinson introduced what he called The Law of Attraction. He mainly wrote about how we attract a reaction by the signals or vibrations we send out. He was referring to how if we send out confident messages about ourselves the other person will treat us with respect, but if we send deprecating messages about ourselves, the other person may denigrate us. His theory doesn't pertain directly to your situation, but Atkinson got psychologists pondering why one person is attracted to another."

Mr. Goldman took a drink of the water from a side table next to his easy chair.

"In my work as a rabbi, people come to me sometimes and ask, 'Why am I attracted to a woman or man who is not my spouse?' A few are brave enough to ask, 'Why am I attracted to someone of my own gender?' It takes courage to ask this second question, but believe it or not, many of us have asked ourselves this in our minds."

"That's interesting. Many have asked themselves that second question?"

"Yes. I asked you those earlier things for a reason. Now theorists are saying we're attracted to people who share our interests. We're attracted to people who show concern for what we think and feel. We're attracted to people who have gone through something like we have. And we're attracted to people whom we deem 'good-looking.' I think that all these factors explain why you are attracted to this person."

After that long speech, Rabbi Goldman took another sip of water. This time, he murmured "Ah" like he savored the refreshing liquid going down his throat.

He folded his arms in front of him and summed it all up. "So, if it's any comfort, many of us have felt this attraction to one or two people of our own gender throughout the course of our lives…"

"You say 'many of us.' Please forgive me if I'm being too personal, but have you felt this way also?"

Goldman shifted in his seat and then he explained, "Yes, in my college days, there was a young man down the hall from me whom I idolized. He philosophized about deep things like I do, he was Jewish, he'd experienced some prejudice like I had, and he was handsome."

He continued, "I thought maybe there was something different about me because I was very attracted to a man, but I realized that the thought of making love to him was something I really didn't consider. So, I just decided I'd accept my feelings for him and see him as a dear friend, although I still thought about him a lot more than my other friends."

"What happened?"

"Nothing. We both graduated and lost touch with one another…and that was fine."

Goldman continued, "This kind of attraction happens to many people and can create confusion. You say you don't have strong sexual, specific urges to do something with this other person." He paused, then said, "But if you change your mind, I see nothing wrong with that. I know our laws don't condone same gender sexual relations but…"

My mind wandered to the Carlson case where our WPA administrator was thrown into jail for being with a man.

"But there are many people who live quietly as homosexuals and seem very happy together."

The cat jumped off my lap, but I appreciated his presence when I needed it most. Mr. Goldman picked up a string. He said, "I get this out to entertain the cat once in a while." He threw the string out, and the cat lunged for it like he was a tiger pouncing on his prey.

Goldman picked up the thread of his thought again. "For some people, having sexual relations with one's own gender is something they choose, but I believe that others are born to be attracted to someone of their own sex. They can tell this from the time they are twelve years old or younger, and I believe they should not be shamed or locked into traditional marriage relations."

I said, "I agree with you that people born in such a manner should not be condemned, but I never yearned for someone of the same sex. In fact, I was attracted to Mary and one or two other girls before I met this person."

"My advice to you, Florian, is to enjoy your friendship with the man. Don't worry about it. For the last ten years of so, you've had to go through so many of life's little and big challenges alone. It will be nice to enjoy the company of someone who listens and cares. Do things together that you both enjoy, and let things happen as they may."

For the first time in our visit, I laughed when I said, "And our friendship has had a positive effect on my wardrobe. I frequently wear a three-piece suit, but to keep up with this man's dashing appearance, I've recently bought more casual clothing that helps me look like a modern man."

Goldman joined in with a laugh himself. "And that could make life more fun."

When he stood by the door with me to say goodbye, his parting words were, "Step lightly in this world, and enjoy each moment."

39

THE GOOD LIFE

I FELT A WEIGHT lift from my shoulders. It was like when the dark cloud disappeared after I quit worrying about my speech problem. Maybe "talking it out" helped again. I hoped that what I felt for Marcel was just close friendship and nothing more. In our society, it was so hard for those who loved people of their own sex.

On Sunday, I went to early Mass, knelt, and prayed, "God, please send a mural to me again. I am rested and ready to go."

The morning's reading was from the Book of Psalms. It said, "Do not fret." That word "fret" described exactly what I often did. I wanted to be more optimistic like Rabbi Goldman.

Two days later I received a call from George Thorp. He said, "I have a new opportunity for you."

Was it divine intervention? In my new effort to be more positive, I chose to believe it was.

This mural was for the Wentworth School at 6950 S. Sangamon. George Thorp and I were invited to a meeting there.

The principal told us what the school had in mind. They wanted three large murals to decorate their spacious fourth floor library.

A woman from the committee introduced herself. "I am Esther Willis, an English teacher here, and I heard from a teacher friend at Newton Bateman about how much they love the gigantic mural you created for their stage. I got a photographer to go with me and take pictures of it. I've shown the photographs to a couple people on our committee, and that's why we specifically asked the WPA for you, Mr. Durzynski."

The principal said, "And I remembered seeing a review of your mural in the art column of the Sunday paper. The critic raved about your 'stylized' depiction of nature. Could you explain what he meant?"

I thought for a moment. No one had ever posed that question to me. "This is the way I would explain it. In the case of painting a landscape, an artist may work in a certain style. Even if the reality of the landscape is different, he makes it fit into the style he has chosen."

Looking at me intently, the principal commented,

"I find that so interesting. Now something else I'd like to know. Do you feel comfortable painting children and adults in action poses?"

"I did two massive murals for Chopin School and must have created at least sixty people dancing and engaging in all kinds of physical activities."

"Impressive," the principal responded.

Then Miss Willis explained that the committee had met previously and agreed they wanted the murals to show children playing or working along with their parents in a cheerful outdoor setting. One mural would depict children from the nineteenth century, another from the turn of the century, and the third from the current era. Overall, they were to portray the joys of childhood and how we can all have a wholesome life by being in nature and working and playing together. The name of the mural project would be "American Youth."

"Another thing," Miss Willis said, "We'd like the artist to adhere the canvases to the wall with glue and then do the painting. I believe you did that for Newton Bateman."

I smiled, "Yes, I have plenty of experience with that process. Painstaking, but piecing the canvases together is the way to create a gigantic mural."

The principal closed the meeting by turning to George Thorp. "I need to talk with the superintendent and Miss Brimley, our librarian, about the logistics and then I will get back to you and inform you of our conclusion. However, I think we will most likely go ahead with the murals, and Mr. Durzynski will be the artist. Everyone seems pleased with his experience. The big problem is money. Wanting to make the murals their class gift, the eighth-graders have already been raising money for the paint and other necessary materials. With the help of the PTA, they will continue to do bake sales and a variety of fund-raisers, but all this will take a little while longer."

On my streetcar ride home, I felt content. I knew I was up to the challenge and radiated that confidence to the group. The first time that someone asked me to repeat something I explained about my cleft palate, and everyone was very understanding. If it became necessary for me to say something more than once, I did it in a relaxed manner. My confidence inspired respect from the committee members. Atkinson's Law of Attraction proved true. However, I was disappointed that we had to wait a while to get going.

Before I opened the door to my apartment, I peered into the mailbox. I saw an envelope from The United States government. After carefully prying open this official-looking piece of correspondence, I saw it was a letter announcing that my naturalization was complete and that I was invited to a ceremony to be sworn in as a U.S. citizen. I took a deep breath and wanted to do a mazurka around our apartment. Actually, I did just that… all by myself.

A few days later, I received the final news that the

Wentworth murals were approved, and I would be the artist even though we'd have to wait for the money. Life felt good. I hoped that sentiment would last.

PART FIVE
1939-1945

40

THE BEST AND WORST

MY KNEES SHOOK, my voice quivered, and my eyes teared up as I raised my right hand and recited The Pledge of Allegiance along with 50 other people before a judge at a courthouse in downtown Chicago. The judge made a big fuss over us, and when I looked around, I saw people of all different national origins who looked just as pleased and proud as I was. Back at our apartment, Kazimierz and Peter popped open a bottle of champagne to celebrate.

Kazimierz said, "Congratulations, Friend. I wish I earned one of those certificates too, but I gotta admit I'm still just too lazy to learn to read better and study for the test."

Peter shook my hand and gave me an American flag pin for my suit lapel.

The house smelled of flowers, specifically lilies, that Marcel had sent in honor of my accomplishment. He called the day before and told me how happy he was for me. Naturally, that delighted me.

This was one of the most momentous days of my life!

~

But just a couple of months later on September 1, 1939, I experienced one of the worst days of my life. At the corner of Milwaukee and Augusta where I waited for my streetcar to go to Wentworth School, newsboys held up copies of Dziennik Chicagoska and yelled out its headlines, WAR EXPLODES! Nazis invade Poland!

Most of us waiting at our stop were Poles, and I'd never heard such an outcry of curse words in my life. It was as if all our loved ones had just been hit by a car at one time. People swarmed the newsboys for copies. Since the Polish newspapers were going fast, I bought an American one. By now, I felt I'd just about mastered the English language.

My streetcar pulled up. I boarded as quickly as possible and sat down.

The paper said that the leaders of Nazi Germany and the Soviet Union had come together recently and signed a pact. It was called The Non-Aggression Pact. Ribbentrop from Germany and Stalin from Russia announced the agreement with a picture of them shaking hands. The words "Non-Aggression" sounded good to many, but in reality Germany and Russia, along with Lithuania, made a secret pact that they would invade and then annex parts of my homeland.

So, Hitler's Nazis attacked the port city of Danzig in Poland. A gigantic, former German battleship called the SMS Schleswig-Holstein arrived in the city's harbor

Not an Ordinary Artist

a few days earlier—purportedly for some kind of goodwill, ceremonial visit. But then at the first glimmer of daylight on September 1, 300 heavily armed Nazi soldiers immerged and bombarded the dock's fort. The Polish army had some soldiers stationed there, but there were too few and they were too stunned to fight back adequately. Danzig fell to the Germans.

And then the "Blitzkrieg" (lightning strike), began. Fleets of bombers attacked Polish airfields and destroyed Polish aircraft. German tanks crossed the western border and shot into buildings on our towns' main streets.

Aloud in the streetcar, I yelled, "I knew something like this would happen!"

No one looked surprised at my outburst because my fellow Poles had similar reactions. Swearing, moaning, crying.

In agitated voices, we all turned to each other—complete strangers—and shared our concerns about our loved ones back home. I contemplated whether my brothers would go to war, if my sister and nieces and nephews would be safe, and what would happen to my dear friend Juri.

When I arrived at Wentworth School that day, it was almost impossible for me to concentrate on my mural. A teacher walking down the hall asked if I was all right.

"Of course, I'm not all right!" I replied angrily. "My country has been invaded!"

She looked at me quizzically but empathetically. "I am so sorry to hear that. What happened?"

I proceeded to tell her the news. She said when her

husband drove her to school, she had noticed that many people on the sidewalks seemed upset. "I'm not Polish, but I can imagine how devastated I would be if the United States was suddenly invaded. I'm the assistant principal. If it's all right with you, I'll inform the principal of what happened and tell him you will not be working on the murals today."

"Thank you so much. I need to try to contact my family back in Poland as soon as I can."

Quickly putting away my paints, I broke into a brisk walk to the streetcar and then to our apartment. Immediately, I put the phone to my ear and asked the operator to make the long-distance call to my brother's number in Poland. Of course, I had to wait until she transferred me to the traffic operator and then the transatlantic operator who put my call in line to get on a circuit. I could hardly sit still as I hung up and waited for an operator to tell me the call had gone through.

When the phone rang and the operator said she had my party on the line, I screeched, "Hello, Ignatz. How are you?"

"Shocked...utterly shocked. We had no idea this was coming. The children are crying. We adults don't know what to do. But we're thinking of going to Brother's house where he has the bakery. Marianna lives close by there too, and we can all crowd into his apartment above the shop." I could hear Ignatz breathing hard. "I don't think they will do anything to us. People always need bread...even the Nazis...but it's all so unfair, so awful!"

"Be careful," I said in a ragged voice.

Sounding utterly despondent, my usually self-assured brother said, "Except for baking the bread, we'll try to go unnoticed."

Then the phone started crackling, and my brother said the lines were probably over- worked because everyone was trying to call at once.

"I better go then." My voice cracked as much as the phone line. "Keep in touch, and especially if you need anything."

Ignatz sighed deeply. "Definitely, Florian. Try not to worry yourself too much. You can't do anything about this anyhow."

Those words rung in my ears, You can't do anything about this.

Being so far away from my family reminded me of when my mother died and I couldn't be with her and of when Mary was taken so suddenly and her family didn't want me around. I felt powerless then. I didn't want to feel like that now.

Unsure of what to do, I rushed to St. Stanislaus. At least I could pray for Poland. As soon as I passed through the church's doors, I heard people praying and weeping en masse. I had never heard such an outpouring of grief. When the 11:00AM Mass began, I was lucky to find enough space to squeeze into a pew. People packed the church and even knelt in the side aisles. As we mumbled the liturgical chants together, it felt like embracing each other at a funeral.

A couple of pews ahead of me I saw the back of Kazimierz's head. Peter might be among the throngs also. Like me and everyone else at the church, they left their jobs when they got the news.

I believed that God heard my incantations, but what could He do about the evil Nazis? I didn't know, but praying seemed my only recourse.

Afterwards, I met up with Kazimierz and we walked back home together, me muttering, "Oh, my God, Oh my God," and him smoking incessantly. Once we arrived, he went to his room, and I went to mine. There were no words for what we were suffering. I plopped down on my bed and tried to go into what I came to call "my nothing state" like I did when Mary and then my mother died.

Two days passed. Polish radio informed us of where the Germans made further inroads. I felt like my family was probably safe in their location.

Certainly by now, Marcel knew about the Germans invading Poland. I wondered why he didn't call. I had hoped that my conversation with Rabbi Goldman would have ended my obsession with Marcell, but here I was again.

I finally broke down and called him. In his special caring voice, Marcel said, "Oh, hello, Florian. How are you? I heard the news about the invasion. So terrible!"

"Yes, I'm devastated." I didn't like to use such a dramatic adjective, but the situation called for it.

"Have you had any contact with your family yet? Making international calls is difficult enough, let alone in these circumstances."

"Thankfully, I was able to talk briefly with my brother. The family is all right now, but I'm still worried."

"I'm sure you are. It's all so heart-breaking." We were quiet for a while, then Marcel asked, "Would you like to go out for a drink next Friday? It might do you good to have a diversion."

"Yes, that would be nice."

Initially, I felt a sense of relief hearing Marcel's caring words and tone. But a little voice in my head asked, Even though he sent you flowers when you became a citizen, how much does he really care if he didn't call you after the Nazis invaded your homeland?

41

IN IT TOGETHER

It was Saturday so I didn't have to go to work. I felt like a shred of a person hardly held together by string. I needed to do something with my free time to keep myself from completely falling apart. So, I decided to call Isaac and see how he and his family were faring. After all, they were Jewish, and the Jews seemed to be the main targets of the Germans' cruelty. Maybe they had family still in Europe. I felt like if we shared our pain it might be more tolerable.

Isaac said, "Why don't you come over? We're all in this together."

Looking out the window of my streetcar, I saw boys in our Polish neighborhood hanging Hitler in effigy. With newspaper in hand, I read that the police were worried there would be battles between German and Polish Chicagoans.

My greeting at the Goldman house was far different than it had been before. The usually carefree Isaac looked like he'd been hit by a ton of bricks. His father and mother's frowns could not turn into smiles no matter how hard they tried.

Mr. Goldman urged me to have a seat in the living room. He immediately launched into the problems that brought us together. "From what I hear, France and Great Britain have finally declared war on Germany, but they haven't done anything militarily yet." He shook his head and said, "I'm afraid that the longer they wait the more the Germans will take over."

Isaac balled his hands into fists. "And how about our country? Why won't Roosevelt do anything?"

Sitting near Isaac, Mr. Goldman reached out and touched his son's hand. "You know we just got over the Great War 20 years ago. I've heard that over 160,000 of our Americans were killed. Many veterans are in their forties now, some with amputated legs or other injuries. So, people seem to think 'Let the Europeans handle their own problems.' That doesn't make it right, but I think that may be the reason for the neutrality."

Mrs. Goldman shook her head sadly. "I heard something this morning when I was buying bread. It's so awful that I hate to share it." She looked at me in particular. "The Nazis have surrounded Warsaw."

I shouted, "Our beautiful city? Why? Why is Hitler doing this?"

Isaac winced.

Mr. Goldman yelled, "Damn!"

Previously asleep, the cat jerked up her head.

"You've studied this stuff, Dad, haven't you?" Isaac asked.

"Yes, and I have heard a German phrase that's been part of Hitler's ideology. It's called 'Lebensraum' or living space. Hitler says he wants to acquire more living space for the German people, and he believes this expansion requires taking over Eastern European territories including Poland."

"What an arrogant piece of…I won't finish the sentence, but you know what I mean" came out of my mouth.

Everyone nodded in agreement.

The rabbi continued, "Another thing that will infuriate you is that Hitler thinks members of what he calls the Slavic race—which to him includes Poles—are racially inferior to the pure Aryan 'master race,' as he calls it. He'd just as soon eliminate them along with the Jews."

"What gives him the right to think he's so great to look down on us Poles? What will happen to my brothers and sister? My nieces and nephews?" I had to choke back the tears.

All three of the Goldmans shook their heads in sympathy.

As sad as it was to express my feelings aloud, I felt

a sense of relief that I had at least partially unburdened myself. Shared pain was more bearable.

We all slumped. The cat meowed for attention, but no one was in a giving mood.

Mr. Goldman slightly changed the subject, "Hitler probably liked the idea of attacking Danzig because they're a lot of Germans in that port city. I'm sure you know, Florian, that it was once considered part of Germany."

"Yes, my family often talked about how happy they were that it was given back to Poland after The Great War."

Mrs. Goldman asked, "And what about Warsaw? Why are they bombing Poland's beautiful capital?"

Isaac offered his theory, "If they take over Warsaw, they probably feel like the Polish people will capitulate."

"My people will never do that!" I responded fiercely. "I'm worried sick about my family, but I'm wondering about your family, Mr. and Mrs. Goldman. Do you have any relatives back in Germany or Poland?"

"Thankfully, no," Mr. Goldman said. "Our relatives came here from Russia a hundred years ago, but I will have to comfort members of my congregation who have family in Europe."

Mrs. Goldman stood up and tried to smile. "This is all so tragic, but perhaps I can offer some distraction. I bought bagels and sweet rolls at the bakery. I will put on a pot of coffee, and we can go into the kitchen, if you like."

We all nodded in gratitude to her kind offer. We had run out of words.

The cat rubbed against my legs. I picked her up and sat her on my lap for a moment. "What did you name him or her?" I asked Isaac.

"Boots. You see that even though she's black she has a bit of white hair on her stomach and that each of her four paws is white."

I said, "I've seen other cats like that. They're like little miracles to have those markings."

In the kitchen, we tried to discuss mundane subjects: how the leaves were turning colors, how Isaac and my mural painting was going, and the how the Cubs were playing so well.

By the time I stood at the door and was ready to leave, Mr. Goldman came up to me. "You remember last time I told you something like 'Step lightly in the world and have a good time.' That's hard to do in this situation, so I'll just say, 'Keep your head above water, try to concentrate at your job, and take each day as it comes.'"

With Germany attacking Poland, I needed every ounce of encouragement I could get. Even though it wasn't the time for it, I would also have liked to talk with Rabbi Goldman about the return of my obsessing about Marcel.

42

EFFORTS TO BE ACTIVE

Although my family consumed my mind and heart, I still thought about other things. Of course, my Friday evening outing with Marcel was one. I was tempted to worry about how things would go, but I tried to take Goldman's advice to take each day as it comes. Also, I still tried to practice the Scripture reading saying, "Do not fret."

I did some active but worthless things to distract myself from worrying. I went to the liquor store and bought a six pack of beer. I even bought a pack of cigarettes. Real smart? but I couldn't seem to help myself.

When Kazimierz and Peter saw me drinking a beer, they didn't tease me.

Peter said, "You must be really suffering over your brothers and sister back home."

Kazimierz commented, "Good for you, Florian! A can of beer will settle your nerves."

I got out my pack of cigarette and lit up, but when I took the first puff, I coughed so hard I almost fell off my chair.

"I think those things are better left in my hands," Kazimierz chuckled.

"Here, take them," I said.

That evening, I wrote a letter to Juri. I didn't have his phone number. I told him how much I thought about him and prayed for his safety. Also, I asked about his friend Otti Berger, the Jewish Bauhaus artist.

In another effort to keep busy, I called Sophia Piotrowski, the young Polish woman who worked with me at the WPA. I happened to have her number because she worked with me on the Chopin mural.

After exchanging the usual niceties, I said, "I remember that you live in Pilsen. Do you know anyone in your neighborhood who needs a roommate?"

She said, "I moved out of Pilsen and live in Humboldt Park now."

"I didn't know that. Were your friends and family disappointed?"

"At first. They thought I was losing my Polishness."

I laughed with more gusto than I had for a long time. "That's what I've been told will happen if I leave West Town. Do you really feel less Polish?"

"I still go back sometimes on Saturdays and occasionally for Mass on Sundays. I like seeing my family and love my mother's cooking. I know I'm still loyal to Poland because the invasion is eating away at me. I have aunts and uncles back there." She paused for a while, then said, "But it is probably true that I've changed a little."

"Is it wrong to change a little?" I said more to myself than her.

"I don't think so. Why not spread your wings?" Echoes of Marcel.

We talked about our latest WPA murals, then hung up.

I rejoiced when the weekend was over and I had to go back to work. My emotions seldom got the best of me when I had a brush in hand. Thorp had called me a couple of times to tell me about all the fund-raising activities the students and the PTA were doing. Finally, now the money was available for the cost of materials, and I could begin.

Wentworth School wanted two of the murals to be 7'10" high and 8'3" wide, and a third mural to be 5'9" high and 10' wide. As usual, applying the glue and placing the canvases together would require a steady hand and an intrepid spirit. By now, though, I was so confident of what I was doing that I knew my assistants would easily follow my directions. I thought Atkinson's theory of Attraction applied here—my certainty would evoke certainty on their part.

43

OLD TOWN

When Thursday morning rolled around and I still had not heard from Marcel about his invitation for Friday, I had to use all my will power to keep from fretting. Relief washed over me when on Thursday evening at about 6:30PM, Marcel called and made the arrangements. So much for trying not to fret.

Marcel asked me to come to his residence and suggested we go to a neighborhood known as "Old Town," not far from Marcel's residence.

Of course, I agreed. I would do anything—or maybe almost anything—for Marcel. I was still putty in his hands.

It was dark by the time we got to Old Town, so I viewed it in the shadows. "Quaint" was the word that popped into my mind. Tree-lined with Victorian homes and interesting little shops, it had a definite appeal.

Marcel saw me looking at a steeple in the distance. He explained, "That's St. Michael's Church. It's one of the few buildings to have survived the Great Chicago Fire."

It was 9:00 PM, and when I looked around, I saw that the partying in Old Town was beginning. Men and women dressed in evening clothes—provocative evening clothes—walked in joyful expectation to the many bars that lined the street. Marcel took me to a place called The Mitre where I was surprised to see behind the bar a magnificent but scuffed up statue of Queen Cleopatra sitting on a throne in all her majesty. *In a bar? What next?* I thought.

A band tried to imitate the sounds of the big band of Benny Goodman (who Isaac told me was dubbed the "King of Swing"). The saxophone screeched. The drum beat. The trumpets blared. People danced and laughed together.

It looked as though the crowd was composed of single people drinking and trying to attract people of the opposite and, in a few cases, the same sex. And here I was again: in the midst of all this uproar, trying to figure out Marcel's sexual preference…and maybe my own.

The combination of loud music and boisterous voices made conversation impossible. So, Marcel and I ended up tapping our feet to the beat and watching people having a good time. Although neither of us danced, I enjoyed being in this raucous atmosphere because it helped me escape from my worries about Poland.

We left at about 11:30. As we stood outside, Marcel said, "Once again I brought you to a place where you weren't comfortable…"

I responded sincerely, "It isn't my kind of place, but I needed it…I needed this…"

"Probably to quit thinking about the invasion, the war. It's got to be devastating for you, Florian. Let's take a streetcar to my place, and you can come up for a nightcap."

Of course, I agreed.

In his suite, Marcel had a little bar with different liquors and liqueurs. Marcel said. "You're welcome to have whiskey or anything else, but I thought a brandy might be nice to close out the evening."

"Brandy sounds delightful."

Marcel encouraged me to share my concerns about my family back home. As I did, he moved his chair closer to mine. Our knees were within an inch of touching.

Then Marcel said, "Not to change the subject, but I know you've been looking for new accommodations. I'm sure you remember when we went to Cyril's party at 40 E. Cedar St. He says there is a former mansion on 46 E. Cedar that has been broken into separate small apartments, each with its own kitchen, bath and all the facilities of a regular apartment. Maybe you could even afford the rent on your own, considering that the landlord may not have as many renters as he'd like in these difficult times. And it's only about six blocks from where I live."

I could feel my face break out in my first smile since the invasion.

"Maybe that will work," I said. "I've saved some money from my earlier portrait painting, and I think the WPA will keep the art program going for at least a couple more years."

After we finished our brandy, Marcel stood up. "I must get up early tomorrow to give a couple of voice lessons at Sherwood, but I have really enjoyed our time. Let's get together again soon." He added in a pensive vein, "In the meantime, I'll be thinking about you and your family, and why don't you go over to 46 E. Cedar and see if the landlord is around?"

At the door, he rested his hand gently on my shoulder as only Marcel could and said, "Good night and God speed."

44

ONE PROBLEM SOLVED

THE NEXT MORNING, I made plans for my weekend. On Saturday, sketch people for my mural. On Sunday, go to 46 E. Cedar about the apartment.

For the sketching, I called my landlord who lived next door to us. "Aleksy, I really hate to impose, but if you and your wife and children have time today, could you come outside and briefly pose for my mural? I will pay each of you. I would appreciate your time so much."

"Of course, Florian. We can come outside in an hour,

but I was so sorry when Peter told me that you fellows are leaving soon."

"I'll miss you folks. I've loved living here in West Town and especially the apartment in your building. You've been a great landlord…keeping everything up so well."

When Aleksy and his family came outside, he asked, "Are you moving far?"

"I don't know yet, but maybe about five miles."

Aleksy shook his head and said, "Too far. You won't feel the warmth of our people there."

"I'll come back often."

"That's what they all say." Aleksy came closer to me, put his hand on my shoulder and said, "but maybe you'll be different. Try to come back as often as you can. We all need each other now more than ever."

Choking up, I said, "I know. This probably isn't a good time to leave West Town, but I will take the streetcar every Sunday to St. Stanislaus to stay close to our people."

"Sounds like a wonderful idea. I will look for you at Mass."

Aleksy's wife Natalia said, "You and Kazimierz and Peter will be missed. Such nice Polish men you are." Then she asked how I'd like everyone to pose, and she got her kids in line so I could sketch them.

I was thankful that the children cooperated, and I was buoyed by the affection I received from these folks. Before I went inside, I got out some nickels for the kids, but Aleksy wouldn't let them take the money. *My Good Polish People*, I thought.

Sunday was more of a challenging day. Marcel had asked Cyril to put in a good word for me, since he knew the landlord.

The building—completely made of light-colored stone—was like three buildings combined. Each had its own front staircase, engaged Corinthian columns, and large, vertical windows.

After knocking at the second front door, I found the owner. He knew I was coming and immediately brought me to a vacant apartment. Just like Marcel said, it had a living room, a kitchen, a bedroom and a bathroom. The rooms were small, but the apartment came furnished, and the lighting from the large windows was superior. I started to imagine how I could develop a niche for a studio.

Then the landlord brought me down to his office where he took out a lease. Everything looked to be in order. My main concern was the rent.

The gentleman said he would give me a bargain price because of the lingering Depression, and he admitted that he still had one more apartment to fill. I didn't think I'd be able to afford an apartment without a roommate, but the landlord's deal was so good that I jumped at his offer and signed on the dotted line.

45

TEARS AND LAUGHTER

Our lease in West Town would be up in a couple weeks. I scrambled to pack. At night, I listened with Kazimierz and Peter to our Polish radio. The news was so bleak I wanted to take to my bed and go into my "Nothing State," but I couldn't. I had too much to do.

On a Sunday afternoon sixteen days after the Germans invaded Poland from the West, the Soviet Army invaded Poland from the East. This crushed any chances that our Poles could hold off the onslaught. My worst fears had come to fruition.

I tried to call my brother, but amid attempting the transatlantic call, I realized that because he moved, Ignatz's phone number would be different—if he got a new one at all. I couldn't imagine the Nazis helping people who relocated to get new phone numbers. Now I feared I had lost all contact with my family.

I froze.

Peter and Kazimierz noticed me sitting next to the

phone table with the receiver in my hand. Just sitting and staring ahead.

Kazimierz yelled, "Florian, Florian, wake up!"

In his gentle way, Peter removed the phone from my hand, took my elbow, and had me stand up. Knowing that I'd been trying to call my family, he said, "It'll be all right. All that trouble will be over soon."

His reassurance made me mad—probably what I needed to snap out of my trance. In an angry tone, I said, "Easy for you to say, Peter, your family is right here! Yours too, Kazimierz."

The fellows knew I was right.

∽

But I had to go to work the next day. Life had to go on.

I brought the sketches I made of the neighbors in their action poses. When I arrived at Wentworth, I was in no mood to be friendly. Since this was so unlike me, my assistants looked at me with puzzled expressions.

After getting out pencils to sketch the children onto the canvas, I started feeling more cheerful. The act of creating had that effect on me. Even though I couldn't control events in the rest of the world, I could unfold a world of humanity and beauty with the strokes of my brushes.

On one of the murals, I started drawing children in an outdoor scene. Boys flew toy planes, built models, sailed little boats, and played with bows and arrows. Girls cut out paper dolls, talked to each other and read. When I sketched the girls, I thought about my little niece back in Poland. She was about seven when I last saw her.

Thinking about my niece made tears come to my eyes. *How is she now? About 14 years old and having to endure God knows what changes!* My heart beat so fast that I could hardly breathe.

With a massive effort to contain my tears and calm my heart, I showed my assistants the sketches from home with my desired colors on them. I asked them to concoct matching paint colors in small batches subject to my approval, but, in the meantime, I said I had to go to the restroom where I would try to stem the tide of my tears. I always went to the faculty bathroom, but the boy's bathroom was the closest one. I rushed into a stall to get some toilet paper. I hardly noticed the recess bell going off. I left my stall door half open. Suddenly, eight or so boisterous boys bounded into the bathroom. One slammed into my stall's door and almost sent me careening into the toilet. I managed to keep my balance, but for the rest of the day whenever my mood started sinking, I thought of the bouncing boys and laughed to myself about how funny it would have been if I'd landed fully clothed in the toilet.

46

A CALL AND A CONCERT

THE NEWS FROM Poland kept getting worse, but I had to know what was going on. In the mornings, I read our Polish newspaper. In the evenings, I listened to our radio station.

The latest news was that the Nazis wanted to get rid of all the intellectuals in Poland. A shocking headline announced, "Nazis kill Polish Elites." They went to the universities and killed professors. I couldn't believe it. At first, I thought somebody might be exaggerating, but then I remembered the Nazis closed the Bauhaus for no reason except that it was full of creative thinkers. Hitler and his Nazis hated people whom they deemed as "intellectuals" because they believed they might organize an insurrection against this man who many Germans now followed blindly.

Since my brother Ignatz was a teacher, I was afraid the Nazis might tag him as an "elite." I was more thankful than ever that he moved to our brother's home and joined him working at the bakery.

Thinking about the Bauhaus made me want to reach Juri. He had not written back to me even though I had sent him a letter right after the invasion. We always communicated by mail, but since I feared the Nazis might not allow the postal system to work in Poland, I dug out my phone book and decided to give him a call. I knew chances were slim that I could reach him this way, but I wafted a little prayer to heaven and hoped for the best.

After one operator eventually connected me with another and I had to hang up to wait until they reached Juri, I almost lost hope. Surprisingly, though, the phone rang, and Juri was on the other line.

"Oh, Juri, I've been so worried about you. How are you?"

Juri answered in a despondent tone, "Terrible. You know my father is a professor. Once the Nazis discover him, they could see him as a threat, and since I went to the Bauhaus and have an art degree, the Nazis might come after me too." Then Juri's voice became more animated and hopeful-sounding. "You remember I am an only- child, so there are only three of us in the family to worry about. That could work to our advantage. My parents and I have hatched a plan that I hope will work."

"Tell me. Oh, I so hope it will work."

"My father's brother lives in France. We have a car. Since the invasion is only about three weeks old, the Nazis still haven't been able to saturate all of Poland with their soldiers. My father knows back roads we could take to my uncle's home in France. Then we could go to the port at La Havre and take a ship to England. We still haven't worked out how the English would let us in if we arrived, but I've heard that they are looking for young men to be soldiers in their fight against the Nazis." He paused for a moment and enunciated with certainty, "I want to volunteer."

I got panicky. "Why? You could get yourself killed!"

"I need to stand up for Poland. The English declared war on Germany when they invaded Poland, and I want to help them defeat those damned Nazis."

Juri made a choice to help save Poland. I was reminded of my choice to immigrate to America. Was I a traitor for leaving because I suspected trouble could ensue with Germany or Russia? Besides praying, attending fundraisers, and buying bonds, I felt like I should do more to help my people.

We closed by wishing each other well, and I urged Juri to stay in touch. "If you go to France and then England, the mail system should work there…no surveillance of what you're writing, if that's the next thing Hitler does. When you have time, send me a letter, and let me know your address. And, by the way, did you ever find out what happened to your friend? What was her name—Otti?"

I could hear Juri sigh. "Yes, she wrote to me from her home in Croatia. Just a few weeks ago—before the Nazis invaded Poland—she said she finally decided to return to take care of her sick mother rather than fruitlessly pursue a visa to America. Personally, I think her Bauhaus friends, especially Ludwig Hilberseimer—her beau—

could have tried harder to sponsor her when they came to America. The problem is that being a Jew anywhere here in Europe is dangerous now. So, Croatia may not be a safe place for Otti. But I'm going to try to stay in touch with her and see how she does."

We talked a little more, and after we said an angst-filled goodbye, Marcel called.

"How would you like to go to the Civic Opera House on October 8th for a symphonic event? It's sponsored by The League of Young Polish Women. The money raised will go towards Polish relief, and it will feature a nocturne by Ignacy Paderewski. My head spins thinking about it."

I hesitated for a moment, since it was hard for me to share my feelings for Marcel, but I did it anyhow. "Seeing you always lifts my spirits. Plus, it will be for a good cause."

"Good night, My Friend," Marcel said in a soft voice that brought back vague memories of my father wishing me a good night when he tucked me in bed.

The concert began at 8:00PM. Marcel and I agreed to meet outside at the front entrance at 7:15. I had never been to this part of the city. Arriving at 7:00, I took a short stroll. The front of the Civic Opera House faced east. The Chicago River was right behind it. I stood on the pedestrian walkway of the bridge behind the Opera House and looked up and down at Chicago's magnificent buildings. Viewing the Opera House from this angle, I noticed that its back was shaped like a gigantic throne. When I walked back towards its front, I feasted my eyes on a side entrance that featured bronze doors with gilt cornices. My guess was that the building was done in the Art Deco style. It looked like it might only be about ten years old—everything looked so new and fresh. A wonderful sight to behold in this time of war and sorrow!

Returning to the main entrance, I paced and looked at my watch. It was 7:55. Feeling deserted, I suddenly saw Marcel hurrying towards me. Out of breath, he explained, "So sorry, my last voice student was very challenging, and then the streetcars were running slowly."

My smile was not the most forgiving, but I never had the courage to complain to Marcel about his being late, as often happened. The problem was that when he was late it made me feel that he didn't value me near as much as I valued him.

When Paderewski's nocturne began, I thought of what a great pianist and composer he was but also about how he had saved Poland. Every good Pole knew how he agreed to be our Prime Minister for a year, how he, as a statesman, toured the U.S. where he met with Woodrow Wilson; how he influenced Wilson to support the creation of an independent Poland at the treaty of Versailles; and how he succeeded in getting Poland to become a free state again. After he had accomplished all this, Paderewski fled politics and went back to composing and playing piano. *What a selfless man,* I thought.

At one point, the orchestra played the Polish

national anthem, and we were all encouraged to stand and hold hands. A thought ran through my mind, *Holding hands with Marcel might be a telling moment for me.* Marcel took my hand firmly; we looked at each other briefly. His hand felt smooth—unlike mine that was rough from working with paint chemicals. I felt shy about sharing this physical touch with him, but it felt good. At the end of the anthem, Marcel gave my hand an extra squeeze. We looked at each other again and sat down.

47

STILL PERPLEXED

AFTER THE CONCERT, I said it was getting late and I'd better head home. Marcel said, "I need to go too, but it was wonderful spending this time with you. Also, you know how much I love music. What a superlative rendition of Paderewski's nocturne!"

It was an interesting evening. The next day I called Isaac's father to request another private meeting.

He said, "Let's meet at Gertrude's Restaurant down the block from me. They have delicious breakfasts."

Gertrude's was a small, homey place. The aroma

of cinnamon rolls and the clanking of coffee cups filled the air. I hoped the noise would keep people from overhearing what I wanted to discuss.

Seeing me looking around and hearing me speak softly, Mr. Goldman spoke quietly also. "My dear wife is ill this week. I don't think it's anything serious. She coughs a lot, is tired, but doesn't seem to have a fever when I feel her forehead. I didn't think you'd want to walk into that house of sickness. I feel fine, but I hope I don't give you anything."

The waitress came to our table, and after we gave her our orders, Rabbi Goldman asked, "Could this possibly be about your friend?"

"Don't worry about passing along any germs, and yes, it is about my friend. You would think that with all that's going on in my life—moving, working and especially worrying about my family—I wouldn't have room in my head to dwell on Marcel."

"I told you I went through that once before, and I understand the…the…obsession."

"I hate to think of it as an obsession, but I guess that's what it is since I can't get my mind off him. When you suggested I step lightly in this world and not analyze things about Marcel so much, I felt good at first. But things have happened, and I've started worrying again."

"What in particular are you worrying about?"

"I guess it's changed a little. I'm not so afraid that I am—" I lowered my voice to a whisper—"a homosexual. That could or could not be true down the line, but I'm more confused now about whether Marcel values me.

I'll give you some examples, since I've thought about these things..."

"I imagine you have...over and over again. Not to be sarcastic but, remember, I know that feeling," Mr. Goldman said in his all-knowing but non-judgmental way.

"True," I smiled. "Okay, a couple of weeks ago Marcel mentioned on a Monday night that he wanted to go out with me on a Friday night, but he didn't call to make definite plans until dinnertime on Thursday. I felt anxious all week waiting for his call. Another example: he was kind enough to send flowers for my naturalization, but a few days later when Poland was invaded, he never called. I finally called him, and he was all kind and thoughtful. Then just a week ago he asked me to go to a concert featuring Paderewski's work. We were supposed to meet outside at 7:15, but he didn't make it until 7:55. All these situations make me feel that Marcel doesn't really care about me nearly as much as I care about him. It shouldn't matter to me that much, but unfortunately it does." I shook my head and sighed.

After a sip of coffee, Rabbi Goldman delivered his evaluation. "The double-message conundrum. On the one hand, he acts so caring when he's with you, but then he's late or irresponsible about calling. When you really care about an individual, the double messages can drive you crazy. If you didn't care so much, you'd probably write it off as that person is irresponsible in some ways, but you wouldn't take it personally."

"True."

Mr. Goldman continued, "Just think of your relationship with your roommate Kazimierz who you mentioned once. If he committed those little inconsiderate acts, you might get angry, or you'd just think 'there goes Kazimierz again.' But you wouldn't lose any sleep over it. Right?"

"Right."

"However, when someone you care about acts like that, it keeps you guessing and wanting their attention all the more. You need that reassurance."

"So, what do I do about it? How do I find peace?"

Rabbi Goldman paused, cut his waffle, and finally said, "First let's go back to your initial problem." He lowered his voice. "You didn't know what kind of feelings you had for this man. I hate to be so forward, but I have to ask: has anything of a physical nature happened between the two of you lately?"

"We held hands during the concert."

Goldman suspended his fork halfway to his mouth and opened his eyes widely.

I laughed. "I thought you would react like that. We only held hands because the entertainer told everyone to do it when he began to sing the Polish national anthem. It felt good to have this human touch, but I didn't feel any sparks fly."

Goldman proceeded to put his waffle bite into his mouth. "Okay, that may help in defining your feelings. At one time, you said you had fantasies of Marcel sitting by your bed and comforting you. Do you have those fantasies now that terrible things have actually happened to you and your family?"

I thought for a moment. "No, not really. Now that a true tragedy has occurred, I'm too absorbed with the actual crisis to look for any comfort."

Mr. Goldman dabbed a napkin on his beard to remove a few waffle crumbs. "It doesn't sound like you have…" Now he whispered, "Any sexual desires for Marcel. But he has you tied up in knots by being somewhat unreliable. My wisdom for you now is this: think when Marcel is late or when it takes him forever to call, 'Oh, well, I guess that's just the way he is.' Don't take it personally. On the other hand, that trait might make you consistently on edge. Personally, I like being in a relationship with someone like my wife who is reliable, true to her word, and strives to be on time. It may sound dull, but that's what I like."

"Thanks for your food for thought, Rabbi Goldman. It almost tastes as good as this last bite of my cinnamon roll."

Again, talking things out seemed to help—at least for the moment.

48

GOODBYE WENTWORTH, GOODBYE WEST TOWN

As usual, my painting kept my worries at bay...at least while I was at the school. I felt satisfied with how the murals at Wentworth were progressing. However, the proper position of one character still illuded me. Luckily, one day I saw a boy of about ten years old who came to the library and looked to be the right size for my mural. So, I asked the librarian if I could talk with him.

"All right," she said gruffly.

I crouched down and smiled at the boy as he sat at his desk. "Hello, my name is Mr. Durzynski. You may have seen me painting this mural." I motioned to it.

"Yes," the boy said shyly, probably wondering why I approached him.

"I hope that you can do me a favor, either today or on another day when you are in the library and have time. I'd like you to pose for me in a particular position."

As had happened so frequently before, the boy looked confused. I knew why.

As distinctly as I could, I said, "I have a speech problem. I'm sorry I'm hard to understand…"

"That's okay," the boy said quickly, probably not wanting to hurt my feelings.

"So, I will speak slowly, and if you don't understand something, please let me know."

"Sure," the boy said with a smile.

"Could you possibly pose kneeling and putting a worm on a fishhook for another boy?"

"I got time now, Mister. Be glad to do it."

And so, this young lad came over to the mural and knelt in the pose I requested. This got the interest of the other students.

I learned that the boy's name was John. Besides the fact that he was the right size for the pose, he was willing to kneel in one position for fifteen minutes on two different days.

The children kept watching, and they clapped when I finished painting John. All the children, including John, looked like they were trying to see if I had painted him well.

The librarian, Miss Brimley, was a stoic woman see. Even though she dutifully picked out books for the children and occasionally helped a student with his or her homework, she rarely smiled. However, Miss Brimley didn't scold the students when they clapped and gawked.

My assistant Ethan said, "I'm glad that boy posed for you, Florian. You've finally cheered up a little, and, by your example, these kids might start taking an interest in art."

When the mural was almost done, Miss Brimley said to the students, "I will give each of you a piece of blank paper, a pencil, and crayons. I'd like you to draw a picture of something… like Mr. Durzynski has done."

The kids smiled, and some whooped a little for this departure from the serious demeanor of the library.

∽

When I completed this three-part mural, I was happy about how it turned out, how the children may have been inspired, and how Miss Brimley attempted to foster their creativity. As I packed up my art supplies, Miss Brimley approached me.

"Mr. Durzynski, I want to say how lovely our library's walls look now. They used to be so drab. My library… our library… is now a cheerful, maybe even inspiring, place for our children to study."

"Good. I'm glad you feel like that, and I liked the way you got the kids to do a little art for themselves. You never know if one might become the next Michelangelo."

Then the principal popped in. He walked around and smiled as he took in the details of my murals. "Great job, Mr. Durzynski. The PTA and eighth grade class want to sponsor an evening open house to which all the parents and kids will be invited to view your work. We would be most honored if you, the artist, would come so everyone can have the honor of meeting you and asking any questions they might have. We'll contact the newspapers, and the PTA will serve punch and cookies afterwards. How does that sound to you?"

"It sounds great. I am so pleased the children and the PTA care enough about art that they raised the money for our supplies…and now the get-together. Wonderful!"

On the night of the event, at least 50 people crowded into the library. And there among them was John. Holding his mother's hand, he took her to where I had depicted him. His mother looked impressed that her son was in a painting. Circulating around the room was a smiling Miss Brimley with her head held high. Her humble library was transformed into an art museum.

A photographer doubling as a reporter captured the evening in photos, and shortly thereafter a short story appeared in the newspaper. I was happy to build to my advertising file of clippings about my creations, but most of all I was happy that the Wentworth children and their parents appreciated the art.

Thankfully, I concluded the Wentworth murals within a few days before I had to move. Packing was a lugubrious process. We had three days left on our lease. Kazimierz and Peter wanted to stay until the last day. Since my apartment was ready, I decided to leave earlier.

My dear uncle brought over a truck he borrowed from a friend. After he came in, I stood with him in the hallway, and he scanned the labyrinth of boxes before us. "We got work ahead of us, don't we, Florian?"

I said, "Thank you, Uncle, for all you've done. You made my coming to the United States possible, and now you're helping me move."

"That's what we do. Poles help Poles, especially family." By now, I could count on ten fingers the times people had said this in West Town.

We went into the kitchen where Kazimierz and Peter were finishing their breakfast. They rose and greeted my uncle.

A difficult silence ensued. It was time for goodbyes.

Kazimierz claimed he had something in his eye. When he put his fist to his eyes, it came back wet. "You have been a good roommate, Florian. All that culture you brought into my life. Whether I wanted it or not." We all chuckled. "And you've been easy to live with. I'll never forget how you helped me after that accident at work."

When emotions got the best of me, like in this situation, it was harder than ever to get out my words, but I tried my best. "And you, Kazimierz have show… have shown me how to be more straightforward. It…it took me a while to see it, but deep down inside, you… you have a heart of gold." My emotions made It sound more like I had a problem with stuttering than with a cleft palate.

Peter's wet blue eyes radiated tenderness. "I love you like a brother, Florian. I wish things wouldn't have turned out like they did for you with Mary, but you've picked yourself up and gone on. And I'm impressed whenever I see your art." After giving me a hug, he added, "Living with you has been like living with a famous person."

I waved away his compliment. "You're too kind."

Peter continued, "We three must stay together… somehow."

I suggested, "How about if we attend St. Stanislaus once a month? Maybe the first Sunday? We can sit together ten rows or so from the back so we can see each other."

That plan seemed to leave us in a more cheerful frame of mind. However, I suspected that our meetings would be few and far between.

49

NEW BEGINNINGS

LIVING IN MY new apartment on Cedar Street unsettled me. Everything was so different from my beloved West Town.

The physical characteristics of the neighborhood (which Marcel called the Near North Side) bothered me more than I anticipated. Big mansions—many divided up into apartments—replaced the three-story brick structures I so loved. Of course, I knew this ahead of time, but actually living in this new location was a different story.

The people were different. When I'd see them in the shops and on the sidewalks, I'd think to myself that they all seemed like the sorts I'd met at Marcel's parties.

Many of the men and women wore stylish, modern clothes you'd see in magazines. Some used fancy cigarette holders. And they all spoke in perfect English. I preferred the atmosphere in West Town where the people were more "down-to-earth," simply dressed, and spoke my beloved Polish. It helped me one day when I recalled an old maxim of my mother, "Deep down inside we human beings are all alike."

At first, I castigated myself for making the choice to move to Cedar Street, but, within a few days, I reminded myself that I tried my best to rent a place in a Polish neighborhood. So, my inner voice said, *Don't be so hard on yourself. You had to move somewhere.*

And then there was Marcel. So near and yet so far. As close as he lived to me, he still hadn't come over or called. After my last talk with Rabbi Goldman, I had hoped that my new insights would help me quit obsessing, but, as busy as I was, I found that in the quiet hours of the night and in the early morning, my thoughts still returned to Marcel. Whether I liked it or not, the man took up residence in my heart. Inner conflict was getting the best of me: I wanted a relationship with Marcel, but then again I didn't.

Five days after I moved in, Marcel called and asked if he could stop by. As usual, I agreed.

Marcel was impressed with how I had fixed up my apartment. I converted my bedroom into a studio by getting rid of the original bed and installing a Murphy bed. And I kept the draperies pulled back so the light from the tall windows would show through. "Perfect for an artist!" Marcel gushed.

After seeing my place and what I'd done with it, Marcel took me to a nearby restaurant. He said, "This place is not very beautiful, but it's sufficient for a simple meal."

It was large, brightly lit, and full of knicked-up, dark wood tables and booths. Waitresses hurried by, dishes clanged, and a cacophony of loud voices created a discordant symphony. I longed for Krystos' small, homey place back in West Town.

After we gave our lunch orders, Marcel leaned forward and said enthusiastically, "I have an idea for you...for us. How would you like to go to Perrin Hall at the Auditorium Theater to hear Augusta Savage speak?"

"Who is that again? Her name sounds familiar, but could you refresh my memory?"

"Florian, please, you should know her! I read about her and the event on the society page of The Chicago Tribune. She's the one who began the WPA program in New York City, and it's the largest WPA art program in the country."

I put down my coffee cup. "I'm so embarrassed! How could I forget her name and everything she's accomplished? I'm so busy painting my murals that I hardly hear about what the other WPA art programs are doing, but now I remember Augusta Savage. She's almost like the founder of the WPA art program, and I loved her gigantic sculpture at the New York World's

Fair. I think it was called 'The Harp.' I saw a picture of it in the paper. It was so realistic and touching with young Negro children lining up like strings of a harp and singing their hearts out."

"She is quite an artist! The program will be in two weeks. Then, you'd like to go?"

When I nodded a yes, Marcel said, "This will be an elegant affair, so I suggest you wear your best, dark-colored three-piece suit, and, if you feel artsy, fling a white scarf around your neck. You'll look the part of the successful artist and socialite!"

"Okay, now I'm excited," I said.

"Better than going to the bars?" Marcel said with a wink.

"Much better."

50

A TURNING POINT

THE LATEST NEWS in our Polish newspapers was that Hitler did something so daring that it utterly devastated me. Following his Lebensraum theory, Hitler had his soldiers order Polish people out of their homes to work and live in nearby factories. At the same time, he ordered Germans to move into the homes taken from the Polish. The gall! I couldn't believe he could orchestrate such a life-changing process and that ordinary Polish and German citizens complied. But then it came to me that people were probably terrified into submission when they saw protesting families dragged out of their homes to labor camps or what were now called "concentration camps."

I hoped that Ignatz and the rest of my family were able to remain at my brother's bakery and the now- crowded apartment above. It would be difficult for the Nazis to replace them with their knowledge of bread-baking. However, because the mail and phone calls didn't go through anymore, I could just hope and pray they were all right.

As I waited for my next mural assignment, I prepared for my evening out with Marcel to see Augusta Savage at Perrin Hall. Now, this was my kind of affair! Getting dressed up, being with sophisticated people, and hearing a well-respected artist. I took Marcel's advice to get a slender white scarf to wear with my dark suit.

This time I went to Marcel's apartment, and we took the short streetcar ride downtown together to the event. The wind just about blew us inside when we opened the large, heavy doors on this cold, blustery evening. Perrin hall was a large recital room situated in the gigantic Auditorium Theater which was right across the street from the Art Institute and on the same block as the Fine Arts Building. I was impressed by the well- dressed, very accomplished-looking crowd. When we sat down, I could hardly wait for Augusta Savage to give her presentation. She stood off to the side before she was introduced. Augusta was small in build but seemed to be of average height for a woman. Although she wore a tailored suit in contrast to the other women's long dresses and furs, I thought she looked sophisticated.

Edward Embree from the Rosenwald Fund introduced her. "Our foundation was honored to grant a scholarship to Augusta Savage some fifteen years ago to study sculpture in France. She has become the first nationally known artist to make a career out of sculpting Negro people. In addition, she has recruited and trained some of our most gifted artists from the streets of Harlem to teach in the largest WPA program in the country. Tonight, she has been kind enough to show and tell us what some of the people of her race are creating. And so, I present to you Augusta Savage, artist of the people!"

Crisp, energetic applause sounded, and people leaned forward, eager to hear what this woman had to say.

At the lectern, Miss Savage began by talking about herself. Her voice was soft and gentle. Her almond-shaped eyes were beautiful but looked somewhat sad. However, she put a smile on her face as she told of her humble beginnings in Green Cove Springs, Florida. She said she was from a large family where the children made up their own games and fun by playing outside.

"I did my chores," she said, "but all I wanted was to sneak to a nearby clay pit and scoop up the clay. Then I'd go to a creek that was next to the pit. On dry days, we kids used an old, leaky bucket to collect water from the creek to throw over the clay so it would be wet enough to mold. My parents yelled at us for doing this because when we went back home our clothes and hands were full of mud. My father became increasingly irate when he'd find me there. He said I was making 'graven images' or little idols out of the clay."

"My siblings didn't want to keep getting punished. Anyhow, they only made mud pies. I never made mud pies. I loved sculpting our barnyard animals, chickens and especially the ducks in the creek."

With a laugh, she said, "My father took a switch to me about three times a week. He just about whipped all the art out of me." Everyone winced, but she said she could laugh now because her father finally realized what talent she had and apologized.

The audience was so attuned to Augusta's story that you could hear a pin drop.

But then Augusta shifted to the present and very nicely said that she and her fellow artists could fall into the category of "starving artists" because no one bought their work. Her closing words were, "My greatest hope is that people will become more art conscious—that they will value the contribution of the Negro as well as the White artist and occasionally buy our work."

At this point, people started shifting in their seats—men examined their neckties and women fingered their purses.

"Thank you very much for your attention tonight," Augusta said brightly. "Feel free to come to the stage, look at our works, and purchase any art you might like."

Roughly half of the attendees came to the stage and examined the pieces. Most of them said to Augusta and each other, "Oh, isn't this beautiful." However, I didn't see anyone buy the art.

I coaxed Marcel to go up to the stage with me. We both looked at the pieces, and I commented on how unique they were. I didn't attend this function with the intention of buying any art, but I ended up purchasing a sculpted brown hand that was the same size as an actual hand. It was so realistic! I thought I'd put it on my desk. It was not sculpted by Augusta Savage, but it was created by one of her contemporaries. Her works, especially the bust of a New York street boy and the two-thirds life-size sculpture called Realization, were very realistic and engaging, but I didn't have the money for them.

When I paid her, Augusta looked at me with her almond eyes and said, "Thank you." Her thank you was sincere, but I felt it was tinged with disappointment because others didn't buy the art. I found Augusta Savage to be very attractive, but she would be returning to New York City in a few days, and I had a confusing enough relationship right next to me in the person of Marcel Roger de Bouzon.

After the presentation, Marcel suggested I come up to his apartment for a drink. We got to talking about the happy and sad aspects of the evening, and I found myself drinking one glass of port wine after another. I started laughing uproariously at things Marcel said that probably weren't so funny. Marcel loosened up a lot also. He took off his tie and unbuttoned the top button of his shirt.

Eventually, I said the unmentionable. "Marcel, I am curious about you. You are very good-looking, and I see you with men as well as women, but…how can I say this…you never have one special person…of either sex."

Marcel suddenly looked alert. He sat up straighter in his chair, and his lips went from a smile to a frown. "Hmm, you are putting me on the spot."

I hemmed and hawed. "I didn't mean to pry or make you uncomfortable. It must be the alcohol. Just forget what I said."

"No, it may be a difficult subject for me, but if we're going to stay friends, I guess you should know."

Marcel took a deep breath and got up to pour himself a glass of port. "Would you like another also?"

"Sure," I said. *Maybe an additional drink would help me handle whatever was to come.*

"I don't know if there is anyone else like me in this regard, but…" Marcel scratched his head. I had never seen him at such a loss for words.

"I am not attracted to men or women…sexually. I don't know why. I've tried to be physical with a woman or two and once with a man, but it made me uncomfortable."

A hush settled over the room.

Marcel got his words back. "This makes me feel like I'm strange, but I can't help it." Marcel sipped his port slowly and then inquired, "Have you ever heard the word 'libido' that Freud has started using?"

"I don't think so."

"It refers to sexual drive. Some people have more

of it than others. He says one factor may be the level of testosterone a person has or it could have to do with other factors."

"Oh," was all I could say.

Marcel added, "I do at times pleasure myself, but I must admit…I think I have a low libido."

I wanted to help my friend; he looked embarrassed. And then I thought to myself, *Who knows? I may be the same way.*

Marcel changed the subject and took on an assertive tone. "One thing I do know is that you are in no condition to go home. Why don't you stay overnight? You can sleep on the couch if you don't mind."

"Yes, I think that would be a wise idea. I haven't been this in…in…inebriated for a long time. My speech is bad enough already, but now I can hardly talk anymore."

We both laughed. Marcel got out the sheets for me to bed myself down on his sofa.

51

Enlightenment

I WAS AWAKENED BY the bright sun bursting through the borders of the drapes. A liquor-induced drum beat in my head, but otherwise all was quiet. After my third drink the night before, I had a hard time remembering much of anything, but I did remember the most important thing.

As I sat up and leaned over for my shoes, Marcel came out of his bedroom. Wearing gray silk pajamas and black slippers, he looked as fresh as if he'd just had fourteen hours of sleep.

We had coffee together, laughed at our alcoholic over-indulgence and talked about how each would try to make something of the day. After I left, I walked the six blocks to my apartment, and even though the sidewalks were slick, I glided over the ice like I was walking on air. I was free, I was finally free of obsessing about Marcel! He had made it easy for me by divulging his truth. Now I didn't have to make a choice!

When I attended Mass the next day, St. Stanislaus' oldest priest read the scripture. It came from Ecclesiastes, a book of The Old Testament. It was the one about how there is a time for everything and a season for everything under the sun.

"To everything there is a season, and a time to every purpose under the heaven:

[2] A time to be born, and a time to die; a time to plant, and a time to sow;

[3] A time to kill, and a time to heal; a time to break down, and a time to build up;

[4] A time to weep, and a time to laugh; a time to mourn, and a time to dance;

[5] A time to cast away stones, and a time to gather

stones together; a time to embrace, and a time to refrain from embracing;

⁶ A time to get, and a time to lose; a time to keep, and a time to cast away;

⁷ A time to rend, and a time to sew; a time to keep silence, and a time to speak;

⁸ A time to love, and a time to hate; a time of war, and a time of peace.

A time for every purpose and for every work."

I loved those verses from Ecclesiastes. Like everyone else, I had seasons in my life. I never thought they would only be seasons, but they were. I never thought I'd get over my obsessing about Marcel, but I did. I never thought I'd get over my grief about losing my father, but I did. I never thought I'd be able to accept my speech difference, but I did.

And then I made a vow to myself: *During a good or bad period, keep your perspective. Remember this is just a season.*

52

WAR TIME

THE WPA COULD not and would not pay for us artists to work forever. The program was only created to exist until the Depression was over. Thankfully, the American economy seemed on the road to recovery. Painting murals for the WPA was a long, wonderful season, but I had to admit it was coming to an end.

I finally heard from my family! They were still making bread, but now it was mainly for the Nazis who had infiltrated the town. My brother hated how they tromped in with their big, noisy boots and acted so superior. They would boss around my family and when they went to pay they'd just about throw the money on the counter and walk off arrogantly like my family should be thankful to do their bidding. After they left, my brother and his wife would swear under their breath until the next Nazi brutes walked in.

When the U.S. was brave enough to join the war, many of my co-artists in the WPA enlisted or were drafted into the military. Because of their artistic backgrounds, they were asked to design posters to motivate men to enlist and women to work in the factories. I thought, *That won't be enough for me.*

With all my heart and soul, I wanted to fight for the defense of my Polish people. I wanted to be involved in actual conflict or even fly war planes, but just like when I went through immigration at Ellis Island, the health inspectors found me wanting. At my physical, they told me, "We're sorry, Mr. Durzynski, but our radio systems play a crucial role in our air and land communications, enabling our pilots and men on the ground to receive vital information and relay it to other airplanes and ground stations. We can't afford to have misunderstandings or to repeat things." And then there was the fact that most of the recruits were only half my age. However, I said loud and clear, "I really want to serve."

They accepted me into the military but with the mandate that I would not go into combat. After looking at my artistic experience on my enlistment papers, they sent me to Camp Robinson in Arkansas. The commander there wanted someone to create a gigantic mural for their service club. I was angry because I really wanted to be of direct service to my Poland.

I got over my anger eventually though because the mural was an opportunity to use my creative energy more than I ever had in the past. Unlike working for the schools where they always gave me a theme, I had complete freedom to plan what would go up on the wall. I felt like the 58' x 20' wall was my "tabula rasa" or blank slate as the new psychologist B. F. Skinner said we were all born with. I thought and thought about what images and ideas I wanted to present. As usual, I wanted my theme to be positive and uplifting. After much rumination, I came up with the concept of the postman's daily mail call to bring much-appreciated letters to the service men and women. I ended up painting a mailman going through towns, factories and farmlands and then ending up at Camp Robinson. The title of my mural was "Mail Call." It took me several weeks of thinking and then seven weeks of actual painting (with assistants) to complete the project.

My supervisors invited reporters out to take pictures and write stories about the mural, and I added the clippings to my advertising collection. However, my greatest joy came from uplifting the soldiers who smiled when they entered the service club and gazed upon my art.

My mural was so well-received that I was sent to Camp Fannin in Tyler, Texas to do a mural for their service club. This group presented me with a theme, "The Life of a Nation for Freedom," but that was quite broad, and again I did a lot of thinking and research to come up with a plan. This mural was to cover the southeast wall from the ceiling of their ballroom to a few feet above the floor. The total area was 30 feet high and 60 feet wide. I painted soldiers in different phases of army life and training, fighting at the Guadalcanal and the Battle of Tunisia. In addition, I depicted the work of the Womens' Army Corps and the Army Nurses Corps. I wanted the viewers to realize that it was only through the hard work of these dedicated people that The United States fought evil and maintained freedom. There were four smaller panels, and in them I depicted the Tyler courthouse, Texas oil wells, and the famous Mimosa trees. Even though I was an immigrant from Poland, I again ended up teaching myself more about American history than a lot of Americans knew.

One night as I lay in my bunk, I experienced a sense of deep satisfaction about my military murals. This led me to reminiscing about the joy I received from doing the WPA murals. However, there was a difference. Doing the WPA murals in Chicago was easier because I could come home to my roommates; I could go to my favorite restaurant; I could attend my beloved church; I could visit with Marcel and Isaac. In Arkansas and Texas, I was basically alone.

My last mural assignment was to depict "The History of Aviation" at Unit 120 of the Army base in Richmond, Virginia. No small task! I figured I needed fifteen separate panels for the job. My superiors wanted the panels to be hung as individual murals anyhow, so they could be separated and sent to other bases if so desired in the future. Off to the library I went again. I began with Leonardo da Vinci and his helicopter inventions; I progressed to the first balloon flight of the Montgolfier Brothers; and I concluded with our current commercial and military planes. I knew that my superiors really valued what I created because they had special lighting installed to highlight each panel. When the service men and women walked by, they lingered and said things like "Nice work" or "Good job."

When I came down from the scaffold on my last day of painting, a small group of officers and privates walked up to me. One man spoke for the group and said, "We want to present to you this plaque for Outstanding Achievement in Mural Decoration." They must have had it made at some little trophy shop, but to me it was like a Hollywood Academy Award. Although I couldn't fight like the other men, I felt I contributed to the morale of the troops.

However, as much as I loved painting the murals and felt good that the Richmond soldiers appreciated my work, I felt "different." I didn't have much in common with the guys in my barracks who were very young and absorbed in their physical training. To gain a sense of belonging, I gladly donned my uniform whenever I wasn't painting.

Searching for companionship and perhaps even love, I went to a few USO dances in Richmond. I met one woman who I dated a couple of times, but I found her to be very persnickety (to use an American term), putting too much emphasis on minor details; not at all like my Mary who loved riding a roller coaster as much as teaching a child to read.

Even though at this time in history, we Americans were most concerned about whether the Nazis would be defeated, we were still individuals with our own wants and needs. I, for one, felt lonely whenever my "leave" time came. Unlike my peers, I had no family eagerly awaiting my visits or return. I recalled the words of the English poet John Dunne: "No man is an island."

Whenever I had a leave, I would rent a car and go by myself to nearby towns or states… always in uniform. I especially enjoyed visiting Virginia Beach. I loved its boardwalk, cafes, and street performers. What struck me the most, though, was the Atlantic Ocean. Living in Poland, Berlin and Chicago, I seldom saw an ocean. The sight of its changing colors, the sound of its roaring waves, and the feel of its gritty sand delighted my senses. Having seen Arkansas, Texas, and now Virginia during my military service, I realized that the United States was a big place with many different geographical regions, and I wanted to see more of it.

And then 1945 arrived! The coordinated efforts of many nations ultimately led to the defeat of Nazi Germany. I felt like I was the happiest man alive. Poland was Poland again.

My family members all lived through this terrible period and returned to their regular jobs and homes. Their letters burst with thanksgiving but also depression from what they had been through.

PART SIX
1945-1959

53

WHAT TO DO NOW?

While I was in the military, Marcel and I occasionally exchanged letters. I fully enjoyed each of them; I felt like someone cared. In his most recent letter, he wrote:

> *Dear Florian,*
> *I am wondering if you have given any thought to where you might live after you leave the service. Gertrude Taylor, who manages my building at 1020 Lake Shore Drive, says she has a couple of vacancies at 1040 Lake Shore Drive which is the complex that adjoins mine. It would be wonderful to have you here, and I think it will be nice for you to know you have a home awaiting you.*
>
> *Give it some thought.*
>
> *Regards,*
> *Marcel*

After we defeated the Nazis, I was elated but unsure of where I wanted to go next. I wrote a letter back:

Dear Marcel,

I really appreciate your letting me know that there will be vacancies at 1040 Lake Shore. I will definitely consider looking into it.

Your friend,
Florian

However, the truth was that I thought about living in West Town again. For me, West Town meant belonging. So, I rented a room at the Lewis Hotel where I had first exhibited my work. I planned to stay until I figured out if I wanted to remain in West Town or try Marcel's building.

"Polonia" was the new name given to Chicago Polish neighborhoods and the hundreds of thousands of Poles living within them. Some said there were more Poles in Chicago than in Warsaw.

West Town was still considered the Polish downtown. I thought that living there again would make me feel at home. I couldn't wait to eat at Nowak's again and, of course, attend Mass at St. Stanislaus.

When I opened the door to Nowak's, I looked forward to hearing Krystos' booming voice and experiencing his warm greeting. However, he was nowhere to be seen. It looked like his children were now manning the restaurant. Vaguely remembering me, they told me their father had very arthritic knees and barely came to the restaurant anymore. My favorite waitress, Kasia, was nowhere to be seen.

When I returned to St. Stanislaus, my favorite priest was still there but just sat in a regal chair not standing up or sitting down. It looked like even those little movements could be treacherous for him. I still was inspired by his devotion as he mouthed the words of the liturgy, but I was disappointed that I didn't recognize one person at the service.

So much had changed!

One possibility remained. I went to see my landlord who I hoped still lived next door to my previous apartment.

Aleksy was outside raking leaves. When he turned and saw me, he didn't know who I was. He eyed my uniform and looked confused. But when I said "Hello" in our native Polish, recognition dawned on him, and he crowed, "Florian, its' been so long."

He gestured towards my uniform and said, "Looks like you've been fighting for our country."

"Well, sort of..." my voice trailed off. "It's so good to see you again." I walked up to him and shook his hand.

A simple handshake was not enough for Aleksy. He smothered me in a giant bear hug and said, "I have some things for you. Wait right here."

He ran into his place and brought out four pieces of mail that had gone to my former West Town residence. I saw one with Juri's name and return address. It dawned on me that I had asked him to write but had not given him my new address when I moved to Cedar Street.

I said to Aleksy, "I'm stunned!" I held up the letter and explained that I hadn't heard from my friend since before the war. "I need to go back to my room and read this. Then I'll return, and I'd like to inquire if you have a place I can rent."

"Sure, sure," he said, "It looks like that letter is very important to you." Aleksy looked almost as emotional as I felt. "Just come back when you can, and it was so nice to see you again, Florian."

Back at my hotel room, I read:

Dear Florian,   *May 30, 1945*

I am happy to share that my parents and I made it to London. Our boat was packed with people, and we wondered if we'd be accepted at the port. Luckily, we were. A kind Quaker family took us in. The Quakers have helped so many of us refugees. I have to pause when I write the word "refugees." It still seems strange to think of myself in that way."

The British would not accept me for military service. Since I had come from Poland, they were afraid I could be a spy. That's okay. At least my parents and I got away from the Nazis.

I am so thankful that the war is over. Your American soldiers finally helped save the day even though it took them forever to enter the melee.

My parents and I will be heading back to Poland within the next month.

But I have sad news. Although you didn't know my friend Otti Berger, you often inquired about her. I think I told you she went back to live with her mother in Croatia. I can hardly write the following words: In 1944, the Nazis stormed her house and took her and her family to Auschwitz. Only one of her brothers who was not home at the time survived. He saw a letter from me and wrote to me that they gassed Otti to death. I couldn't believe it. How cruel to just enter an innocent family's home and drag them to the gas chambers because they were Jewish!

My heart ached when I found out that they killed some of my other friends from the Bauhaus who were Jewish. I hate the Nazis!

But I want to heal my soul and move on. I plan to go back to Kraków or what remains of it. I never got a chance to see how my new artistic style would "sell" in Poland.

I hope you are doing well. At least, you are in the United States where you don't have cruel countries breathing down your borders.

Looking forward to hearing from you.
Juri

When I read about Otti Berger, I felt like someone ran a dagger through my heart. It was so demonic of Hitler and the Nazis! So unjust! I couldn't believe that humans had sunk to such depravity.

My hope was that humanity would learn something from this and would never let it happen again. But I was mostly grateful that Juri was unscathed.

54

LOOKING FORWARD

EVEN THOUGH I told Aleksy I would come back about possibly renting an apartment from him, I realized that West Town was not for me anymore. Aleksy was still the same, but everything else about the neighborhood felt different.

More new Polish immigrants flowed into the

neighborhood after what we began calling the Second World War. With babushkas, tattered clothing, and barely functioning suitcases, they tumbled in, looking shell-shocked. Many of my peers who had arrived in about 1929 when I came had learned English, had achieved an occupation, and had moved out like Mr. Cieplak did. I loved West Town, but I realized I no longer needed the familiarity of Polish customs, Polish Mass and Polish conversation.

If sighs could solve problems, I would be a happy man, but I sat at the desk in my little hotel room sighing and wondering what to do next. Finally, I decided to consider Marcel's offer to live in a section of his building. I hoped I wouldn't get all obsessed about Marcel again—living so close to him—but this was the best option I felt I had.

So, near the end of my short stay at the Lewis hotel, I took the bus to meet with Gertrude Taylor, who, according to Marcel, was the building's caretaker.

Miss Taylor was friendly but cautiously so. You could tell she meant business and would not put up with any shenanigans.

She explained, "There are mostly women in this part of the building. They are all what we now call 'career women.' They are teachers, secretaries, and even a nurse. What happens to be your career, Mr. Durzynski?"

I hesitated for a moment. When I first came to the U.S., I called myself a portraitist. Since I had worked for the last twelve years or so painting murals, I felt I had to respond, "I am a muralist."

Gertrude Taylor cleared her throat and looked at me like she hoped I could pay the rent with such a career.

Nevertheless, she continued, "Each individual has their own little apartment. Our cook prepares breakfast and dinner for everyone, and we eat together at a large table in the dining room. Is that satisfactory to you?"

I said, "Of course," but I wasn't sure if this situation would be to my liking. There would be a lot of togetherness with people who I didn't know and might not like. Then I told myself *If I could live in the barracks with a bunch of men with different personalities, I could handle this.*

∽

When I moved in, Marcel was ecstatic. I didn't have much to unpack this time. Just some clothing and, of course, my art supplies.

I found I wasn't obsessed with Marcel anymore. What a relief! Once he'd made it clear where he stood, I relaxed.

Like many other veterans of the war, it was hard for me to get re-established. There was no market in the Chicago area for murals.

I was able to support myself with my art—but just barely. I lost most of my connections as a portrait painter due to my time away in the military, but occasionally one of my past clients referred a new customer. Cameras were a problem. The new and improved ones captured every detail, and they were affordable. Now most people just took pictures of each other or had their "portraits" done at a photography studio.

Occasionally, I got together with Kazimierz and Peter along with their new families. They had a piece of my heart because we'd struggled together as young men to find a place in the world. We loved to reminisce, but I had to admit I felt jealous because they both had wives and children.

I grew restless.

Isaac and I had stayed in touch. He was still single, and I was glad to have an unmarried friend. We occasionally had lunch together at our favorite Jewish deli. His formerly curly mane was receding, and he even had a bald spot on the back of his head. But he was still the same lively Isaac.

"I need to move on," I told him.

"What are you looking for?"

"It may sound crazy, but I'd like to try living in a new part of the United States. It will be very hard because I won't know anyone, but it could be exciting."

"'Exciting,' I've never heard that word come out of your mouth. I'd miss you if you left again, but let me think about what might be a good place."

During this time, I regularly visited with Marcel since we were both in the same building. He was older than me—19 years older—and it began to show. Wrinkles lined his face, and his gait slowed.

One day Marcel said, "I feel like I'm not valued as

much as I used to be at Sherwood. I think Sherwood is going more in the direction of piano and violin instruction. My gifts don't seem to be appreciated anymore."

I couldn't console him. It sounded like he was being realistic.

"In the past, whenever schools didn't need my talents because they were going in a new direction I would move to a new school—usually in a whole different state, but I'm getting older now. I don't feel like moving. I must find something else to do."

"You can't abandon your gifts!" I just about shouted in dismay.

"A man must make a living," Marcel said. "Sadly, I don't have much saved. I hope you have a better future in the arts. I may have to look elsewhere for an income."

When I returned to my little apartment that night, I was despondent. *Such a wonderful, gifted man not fully appreciated in this stage of his life.* Marcel was in his late sixties.

A chill ran down my spine. Perhaps the same could prove true for me.

A couple weeks later, I celebrated my 50th birthday—alone. I wasn't the kind of fellow who wanted to advertise, "Hey, it's my birthday. Let's do something." My tiny circle of friends didn't know it was my big day, but it made me pause.

I thought, *This latest stage of my life has been my in-between stage, and I don't know what will come next.*

Rather than letting my next stage just happen to me, I sought in earnest for a way that I could define it.

And, much to my delight, my friend Isaac came up with an idea. He called me. "Florian, remember that guy Ethan from the WPA?"

"Sure, he was a great assistant."

"He says the place to go for artistic opportunities is Pasadena, California. They have a very active art league, and some artists get commissions to do murals. There's a lot of money out there, and supposedly people have big, sprawling mansions. Ethan says they commission murals for their walls."

Ta-da! My next stage of life would be in Pasadena!

55

GUTS

"Guts." That's the word Rabbi Goldman used when I went to say goodbye.

Mr. and Mrs. Goldman were in their late eighties now. They shuffled more than walked, but their minds were as sharp as the proverbial tacks.

Boots, the cat, was not quite as sharp. She slept a lot, and when she occasionally got up, she squeaked more than meowed, but her motor ran as strong as ever.

For my afternoon visit, we all sat in the living room. Mrs. Goldman put out cheese and crackers with bottles of Pepsi. Apologetically, she said, "I'm not much into elaborate entertaining anymore. I have to slow down, but I thought you might like these."

Although I wasn't hungry on this hot afternoon when even fans couldn't cool the house, I forced myself to nibble on her thoughtful fare. Then I announced, "I'm going to Pasadena!"

"No!" frowned Mrs. Goldman.

"Guts! That's what you've got, Florian. That's a big change, but I give you a lot of credit," said Rabbi Goldman.

After I inquired about how they were doing and they asked me about my trip, I sat forward and said, "Well, I need to get packing. Isaac said he'd help me, but my little car won't hold much. So, I must be very spartan in my choices."

Then I got choked up. It was time to leave.

Looking at both Mr. and Mrs. Goldman, I said, "I don't have enough words to tell you how much I've appreciated your hospitality over the years. Your youngster Isaac …" We all had a laugh at the word "youngster." "He's been such a friend, and we'll continue to stay in touch."

"Mrs. Goldman, you've been like a mother or aunt to me, and I appreciate how special you've always made me feel in your home."

"Mr. Goldman, you have helped me deal with so many of my secret thoughts that would have driven me crazy if I'd kept them bottled up! And you've shared a goldmine of insights that I'll never forget."

My throat tightened, but I had to finish. "And I know those insights will help me as I step forward into my future. You've helped me realize that I, like everyone else, will be confronted with occasional problems and I shouldn't get stuck in the mire of thinking 'poor me.'"

As we stood by the door saying our final goodbyes, we all smiled and fought back tears at the same time. I hugged Mrs. Goldman, feeling her well-worn apron next to me and enjoying her little pats on the back. I shook Mr. Goldman's hand…that chubby, smooth hand whose main labor probably consisted of turning pages. Then we half- embraced as men do. I noticed that Mr. Goldman had lost inches in height. I thought, *He may have become smaller physically, but he is gigantic when it comes to wisdom and kindness.*

Isaac looked like he was trying to hold back tears, although he was coming with me to do the packing.

56

ON THE ROAD

WHEN I GOT out of the military, I learned how to drive. From my savings account, I purchased a Ford. During the war, automobile factories were re-purposed to build tanks, trucks, airplanes, Jeeps, torpedoes, and even helmets. So, I had to buy a car that was manufactured before the war. Despite it being a few years old, my Ford ran well, and I was eager to take it on the long road trip to California.

While I had faith in my car, I didn't have as much faith in myself—specifically in my ability to follow directions. For two weeks, I studied maps and figured out my route. I discovered that if I followed the highly traveled Route 66 that started in Chicago, I would get to Pasadena.

Before I left, I said one final goodbye to Marcel. How much of my thoughts and feelings had revolved around this man for so long!

Marcel announced, "I finally got a job."

"Great! What's it like?"

"I am now an office manager at a steel treating company. It's a good enough job, and I'm proud that I can keep supporting myself in a respectable way, although you know that it doesn't make use of my true talents."

I said, "I admire you, Marcel, for landing that job. What an accomplishment! When you interviewed, you probably won them over with your good looks, voice, and confidence."

Marcel shrugged and smiled, like he knew it was true.

We hugged, looked in each other's eyes, and echoed, "Good luck, and let's keep in touch."

I felt like I was deserting Marcel. Not only he but also his friends were getting up in age. *Who would look after him if he needed it?* However, in my desire to enter a new phase of life, I ignored that question.

On my trip to Pasadena, Route 66 took me across the agricultural fields of Illinois, to the rolling hills of the Missouri Ozarks, through the mining towns of Kansas, across Oklahoma, to the open ranch lands of Texas, to the mesa lands of New Mexico and Arizona, and to the Mojave Desert until I reached my destination. I stayed at YMCA hotels as much as I could because they were clean, safe and cheap.

I left Route 66 a couple times. Once I went 50 miles out of my way to see the Grand Canyon. I got lost on my little detour, but what I saw was well worth it. With every step I took on the canyon's ledge, the colors and striations on the rock looked different. I never imagined there could be so many different shades of red, green, gray, brown, yellow and even gold. I could have stayed there forever feasting on the canyon with my artist's eyes.

However, I journeyed on. When I finally reached the outskirts of Pasadena, I was weary, hot and sticky. Although I had my car windows down for the whole trip, my clothes were rumpled, and they stuck to my body like glue.

57

SO NEW

BLINDED BY THE light! That's how I felt when I drove on Route 66 into Pasadena.

Was the sun really capable of emitting so much light? I asked myself this after living all my life in cities where the dirty air plus the tall buildings obscured the sun's brilliance. Of course, I had seen the sun shining brightly when I drove across the deserts of the United States, but sill I was impressed, thinking that my destination would hold so much light.

The sun's rays glinted off the fender of the car ahead of me. The sun's masterpieces—roses, bougainvillea, and geraniums—shone brighter than those in any artist's paintings.

I thought that this ethereal brightness would be a part of each day in Pasadena, but the truth was that I drove into the city on one of its clearest days. As time went on, I found that Pasadena was in a valley—specifically the San Gabriel Valley—and that it wasn't always sunny. Located between the foggy San Gabriel mountains and smoggy Los Angeles, the city sometimes was hazy, but it was usually warm.

On my first day driving through Pasadena, I saw that Route 66 was labelled locally as "Colorado Boulevard." Along with what I call regular trees (I wasn't a botanist), I saw a few palm trees for the first time. I loved the way their green fronds gently waved in the wind.

While on Colorado Boulevard, I checked into an inexpensive motel and decided to stay there until I figured out a more permanent living space. That evening, as I sat by the motel's little pink pool, I felt like a fish out of water. Pasadena was like a bit of heaven. I was used to the hard scrabble life of big city living. Did I deserve this? Would I ever be motivated to work in this environment or would I prefer to sit around pools drinking cocktails all the time? After all, I WAS A MAN WHO LIVED TO WORK, NOT WORKED TO LIVE. Most anyone else would jump for joy to be in such a lush environment, but being the serious guy I was, I didn't know if I could embrace it.

I decided to let my ruminations rest and planned instead to follow Ethan's advice: "The first place you should go is the Pasadena Society of Artists." I remembered how Kazimierz and Peter urged me to join the many organizations and teams that St. Stanislaus offered. "Not for me" I would tell them. Nevertheless, even though I was not "a joiner," I knew I should go to the society for at least one meeting.

When I finally summoned the courage to attend, the other artists greeted me warmly. They were planning an exhibit of their members' works. During a break, someone struck up a conversation with me.

"So, what kind of art do you create, Florian?" he asked.

"I love to do portraits and have done many over the years, but murals are also my expertise. I couldn't begin to count the number of walls I painted for the WPA and the military."

This man, who introduced himself as Joseph, gave me that familiar, puzzled look. Then I explained about my speech difference. He relaxed and had no problem asking me to repeat things if he needed the help.

Joseph told me about a wealthy woman who approached him and asked him to do a mural for the interior of her house. He had told her that he was an easel painter and, regrettably, did not think he could do a painting on a wall.

"Actually," he said, "I really have no interest in doing mural painting anyhow. Would you like me to tell her about you?"

"Oh, yes," I responded, "Please do tell her." I got a small piece of paper and a pencil from my coat pocket and wrote down my phone number.

A couple weeks later, I returned to the Pasadena Society of Arts. People remembered me and were very cordial.

Joseph was at the meeting again and went out of his way to greet me. Looking to be about forty years old, Joseph was a slender man, about my height, with black curly hair and dark eyes. He wore a leather jacket and, like many of the members, he had a thin scarf draped around his neck.

When the meeting concluded, Joseph walked out with me. "Since you are new in the neighborhood, I thought you might like to go to one of *our* bars with me."

I smiled, but then decided to gain clarity. "When you say *our* bars, what do you mean?"

Joseph squirmed, then lowered his voice. "You know, our bars are for men only…of… of a certain disposition."

I stopped midstride. *What made him think I would want to go to a bar like that?* I never wished to hurt anyone, so I tried to lace my words with kindness. "I'm sorry, Joseph, but I don't like to go to bars, and I don't like to drink much. But thank you very much anyhow."

Joseph "Understandable. That's quite understandable. Maybe I'll see you at the next meeting. Have a nice evening, Florian."

"You too," I said as Joseph increased his pace and walked away.

58

LIFE STAGE REPEAT

I'D FINALLY LEARNED that I, like every other human being, would often experience problems and would go through various life stages. However, I wasn't prepared for the same issue from a previous life stage to crop up again.

When Joseph asked me to go to what I assumed was a homosexual bar, a thunderbolt ripped through me. I asked myself, *What signals was I sending?*

I thought I had this homosexual-heterosexual thing all figured out. But I wondered again if Marcel had made it easy for me by revealing that he didn't want intimate relations with me or anyone else no matter what my proclivities were.

For the next several nights, I slept badly. Confusion gathered strength in the dark.

But one day, I woke up clear-headed and made a choice: I would remain a heterosexual or maybe a nonsexual male. Perhaps I had a low libido like Marcel or perhaps I was one who could go either way. However, because of my Catholic upbringing and of how I wanted people to perceive me, I would remain as I was…lonely or not.

I ended up purchasing a simple home on Colorado Boulevard on Route 66, the main street of Pasadena. Although my house was a humble one, it was a popular spot to view the Tournament of Roses Parade every year on New Year's Day. I loved smelling the roses and other flowers that permeated the air while people constructed floats on a nearby side street, and I enjoyed watching the bands, horses, and floats as they streamed by my front yard.

The woman to whom Joseph had referred me called me and had me paint a mural in her living room. It was like an advertisement of my skills to any of her friends who came to visit. Regular commissions started flowing my way from homeowners in Pasadena as well as its bordering towns—Altadena, San Marino, Alhambra, San Gabriel, Duarte, and others.

In addition, I approached banks, hospitals, and other institutions to inquire as to whether they had any vacant walls where they might want some art. There, too, I garnered commissions.

Although I initially feared that the persistent warm California weather might make me lazy, I worked like the busy bee I always was. I began thinking of Pasadena as my home and not just a temporary domain. I felt proud that I had summoned the courage to make this move.

And then on December 17th, 1953, I received a phone call from Cyril, the man whom I first met at one of the parties to which Marcel invited me.

Uh, oh, I thought. *This can't be good.*

"How did you get my phone number?" My tone was surly. I was already angry, dreading what was to come.

"You don't have to bite my head off, Florian." Then Cyril's voice turned gentle. "I got it from Marcel's phone book."

"He's dead, isn't he?"

"To put it bluntly, yes. It was a heart attack. He went quickly."

"I'll fly in."

"My friends and I are making the arrangements. It's difficult for me to say these words, but we will have a service for him in a few days. I'll call you back with more details." Cyril paused and took a deep, anguished breath. "I know he meant a great deal to you, as he did to me."

Although Marcel and I lived thousands of miles from each other, I couldn't imagine a world without him. I returned to Chicago in a melancholy haze and attended his funeral.

Lying in his coffin, Marcel still looked handsome. I touched his cold hand and felt a chill run up and down my spine. He'd been such a force of life and vigor, and he'd been such an important person in my life. I still loved him dearly.

Cyril had everyone up to his apartment after the short service and, in hushed tones, we picked at the catered food. Marcel may not have had a wife and children, but he did have many friends who treasured him.

Despite feeling numb, I wanted to do a few things before I returned to Pasadena, but being in Chicago again was a challenge. The many people, tall buildings, trucks and cars still fought for space and air. Plus, it was December, and I was not used to cold weather anymore.

I stayed at the Lewis Hotel in West Town. I made sure I attended Mass at St. Stanislaus. As usual, the pews were full. The oldest priest was still there sitting on a throne-like chair off to the side. But again I recognized no one. I missed that easy familiarity when I could tell who was sitting five rows ahead of me by seeing my neighbor's babushka or knowing that it was the baker three rows ahead by the way he gingerly placed his legs on the kneeler. So much change. I sobbed quietly for Marcel during much of the choir's chanting.

I went to Nowak's after Mass. Now Krystos' children told me their father had moved to Florida. I ordered my kielbasa, eggs and Paczkis like I did in the old days. It was wonderful to eat Polish food again, but I still missed Krystos and Kasia.

I stopped by the Polish Museum of America, as it was now called, and, along with their permanent collection, I saw they had some new exhibits. I introduced myself to the curator, and, when she heard my name, she overflowed with enthusiasm. "You are Mr. Durzynski? In our art gallery, we have a portrait of yours that we recently obtained. It's of Leon Walkowicz's wife, Felice!"

She took me to the portrait and said, "She bequeathed it to us upon her death."

I didn't know Felice had died. I thought, *Has everyone in my previous life passed away?* I forced back tears over the loss of this wonderful woman who was the first person to help me feel comfortable with my speech difference.

I didn't know why, but something told me to take a taxi to Newton Bateman School. I asked the school secretary if I could look again at the mural I'd made for the back of their stage. The mural was still in fine shape. I became sentimental looking at the children below running around during recess. I thought about little Ella Leonhart and hoped my encouragement inspired her and some of the other children to pursue a career or hobby in art. Being reminded of my mortality over the last two days, I realized my visit to Newton Bateman was a way of affirming that my life mattered.

I didn't have time to see the Goldmans, Isaac, Kazimierz or Peter. I had to leave on Monday afternoon to be back to work on Tuesday morning, but I knew I'd return to Chicago. Next time for a longer visit. Polonia and my dear friends here held such a place in my heart!

59

TIME TO PAINT AGAIN

I DISEMBARKED FROM MY plane at about 6:00PM Pacific Standard Time. Even though it was early evening, the sun was beaming brightly. If I were still in Chicago, it would be dark and cold. California's temperate climate was a part of my welcomed existence now.

Before I left for Chicago, I did a mural for the Sheetz Candy Shop.

A man admired my mural so much that he called to see if I would consider doing one for his specialty liquor store. It was named The Golden Keg and was in the nearby town of Duarte.

And so, I met with Case, the owner of The Golden Keg. He motioned for me to sit down with him at his bar.

Case pointed to the wide variety of wines, cordials, liquors and beers lined up on shelves in front of a mirror that reflected the glass bottles and their glimmering liquids. "I want people to know this isn't just any old liquor store. It's one with class and with the best of alcoholic specialties."

A big man with a commanding voice, Case continued, "I'd like you to do a giant outdoor mural on my building's east wall depicting a hand-carved keg that was brought to America around Cape Horn from Germany in the late 1800s."

Case had me walk with him to a corner of his store. "This is the keg. You can see that it's unique because one side is made of glass so that people can view the beer and its aging process. If you could paint the keg and its contents in such a way that it would make a thirsty man want a drink, I'd be willing to pay you good money."

I returned to the liquor store the next day with pencil and paper in hand and did a sketch of the cask. Then I went home and used watercolors to capture the keg's brown, amber, and gray striations, and especially the liquid's golden glow. Although I was more of a cocktail guy, it made even me want a beer.

Case was thrilled with my picture. And, so, my work began.

In California, I painted on new types of surfaces unlike those I did at the WPA and the military. In people's houses, it was plaster. At the Golden Keg, it was brick.

Pasadena was an outdoor mural painter's Mecca. Since its residents spent as much time outside as inside, they seemed to want their art outside too. One day, I happened to see an artist painting a wall. So, I asked him for advice on doing an outdoor mural on brick.

With a slight Spanish accent, he explained, "It's all about the preparation. First, you must clean the surface and repair anything that isn't right, so the wall will be smooth. Then you need to use a white primer. To put down the primer, I'd suggest using a roller with a thick nap. That way you'll be sure to sure to get the primer into all the grooves."

"Then what kind of paint do you use?" I asked.

"Acrylic paint, definitely acrylic."

"Why acrylic? Those paints haven't been out for long."

"They bond very well with concrete or brick. They stand up to the elements. Wind and rain won't hurt them."

"Thank you so much, and may I ask what your name is?"

"My name is Roberto, and yours?"

"Florian."

"I've never heard that name before, but it sounds like a good one. Well, back to work. Hope to see you around, Florian."

"If you go to the Golden Keg liquor store in the future, you'll see me working. I like what you're doing here with your brilliant animals…I guess that's what they are."

"We call them Alabreijes—special creatures we made up. We carve them out of wood and then paint them in various bright colors. In Oaxaca mainly. We sell them as souvenirs to the tourists."

"In Mexico?"

"Yes, Mexico."

Ah, another place I could explore...

60

CHANGE

It was 1959, and I was 57 years old. By that time, I had accumulated a handful of good friends in Pasadena, and I was thankful for them. When I finished my mural for the Golden Keg, I invited these friends to the bar to celebrate.

A friend named Michael who at times posed for my murals said, "You are really something, Florian, with all you've accomplished as an artist!"

I shrugged. "No, I'm just an ordinary artist who has hopefully brought a little beauty into the world."

Sitting next to me, my friend Agnes immediately twisted in her stool and looked at me with fire in her eyes, "Don't say that, Florian! You are not an ordinary artist. You are a remarkable artist!"

The others said things like "Yes, yes, Agnes is right!"

My voice said, "You're being too generous," but my heart told me, *Maybe you're right.*

Not an Ordinary Artist

The next day I received a call. "Our church in Alhambra is looking for someone to paint a mural for the lobby." Of course, I expressed interest.

The church, namely The Church of Religious Science, was very different from my Catholic church. The man who called me was on the mural selection committee, and he explained the church's religious views. From what I understood, their church saw God as a universal force without a specific identity. Within a week, I got an idea. It came from a dream I had years earlier. In the dream, I saw a figure who I thought was Christ surrounded by rainbow colors within an outline. In the background was a beautiful pastel-colored landscape that I felt represented the creation of the world and eternal life. I always remembered that dream and wanted to paint it someday. This was my golden opportunity! I decided to leave the face of my Christ blank so people could insert their image of what they thought God looked like. The church committee loved the concept, and I set to transforming the gray walls of their lobby.

On a late Sunday afternoon, I went to do my final touch-ups. I looked around and admired what I'd created. When I got home, I chuckled—thinking that Peter would have said I'd become a true Californian to do such a form of "religious" art and Kazimierz would have despaired that I'd finally, irrevocably lost my "Polishness."

I could laugh at their supposed comments because I realized I had changed. My worries about who I was and where I belonged had floated away as gently as autumn leaves fall to the ground.

As much as I treasured my times in Poland and West Town, I wasn't worried anymore about losing my "Polishness." I embraced my past but enjoyed the present and looked forward to the future. I lived alone, but was I really lonely? For so long, I thought that being married was "the be all and end all" in life. However, now I liked moving to my own rhythms. I had my religion, a circle of friends, and my art. One evening, I turned on the TV (I so loved this modern miracle of entertainment) and found that Louie Armstrong was a guest entertainer on the Ed Sullivan Show. Remembering when Isaac introduced me to Armstrong's music, I called my friend, and we talked about how Armstrong's trumpet playing was as exquisite as ever. Then I went to the refrigerator and got out a beer to enjoy one of the many new things I began enjoying in my life's next season. The blended palette of my old and anticipated new life created a vision the made me excited about the future regardless of its inevitable bumps.

EPILOGUE

Florian stayed in Pasadena, remained single, and died nine years later at the age of 67 in 1969. Like with everyone else, Florian probably experienced a few challenges along the way, but the final chapter of his life was one in which he kept creating beautiful art.

Along with murals for a hospital and a bank, Florian

painted a highly acclaimed mural for the prestigious Collins family in Altadena. Then he did an outdoor mural for the classical garden of the Weatherby Home in San Marino. One hundred and fifty guests were invited to its unveiling on a specific date between 9 and 11 PM when the moon was forecasted to shine on the mural perfectly to highlight a scene chosen from the little country of San Marino next to Italy.

Death may have taken Florian by surprise. His autopsy said he died of arteriosclerotic heart disease. Perhaps he had what we laymen call "a heart attack." I say that his death may have been a "surprise" because a newspaper article said Florian promised pieces of his art to various people, but it had to be auctioned off because he didn't have a will. His friends organized services for him at Stumps Funeral Home in Pasadena.

Resurrection Cemetery in Montebello, California is his final resting place. His grave was unmarked until an administrator named William Benedict applied to get him a headstone available for members of the Armed Forces. Florian's headstone lies flat on the ground. On its top is a small cross. The stone reads as follows: "Florian Durzynski, Germany, Pvt. 120 Base Unit AAC, World War II, March 2, 1902-July 21, 1969." Mr. Benedict probably did not know Florian personally because Florian would have never wanted his birthplace, "Germany," to take up space; he probably would have preferred "Poland" after his name.

AUTHOR'S NOTES

I WRITE HISTORICAL FICTION books to illuminate artists who once accomplished great things but are now little known: artists whose work is awesome but unsung, whose lives teach us about history, and whose personal challenges are ones to which we can relate. Florian Durzynski filled the bill on all three counts. I discovered Durzynski when I admired the portrait of my close friend's grandfather who is the real John Cieplak. She showed me the signature of the artist on its bottom corner—Florian Durzynski—and she said that she and her husband were always curious about who this artist might be. When they went to a presentation about the WPA murals at the Chicago public schools, they discovered that Durzynski was one of the creators of the murals, and they bought a book called <u>Art for the People</u> which showed how the murals were restored. My friends—the Spiegels—suggested I consider writing a book about Durzynski and offered to help me with the research.

So, Peggy Spiegel, her husband Elliot Spiegel, and her sister Kathy Owens and I dove down the rabbit hole of research together. Elliot did the lion's share of researching all the ancestral facts about Florian from the time he was born in Berlin until the time he died in Pasadena. This was no easy task.

For all my books, I make every effort to visit the places where the artists lived and worked. Kathy, Peggy and I visited West Town and several other neighborhoods in Chicago where Poles first settled. This included churches, restaurants and, on the South Side—the Stockyards. We visited Chopin and Newton Bateman Schools. Then I visited Pasadena with Barb and John Miklos when we were vacationing in Palm Springs.

To aide us on our research journey, the Polish Museum of America was a great source of information. The curator, Julita Siegel, and the staff were extremely helpful, and we visited the museum several times as we delved into details of Polish history that played a part in Florian's life.

I felt reassured that I understood Florian's personality (inasmuch as we can understand anyone) when towards the end of my research, I read one of many newspaper articles about him. Eve Adams, from a newspaper in Little Rock, Arkansas where Florian did a military mural, described him as follows: "Florian Durzynski is a small, soft-spoken man with a certain gentle manner that somehow does not conceal an intensity of feeling for his work."

A famed writer in the historical fiction genre, E.L. Doctorow once said, "The historian will tell you what happened. The novelist will tell you what it felt like." Readers of historical fiction books usually enjoy learning about history through real and imaginary people who experienced it, but they often ask if this or that really was true. So, I will try to answer that question.

Florian's immigration papers and military records both revealed that he had a cleft palate. Elliot dug up information which showed that Marcel was his reference on Florian's naturalization application, that Florian eventually lived in the same housing complex as Marcel, and that Marcel remained single throughout his life.

All the background information about Pola Negri and Felice Walkowicz is straight from historical accounts, and Florian did paint their portraits.

The following were fictional characters I created to help tell the main character's story: Peter, Kazimierz, Isaac, and Rabbi Goldman. There was no "Mary." I invented her as a person to whom Florian could tell his immigration story (for all of us to hear). Also, Florian's activities with "Mary" helped describe life in Polonia (Polish Day at Riverview Park, the parades, the great female Polish activists, etc.).

The administrators with the WPA, from Increase Robinson to George Thorp, were all actual people. Carlson was real too. The names and conversations of the teachers, students and administrators at the various schools where Florian created murals were fictional.

I took some liberties with time. John and Rosealia Cieplak were real people as were their children Emil and Jeanne, but the children were actually much older when I had Florian visiting the family. I mainly wanted to make the point about the values of many Polish immigrants and the way that John Cieplak probably wanted his portrait to reflect his ideals.

Juri was also a fictional character, but Otti Berger was not. Her sad fate was just like "Juri" described in his letters.

I found it interesting that St. Charles was, in fact, doing a massive rebuilding at the time I had Florian going there to visit. However, the visit was fictional.

I hope I have blended the facts with fiction in such a way as to entertain, educate, inspire and to act as a tribute to Florian Durzynski.

SS Lapland

Traditional Residential Architecture in West Town

Tiffany Lamp from St. Stanislaus

Portrait of John Cieplak

Saint Barbara's Church

Portrait of Benjamin Kane

Portrait of Felice Walkowicz

Foster Mural at Chopin School

Chopin Mural at Chopin School

Detail of the Newton Bateman Mural

Stage at Newton Bateman School

Durzynski at Camp Fannin

Photo of Durzynski in His Early Fifties

ACKNOWLEDGEMENTS

First and foremost, I thank my friends Peggy and Elliot Spiegel and Kathleen Owens for their tremendous expenditure of time given to research for this book and for their contribution to the editing process.

My heartfelt thanks go to Chopin and Newton Bateman schools for allowing Peggy and me to view Durzynski's murals—up close and in person.

The list of those who furnished information is very long: Julita Siegel and everyone at The Polish Museum of America; Young Phong from the Pasadena Library; Robert Crook from the Pasadena Society of Arts; Eric Edwards from the Illinois State Library system; Dominic Pacyga who wrote several books about the Polish in Chicago and was kind enough to answer my questions over the phone; the Abakanowicz Research Center of the Chicago History Museum that responded so quickly to my many inquiries; the Sherwood Music School Archives; The Back Home: Polish Chicago Exhibit at the Chicago History Museum; a book entitled The Federal Art Project in Illinois, 1935-1943 by Mavigliano and Lawson; Barbara Bernstein, the Public Art Specialist for The Living New Deal; Margaret Rung and Susan

Weininger from the New Deal Art group; Margaret Nowosielska, former head of mural conservation for the Chicago Conservation group; John Sedlacek and Rick McCallister, lifelong Chicago residents with Polish roots, who were kind enough to meet with me, read my first draft, and give me insights into Polish culture in Chicago; Barb and John Miklos who accompanied me to Pasadena to find Durzynski's former address which is now a Denny's restaurant and The Church of Religious Science which is now a Catholic retreat; James Klotz who helped in the final editing process and shared ideas about the book's beginning and ending. If I have left out anyone, I am truly sorry. Many individuals and institutions contributed to the information in this book.

ABOUT THE AUTHOR

Gail Tanzer obtained her master's degree in social work from the University of Chicago. Midway through her career, she returned to school to pursue her love of art. She went on to teach art history at two universities and has written five historical fiction books about artists—Duccio and the Maestà; Across the Alps: The Secret Life of Albrecht Dürer; Graven Images: The Tumultuous Life and Times of Augusta Savage, Harlem Renaissance Sculptor; and Blame It On the Bauhaus?

gailtanzer@yahoo.com
Facebook: gailtanzer, Author
Instagram:Gail Tanzer, writer
Blog: gailtanzer historic fiction

www.ingramcontent.com/pod-product-compliance
Lightning Source LLC
LaVergne TN
LVHW021758060526
838201LV00058B/3142